THE
SECOND
SON

A Vireo Book | Rare Bird Books
Los Angeles, Calif.

MARTIN JAY WEISS

THE
SECOND
SON

This is a Genuine Vireo Book

A Vireo Book | Rare Bird Books
453 South Spring Street, Suite 302
Los Angeles, CA 90013
rarebirdbooks.com

Set in Dante
Printed in the United States

10 9 8 7 6 5 4 3 2 1

Publisher's Cataloging-in-Publication data
Names: Weiss, Martin J., author.
Title: The Second Son / Martin J. Weiss.
Description: First Trade Paperback Original Edition | A Vireo Book |
New York, NY; Los Angeles, CA: Rare Bird Books, 2018.
Identifiers: ISBN 9781947856158
Subjects: LCSH Twins—Fiction. | Electronic surveillance—Fiction. |
Stalking—Fiction. | Privacy—Fiction. | Information technology—Fiction.
| Secrets—Fiction. | Suspense fiction. | Psychological fiction. | BISAC
FICTION / Psychological
Classification: LCC PS3623.E45553 S43 2018 | DDC 813.6—dc23

For Elisabeth, Jasmine, and Jake

We are all alone, born alone, die alone.

—Hunter S. Thompson

If I ever had twins, I'd use one for parts.

—Steven Write

CHAPTER 1

E THAN STONE HAD NEVER been alone, not even in the womb.
He and his twin brother Jack navigated their first three
decades of life together, unwaveringly, in spite of enormous obstacles,
despite prodigious differences.

That was all about to change.

"We need to talk," Jack said as he ambled into the office after ten,
rushed and harried as ever. "Where's Bailey?"

"His plane was delayed," Ethan told him. "He should be here
any minute."

"Let's hit the pit. We need to talk before he gets here."

Ethan followed Jack into the pit, a four-walled glass box
with a sunken floor that they used as a conference room and for
private conversations.

"I don't know how to say this," Jack said as he shut the door and
began to pace, a sure sign that he was going into panic mode. "I know
what this company means to you. But you're going to have to continue
on without me. I can't do it anymore. I'm moving on."

"Moving on," Ethan repeated dismissively as he glanced down at
an incoming text.

"I'm serious."

"You freak out every time we have a little setback," Ethan
said, trying not to sound condescending. "But we'll figure this out,
I promise you. Everything will work out."

"I've given this a lot of thought—"

Ethan cut him off, "You need to remember, every start-up experiences growing pains, but the ones that endure can revolutionize the way we live."

"I really don't need one of your insufferable pep talks—"

"Think about what Uber did for commuting, what Airbnb did for travel, or what Ashley Madison did for affairs. We're going to transform the way people stalk. We're going to be huge."

Yep, that's right, their company, aptly called Stalker, used advanced search technology, including biometrics, to make stalking easy, accessible, and affordable. Think there aren't a lot of people who want to know how much their boss makes, the whereabouts of their children, if their spouse is cheating, or why an ex really left? And that was just the tip of the iceberg of what their company was designed to do. Ethan was determined to make Stalker a portal of full exposure, a beacon of truth that could prevent deceptions and explain betrayals; the go-to site for anyone who has been bamboozled, double-crossed, or inexplicably dumped. He believed wholeheartedly that the truth would set them free.

Unfortunately, Stalker's face recognition software—the most anticipated feature on their mobile app—had been cursed with delays and obstacles, leaving them in desperate need of an injection of working capital to keep them afloat while they ironed out the glitches. Their CFO, Bailey Duff, had gone to London over the weekend to explain the situation to their angel investor, and hopefully bring back a check so they could make payroll.

"He's here," Ethan said, noticing the commotion in the lobby. "Let's discuss this later."

Bailey rolled in, his Burberry luggage in tow, as if he were walking a designer dog, a pampered poodle like himself. He was still wearing his London Fog raincoat for full effect, despite temperatures in the nineties. "Guess who's back from the Big Smoke?" he announced.

Ethan hadn't advertised the reason Bailey went to London— or their perilous financial situation—but those kinds of secrets are difficult to keep at a small company. And so the team of twenty-some twenty-somethings abandoned the coffee station, juice bar, Ping-Pong and foosball tables, like teenagers caught mashing in their parents' game room, mumbling salutations as they drifted back to their workstations, taking refuge behind their computer screens. If layoffs were imminent, none of them wanted their bosses to think of them as foosball-obsessed, coffee-sipping daydreamers when deciding which of them had to move back into their parents' basements.

Emily Tak, a mousy coder with tattoos drifting from her sleeves and leggings and a platinum pixie-do that made her amber-gold eyes stand out even more than they already did, greeted Bailey as he moved inside. "How was London Town?"

"Foggy, dreary, and congested," Bailey quipped. "Prince William and Kate are having another baby. And bloody hell, I had a crying infant next to me on the plane, didn't sleep a wink."

Bailey's dry humor and unremitting quirkiness amused the techies. Their token Englishman was over forty, shamelessly unhip, inappropriately vulgar, and unabashedly honest—often referring to himself as "the most un-LA bloat living in Los Angeles." He wore his out-of-shape paunch and crusty gait like an entitlement and took pride in his disdain for exercise, sunshine, farmers' markets, vegans, nonsmokers, happiness, and false praise.

Very un-LA.

"They started the Monday morning meeting without you," Emily whispered as she took his coat. "They're in the pit."

"For the love of God," Bailey called out as he passed nervous eyeballs peering over workstation cubbies, "would one of you gorgeous geniuses please fetch me a double-shot mocha before my head explodes?"

———

"WHO DIED?" BAILEY SAID, mocking the doleful expression on Jack's face.

Ethan forced a smile. "Welcome back, Bailey. How did it go?"

Bailey set his suitcase down in the corner and said, "We'll get the money as soon as we launch our Face Match Mode."

Ethan felt his stomach sink. Since Apple, Facebook, and Google were battling privacy lawsuits over their facial recognition systems, Stalker had to limit the ways they collected, stored, and shared data—the reason their face recognition feature was fraught with technical issues. "Did you tell him that we have to work around the privacy restrictions and it could take another six months?"

"I gave him the whole spiel."

Jack put his hand on Ethan's shoulder. "I'm sorry. I know what this meant to you."

Ethan looked at Jack like he was speaking Farsi. "We'll find the money somewhere."

"The contract specifies, Stalker can't raise money anywhere else for another year. We've been over this."

"There has to be a way around that."

Bailey pulled a check from his billfold and waved it in the air like a flag.

"You don't have to find a way around it."

Ethan reached for the check. It was from the angel's anonymous shell company, Highpoint Corp, and it was for the full amount. "You got the money?"

"I got the money."

Ethan hugged Bailey, his six-foot-five frame engulfing the portly Brit. "Why didn't you just say so? You almost gave me a heart attack. My brother was about to quit."

Bailey laughed. It was a nervous laugh.

Ethan was so relieved he couldn't let go.

Bailey grunted. "You're squishing me."

Jack sighed, clearly vexed. "What's the catch, Bailey?"

Bailey escaped Ethan's overpowering grip and sheepishly admitted, "There is one little rub."

The brothers shared a look.

Bailey cleared his throat and told them, "We have to upload Face Match Mode now, as is."

Ethan frowned. "I had a feeling you were going to say that."

"I showed him the demo," Bailey said, "and he feels that it's working well enough—"

"Well enough?" Jack scoffed. "The point of that demo was to show how inaccurate it could be, so he would give us more money, not tell us how to run our company."

"We need to stay solvent," Ethan said with a conciliatory tone, staring at the check, "which means we need to keep our investor happy. It's called compromise."

Jack sneered. "Zuckerberg hasn't ceded control. Elon Musk won't kowtow to anyone. And Sean McQueen doesn't compromise. Ever."

Sean McQueen—aka the Wizard of Silicon Valley—was the founder of Stalker's biggest competition, a company called Hounddog, and the sound of his name made the hair on Ethan's neck rise.

Ethan sneered back at his brother. "Why are you being so negative?"

Jack moved closer to Ethan and said, "You and I have never even met this nameless angel and Bailey signed a confidentiality agreement to keep it that way. Now the moneyman is trying to turn Stalker into the next FindFace."

FindFace was a controversial Russian app that allowed users to photograph people in a crowd to find their names, phone numbers, and social media profiles, often exposing and shaming them, with less than 70-percent reliability.

Bailey chimed in, "Our angel just wants us to do what we promised before anyone else does. Being first matters. Instagram uploaded pictures faster than any other photo sharing service. Spotify loaded stations faster than any other music service. Netflix produced premier content before any other streaming service."

Ethan added, "The big five were also built on beating the clock."

"Quite right," Bailey said, "and that's why we shouldn't dillydally. We have great buzz. Projections show us having a profit by year-end."

"Exactly," Ethan agreed, "and then we can exercise our option to buy the angel out, and we won't be beholden—"

"Those projections didn't account for complaints and crappy reviews when the face recognition feature sucks," Jack said.

"Throw a spanner in the works," Bailey spewed as he grabbed the check and placed it back in his billfold. "I can cash this as soon as you get the feature up and running."

Ethan assured him, "We'll have it done by the end of day."

Just then, Emily Tak burst through the door. "Per His Highness's request," she said, delivering a steaming mocha espresso drink. "I hope this cures Sir Bailey's jet lag." Unlike everyone else who poked fun of Bailey behind his back, Emily unabashedly teased him publicly and praised him in private.

"Mmmm…" Bailey moaned as he took a sip. "How I've longed for my delicious American indulgences." He winked at Emily and added, "Especially my favorite *tart*."

"Thanks." Emily blushed. "I think."

Coworkers called her Bailey's puppy dog. Ethan had another thought about why she followed Bailey around so much, but it would have been inappropriate, and possibly legally actionable, to say so.

"Thank you, Emily." Ethan said, glaring at his brother, who still looked uneasy.

Emily took the cue and headed back to her workstation. "Adios, amigos."

Once the door shut, Ethan asked, "What is it, Jack?"

"I meant what I said before. I can't do this anymore."

"Can't do what?" Bailey asked.

Ethan stared at his brother. "You're serious."

Jack nodded. "I've made up my mind."

"About what?" Bailey asked.

"I'm moving on," Jack said.

Bailey choked on his mocha. "Why?"

Jack cleared his throat and delivered another bomb: "Hounddog made me an offer."

Ethan's jaw dropped further south. Everything he had heard about Hounddog—all unverifiable rumors—had them snapping at their tail, ahead in staff size, growth, and development. "They're our only real competition."

"There's room for everyone to succeed," Jack said, mocking one of Ethan's favorite proclamations. "And you have other good programmers—"

"You're an exceptional programmer and we need you," Ethan said. "Even the slightest difference in execution could give two similar tech companies completely different results—think Facebook and MySpace."

"Hounddog and Stalker are dissimilar enough to coexist," Jack countered, "like two different dating sites, think JDate and ChristianMingle."

Ethan groaned, which made Jack chuckle.

"You signed a nondisclosure," Bailey charged. "You can't share anything about our software or strategies—"

"I would never do that," Jack said, "and they're not asking me to."

"You walk, you get nothing."

Jack headed for the door. "I know the deal. I have to vacate the premises immediately. I'm leaving now."

"You'll be giving up ownership," Ethan blurted, desperate to change Jack's mind. "You'll go from entrepreneur to intrapreneur."

"The world needs both." Jack looked back at his brother. "I knew this wouldn't be easy, but I really think it's for the best. You and I haven't been the same ever since we started this thing. It's just not worth it to me anymore."

Ethan had to ask, "Is that where you've been sneaking off to every weekend, Silicon Valley?"

Jack nodded.

"I thought you had met someone."

"I know you did." The corners of Jack's lips twitched, another nervous tick Ethan knew all too well. "Hounddog is sending movers this afternoon. I'll be gone by the time you get home." Jack pushed the door open, paused, and then turned back. "For better or worse, I hope you do change all public and private transparency forever and it all works out the way you want it to. Good luck."

Ethan watched Jack leave, his mouth agape.

Good luck?

In nearly thirty years, his brother never wanted to leave his side, almost to a fault. Now he was walking out the door and moving up the coast, just like that.

The door slammed shut and reverberated.

Ethan went aphonic.

Bailey flapped his hand and shouted, "Do something!"

Ethan ran after Jack blindly.

CHAPTER 2

Ethan cut off Jack at the reception desk. "This is what we always wanted. Why would you give up now?"

"I have my reasons," Jack huffed.

"You owe me a better explanation than that."

The harsh light from the wall of windows overlooking the Third Street Promenade shed a spotlight on the statuesque twins, turning the open, airy floor plan into a stage to air their dirty laundry. The staff couldn't hear their conversation, but Ethan's frenzied body language and Jack's hardline stance said it all.

Jack looked away and mumbled, "It's just too much."

Ethan tried his wonted upbeat spin. "All start-ups have growing pains, unexpected hurdles, but once we get to the next level—"

"I want to have a life."

"I don't know what that means."

"I know you don't."

Ethan felt as if his right hand had said it no longer wanted to clap with his left. He and Jack had been obsessed with the tech boom in California since their first coding club in elementary school. Growing up in the suburbs of Minneapolis, the twins from the Twin Cities had dreamed of becoming Internet entrepreneurs—always together—changing the world for the better, like Jobs and Wozniak or Page and Brin. Ethan was a visionary, the idea guy, and he was driven. Jack was a great programmer, loved solving technical problems and the solitude coding required. This was their shared destiny. Now Jack was pulling out, without warning. And worse, he was going to go work for their rival.

Ethan stepped closer, nose-to-nose; the two tallest guys in the room squaring off, an unimaginable faceoff. Identical twins usually can't help feeling like they're looking in a mirror.

This wasn't one of those times.

"Talk to me, Jack. What is this really about?"

"It's about me putting myself first for once, getting what I want, what I deserve."

"I see therapy is working."

"Self-awareness can lead to change," Jack said. "You should try it sometime."

"I already know who I am. I just have to look at you and think of the opposite."

"Lucky you."

"Lucky me."

The staff pretended not to pay attention, but the Stone brothers were getting louder than they meant to be; a lifetime of trying to be heard in stereo will do that.

"So that's it?" Ethan said, discontented. "You want to have a life and put yourself first. Did I get that right?"

"Pretty much."

They both fell silent. Combustible twin towers. You could hear a pin drop.

Ethan nodded because he knew what his brother was really saying. They were housemates, business partners, and identical twins, but all things were not equal, and never had been. Ethan now had a bigger role in the company.

And he had Brooke.

Ethan nodded. "This is about Brooke, isn't it?

"Get out of my way." Jack shoved past Ethan and headed outside.

Ethan followed after him, shielding his eyes from the blinding late-morning sun, considering the possibilities for such an angry reaction.

It has to be about Brooke.

Brooke Shaw was Ethan's stunning English girlfriend. He had met her at the Stalker's corporate retreat in Big Sur last year and she had been living in the twins' bachelor bungalow ever since. Ethan had wanted to tell Jack that he had been ring shopping and preparing to pop the big question, but he hadn't found the right time.

Maybe he knew.

Ethan caught up with Jack in the parking lot. "I'm okay with you leaving," he said, "if that's really what you really want."

Jack kept walking. "Now you don't have to ask me to move out."

He knew.

"I wasn't going to ask you to leave," Ethan explained. "Brooke and I will get our own place."

"Now you don't have to."

Jack reached for his car door. Ethan blocked him and said, "I want to marry her, start a family, the whole nine yards."

"I'm happy for you."

"But it doesn't have to change us, you and me. And you certainly don't have to leave Stalker."

"I want to leave Stalker."

"Let me put it another way—"

"No."

"No?"

"You're trying to talk me out of doing what I want, like you always do, as if I should want what you want. But I'm not you."

"I never said you should want what I want."

Jack laughed sardonically.

"Give me one example."

"When I wanted to study business with you at Stanford—"

"That's not fair," Ethan protested. "You got accepted in the engineering school. That's your strength. We were going to build a tech company, it made perfect sense."

"To you."

"If I'd known you'd harbor resentment—"

"Oh please, you have plenty of resentments, too."

"Oh really?"

"Really."

"Like what?"

Jack squared off, looked him in the eye, and said, "Like Barry."

Barry was their mutual best friend who killed himself in college.

Jack said, "You blame me."

"What?"

"I spent that last summer with him and you think I should have known."

"I never said that."

"You didn't have to. If you didn't think I felt bad enough..." Jack wiped a tear and moved on like he was reciting a rehearsed list. "When Dad died, you took his entire baseball card collection, which I later learned was worth a small fortune."

"He and I shared an interest," Ethan tried to explain. "Those cards are worth a lot, but I'm never going to sell them. He wanted me to have them."

"Yeah, right, you were a much better athlete. And I remember your love of the game. Like when I served your detention so you could play."

"Seriously?" Ethan said. "We were like sixteen, and it was a playoff game. They needed me. You took one for the team."

Jack took a step back, looking satisfied, as if Ethan had just proved his point. "Now it's your turn to take one for the team."

Jack got inside his car. Ethan let him go and watched him drive away.

On one level, Ethan felt relieved. He and Brooke were now free to start their life together, and he could run Stalker without Jack's restraints and complaints.

On the other hand, his heart ached more than he could ever have imagined.

Monozygotic twins, brothers of the same mother (and egg), are nothing like other siblings. Their genetic reflections make them feel a connection like no other.

After three decades of sharing everything, they were finally parting ways.

Ethan thought about their father on his deathbed, asking him to watch over Jack, as if he were the big brother. Their father knew that Jack was too sensitive for his own good, but maybe there was more to it. Brooke once asked Ethan if Jack was the second son. He told her what his father once told them, that confusion in the delivery room prevented anyone from noticing who was born first.

Brooke didn't believe that. "Your father knew," she said. "Birth order and birthrights shouldn't matter, but they always do."

Ethan would soon learn what she meant by that.

CHAPTER 3

ETHAN CALLED BROOKE AS he walked back to the office. He explained everything that happened in the meeting and told her that Jack was on his way home to move out. He expected her to be as shocked as he was. She and Jack were close. They had spent a lot of time together, especially when Ethan put in insane hours at work. But she didn't comment on Jack's departure at all.

"You can't upload the Face Match Mode," she said, "it's not ready."

"We have to."

"When?"

"Now. This afternoon."

"What?"

"Did you hear the other part that I just told you? Jack is moving out. Today!"

"I heard you," she said in a wispy voice.

Did she already know? Did he tell her he was leaving before he told me?

Brooke switched the subject back to the face recognition issue. "You said that feature was several months from working correctly."

"Why are you so concerned about that—?"

"I do want to see Jack," she interrupted. "I'll be home in a little while."

"I figured you would."

"Will you be there?"

"I think he wants some space, and to be honest, I don't want to get into it with him again."

"I get it," she said. "You should take some time after work. Blow off steam. Do what you have to do to process this." She paused and then said wistfully, "I'm sorry, Ethan. I'm sorry it didn't work out."

Odd way to put it.

"I think he'll regret this," Ethan said, "but this is what he wants and I can't change his mind. We just don't see eye to eye anymore."

"You and your brother are as different as chalk and cheese," she said, "but that's not what I meant..."

Unlike Bailey, whose British accent and colloquialisms sounded amusing, hers came off as profound, and her insights about people were usually spot on. "Go on," he prompted. "What did you mean?"

"I know you always feel responsible, but sometimes there are other factors you don't know about and there's nothing you can do."

"What other factors?"

"Point is," she continued, "the world has been kinder to you and you feel guilty about it sometimes. But don't. Your brother likes exactly who he is, and he should. Let him be happy. It's his time."

A bit overdramatic, he thought.

And then she whispered, "I love you."

Ethan could feel her heavy heart through the phone. And when she hung up, he'd never felt a deeper void.

———

THE FACE MATCH MODE feature took a few hours for the Stalker team to upload. Ethan configured a warning banner to explain the possible hiccups users may encounter, and then he wrote and distributed a press release announcing its launch.

Bailey dipped into his office and asked, "Are we good to go?"

"Good to go." Ethan confirmed.

"It's the right thing to do, Gov."

Ethan forced a smile. "I know."

Ethan liked and trusted Bailey because there were no pretenses and he was as committed to Stalker's success as he was. Ethan was also well aware that Stalker never would have been launched without the seed money Bailey brought to the table. Two years prior, Bailey had approached Ethan at Pitchfest, a convention like *Shark Tank*, where entrepreneurs practice their ideas on venture capitalists searching for a diamond in the rough. Ethan had been pitching his concept for Stalker all day. Bailey came along and told him he was searching for a tracking app for an angel investor in London. It was a perfect match. Only after contracts were signed did Ethan learn that Bailey didn't even know his well-heeled angel's real name, only his shell company—Highpoint Corporation—and his rules: the angel would only communicate through Bailey, only when necessary, and always on his terms. At first Ethan didn't mind the arrangement. He knew that venture capitalists often required discretion for the same reasons tech companies don't want competitors to know how they were funded. But now they were heading toward a desperate turning point; their angel was a ghost, and they were completely dependent on this phantom.

Bailey headed out to deposit the Highpoint Corp check before the bank closed, and the Stalker staff left early. Ethan grabbed the extra surfboard he kept in his office and hit the beach.

———

ETHAN RODE THE WAVES just north of the Santa Monica Pier until sunset and realized that Brooke was right, he really did need some time alone to process what his brother's departure would mean—to Stalker, to him, and to their relationship.

His first reaction, like Brooke had said it would be, was to feel responsible, and his mind raced with questions:

Did I shut Jack out when Brooke came into my life? Was I too preoccupied by her and Stalker?

Then he started to think about what life would be like without his brother. Jack had been his reflector, shadow, sounding board, advocate, and devil's advocate. When Ethan and Jack were at their best, they mastered the bait and switch, knew each other's thoughts, and even spoke for each other. They got twice as much done, could be in two places at the same time, and always knew the other had their back. Can you imagine how much you could get done in a day if you could clone yourself? It had always been them against the world, *simpatico*, two sides of the same coin.

But Jack had also been a perpetual thorn in Ethan's side. All siblings deal with favoritism, jealousies, and entitlements, but twins have to deal with a unique set of rules. There are expectations to live up to: expectations for each other and expectations from others. Ethan always felt that there were too many expectations.

He didn't feel that way with Brooke.

Brooke was about to become his new life partner, the one he chose. And somehow she understood the twin dilemma better than anyone. She once told Ethan that having a counterpoint in life was a gift because it allowed him to make sense of the world, but it also could distort the truth.

She understood. Somehow, she knew.

Ethan rinsed off at the public beach showers, threw on a change of dry clothes he kept in the trunk of his car, watched the sun dip below the horizon, and came to the conclusion that the timing of Jack's departure was a blessing, for all of them. He and Brooke could start their life together. He and Jack wouldn't bicker over the details of the business anymore, and they could be brothers again. Jack could get a life, his own life, and do it his way.

Let him be happy. It's his time.

Ethan figured another hour or two should be enough time for Jack to have cleared out of the bungalow, so headed over to James Beach, an upscale hangout on Market Street in Venice, to kill some time.

He grabbed a stool at the bar and ordered a beer. He didn't want to be alone but he didn't want to talk to anyone either. Unfortunately, this wasn't a place he could be a fly on the wall.

A gorgeous redhead sat on the stool beside him.

"Do I know you?" she asked him, her emerald eyes impossible to ignore.

"I don't think so."

"I'm Julie."

"Ethan."

"Are you meeting someone?"

"No."

She moved closer. "Would you like some company?"

He reached for his wallet and waved for a check. "I actually have to get going."

She put her hand on his. "I just broke up with someone. I could use a little company." Then she whispered, "No strings attached."

"I'm flattered," he told her. "But I couldn't do that to my girlfriend."

The redhead didn't relent. "Did you hear the part about 'no strings attached'? I have a place just up the street."

"I'm sorry. I can't."

"Because of her?"

He didn't hesitate. "Because of her."

The redhead pulled back. "She must be something special."

"She is."

"Lucky girl."

"I'm a lucky guy."

"Now I feel like a creep," the redhead said. "I got so used to dealing with jerks, I've become one. Where can I find a guy like you?"

"I'd introduce you to my twin brother but he just left town."

She laughed.

He wished he were joking.

———

ETHAN LEFT JAMES BEACH and headed home under a dim waning crescent moon, looking forward to seeing Brooke's warm smile and spending their first night on their own. Hill Street was just a five-minute drive and he found a parking space right in front. Maybe his luck was about to change, he thought as he approached the cozy bungalow. How great it would be to have the run of the place—just him and Brooke—and not have to close doors for privacy anymore.

When one door closes, another door…

Unfortunately, when he went inside, another door was about to slam in his face.

CHAPTER 4

THE BUNGALOW WAS DARK and dank. The windows were all shut, sans the usual cross breeze that masked the mold. When Ethan flipped the lights on, he saw that all of the furniture was exactly where it had been when he left for work that morning. Since the twins had split all the expenses of furnishing the home, Ethan had assumed Jack would split it fairly and take what he wanted.

Apparently, he wanted nothing.

Ethan went into Jack's bedroom, which was on the first floor, expecting it to be emptied, but only his clothes and personal knick-knacks were gone. The bed, the sheets, the dresser, even the plants were left behind. Ethan peeked out the window just to make sure Jack's car was gone. It was.

"Brooke!" he called out.

There was no response.

Whenever Ethan would work late, she would usually wait in bed and read. Sometimes she would fall asleep. So he ventured upstairs, quietly, hoping to sneak under the covers to consummate this new beginning, their first night living together alone, but when he arrived at the hallway landing, he had a strange feeling. Something about the house felt desolate, cold, and uneasy; the evening's crepuscular charm began to turn sibylline; every creek in the hardwood floorboards seemed to forewarn malevolence.

When he entered the bedroom, he saw what it was, and it rendered him immobile. He couldn't move, couldn't feel his hands or feet. And he knew that his life would never be the same.

Brooke had left him, too.

All of her clothes were gone. The only thing she had left behind were some of her paintings, a dozen or so watercolors she had been working on, stacked in the corner, possibly forgotten, more likely abandoned.

And there was a note left on the floor beside them. Ethan picked it up and sat down on the bed to read:

Dearest Ethan,

> *You once said that my happiness was the most important thing to you. If you meant that, please respect my decision. There's nothing you could do to change my mind. Please do not search for me, or contact me. I love you and always will. I am truly sorry. Unconditional love is, unfortunately, always conditional. Please be mindful.*

xo,

Brooke

Ethan went numb.

Please be mindful.

Mindfulness was one of the first things Ethan ever heard Brooke talk about when he first laid eyes on her at the Dancing Rabbit retreat in Big Sur, and that indelible moment played back in his mind.

—

BILLOWING MORNING MIST ROSE from the glassy ocean surface to a sea of vibrant wild flowers. She emerged like a dream, the warm sunlight cascading over her swarthy, silky skin; the soft breeze fluttering through her long black hair. The angel with piercing azure eyes and a Mary Poppins accent chose her words thoughtfully, an oracle's soliloquy with a sexy Brit brogue. "We try to make sense of the world as a place of binary opposites," she began, somehow coming off more poetic than pompous. "Earth and sky, light and dark, good and bad. But when it comes to human nature, we're less clear. Our differences make each of us unique and yet we still hide who and what we really are. Why? Why is that...?"

Jack nudged his elbow into Ethan's ribs and said, "Stop staring, you putz."

"I'm just listening," Ethan lied, trying to play it cool, an ardent grin taking over his face.

"You're looking at her like prey, like she is a naked Victoria Secret model that just told you she had a master's degree in business and knows how to code."

Brooke turned toward them and dipped her sunglasses, as if the alignment was causing her to see double. The twins were used to all kinds of reactions when people first noticed them. They couldn't hide their identical features, or their height. (At six foot five, they almost always stood out in a crowd.) Ever since they started Stalker, people called them "the other Winklevoss brothers," referring to the very tall and athletic twins that claimed to come up with the idea of Facebook, settled with Mark Zuckerberg for millions, and went on to Bitcoin, making billions. To avoid further comparisons, the Stone brothers had done their best to differentiate themselves with shears and blades. Ethan always wore a full beard and long, rock-star locks. Jack was always clean-shaven with a closely clipped Caesar cut. But those differences were never what fooled anyone. Especially Brooke.

"Some say people can't really change," she continued, "that they reveal themselves over time. But we don't believe that here. Dancing Rabbit is not only an educational center and leadership forum, but also a place to reflect, renew, and transform. Our goal for this weekend is to inspire you to set new intentions, explore spiritual possibilities, and pioneer new paths for change…"

"For the love of God," Jack mumbled, "what on earth is she going on about?"

"Who the hell cares?" Ethan moaned lustily.

"As a self-sustaining community, we harvest nine thousand pounds of lettuce, broccoli, and kale, and compost five tons of organic waste every month. Does anyone know what we do with all that compost?"

She nodded toward the twins. "Any idea over there?"

Ethan tapped at his chest and his voice cracked. "Me?"

"No," she said with a flirty grin, "the handsome one on your left."

When the laughter faded, Jack said, "You use it to fertilize, I suppose."

"I guess that one got the looks and the brains," Brooke joked. "Binary opposites."

Bailey's throaty laugh echoed noticeably over the others, as did his bright color-coordinated Patagonia outfit that he had likely bought just for this weekend, never to be worn again. He turned to Emily and explained, "'Cause they're twins."

Emily looked up at him, bugged. "We get it."

"They all get it, Mr. Duff," Brooke teased. "Is that not why we hire people smarter than ourselves?"

Bailey and Brooke already had a good rapport from their dealings in organizing the retreat, but those interactions were limited to phone calls and emails. This was the first time Bailey had seen what she looked like and it rendered him more awkward than his usual ungainly manner. And less witty.

Bailey snickered and his complexion went flush. "Good one."

A cell phone rang and Ethan realized it was his. Jack glanced at his caller ID and gushed-whispered, "It's that bimbo you've been shtupping. Answer it."

Ethan picked up. "I'm in a thing. Call you back—"

Brooke advanced with a seductive gait and said, "We are going to completely unplug this weekend. We call it mindfulness."

Before Ethan could excuse himself, apologize, or say goodbye, Brooke grabbed his phone and told the girl on the other line, "He won't be available for the rest of the weekend. Maybe ever."

As if she already knew.

Everyone awaited Ethan's response.

"That's one way to break off a doomed relationship," Ethan joked. "Mindfully."

Their eyes locked, and time stood still, irresistibly.

—

ETHAN SAT ON THE edge of his bed staring at the note she left behind.

Please be mindful. WTF!

At Dancing Rabbit, they talked about mindfulness with utter awe, as if discussing the wind, gravity, or evolution; the notion that every living thing looked through a different prism and that honoring every point of view was the only way to manifest true understanding. Now he had to look through a different lens to make sense of his new reality.

Ethan went outside and sat out on the porch for hours that night, cursing mindfulness and the horse it rode in on. He couldn't find a reason why Brooke would leave, or his brother, and why he couldn't see either abandonment coming. He blamed them both, separately and together. He had once prided himself on his optimism and unrelenting faith—faith in God, love, loyalty, business fundamentals, and hard work.

Now he doubted everything, even himself.

Was I blind or was I just blindsided? Had I been selfish and self-involved? Did my ambitions leave Jack and Brooke each with a void? Had I betrayed my brother by wanting him to go away, to be with Brooke...alone?

His thoughts grew darker as the night grew long.

Betrayal; premeditated and cruel; temptations justified; loyalties shunned; too ashamed to face the truth, or me; both of them knowing how they would leave me. Did they know what they would be doing to me once I was left behind, alone, without explanation? Did they care? Could I get them back? Would I want to?

The two people closest to me, whom I trusted and loved the most...

He drifted off, slept better than he should have, and dreamt vividly of a fatal car accident.

In the dream, a car was racing up a winding road. The road was slick. It was raining. Oncoming cars were wailing on their horns as the car sped by, skidded, spun out of control, and went up and over a barrier. It fell and fell and fell. There was a thunderous explosion. Then nothing. Nothing but silence. Deadly silence. He couldn't be sure who was in the car.

He only knew that it wasn't him.

CHAPTER 5

E THAN'S BODY SHUT DOWN. Fortunately, he had crashed so hard that he slept through the night and awoke well rested. Unfortunately, when he remembered what he was waking up to, he had to experience the entire ordeal all over again.

He was grief-stricken and overwhelmed; his gut wrenched with an ache in his stomach that felt like his world had collapsed, which it pretty much had. He went for a five-mile run on the beach to clear his head, which it didn't, and then decided that the best thing would be to get to work and act normal, like nothing had happened, so that the staff could stay focused on the Stalker mission, not his personal life.

Wishful thinking.

He took a long scenic route to work, up Ocean Avenue, past the gateway to the beachfront city, the Santa Monica Pier and its multicolored Ferris wheel, Muscle Beach, the crimson Palisades Park skyline. He passed by the seaside bars, restaurants, music venues, and artisanal shops—all the reminiscences of the city on the beach he had come to conquer with his brother, and then Brooke; all the experiences they had shared whirled by like the constant motion of joggers, bikers, and rollerbladers; the visual triggers he was left with, now a backdrop laced with fading memories; the warm tech bubble by the ocean Ethan had once seen as paradise now felt like a lonely ghost town.

He turned up Montana Avenue, driving past an upscale strip of bistros and boutiques that he used to stroll with Brooke on weekends. Sometimes they would walk north, all the way up to the

Pacific Palisades, admiring the magnificent Tudors, Cape Cods, and Mediterranean villas on large lots—some of the most desired real estate on the Westside. Brooke had told him that the natural beauty reminded her of the coast of Spain and Italy, and that she always dreamed of starting a family in such a place.

Ethan stopped at one of Brooke's favorite up-market haunts, Cafe Montana, where they used to talk about their future plans while sipping cappuccinos and watching young couples push strollers past them. This was the life Brooke wanted.

Why would she leave before we even began?

Cafe Montana was a healthy gourmet brasserie that guaranteed purely organic fare grown locally, which Jack once joked only guaranteed heart failure when you realized the dent it put in your Apple Pay.

Ethan laughed about it as he ordered an egg white and vegan cheddar on a croissant, mixed Vega-shake, and double-shot mocha for the same price as a month's worth of groceries in Minneapolis; then he headed back to his car, remembering how his brother would so often make fun of the SoCal lifestyle. Almost everyone in Los Angeles has a story about how they came for the sunshine but stayed for the lifestyle.

Not Jack.

He never considered himself an Angeleno, and never cut LA transplants any slack that did. He was especially tough on New Yorkers who acted elitist about their East Coast pedigree but never moved back.

The perfect weather, year-round surfing, and close proximity to the desert and mountains weren't enough for Jack to put up with the celebrity worship, lack of intellect, contagion of narcissism, and unrelenting congestion. He reduced the tech renaissance on the beach to "the new black"; Hollywood *redux*; high school with money; passion without spirituality; social mobility without regard.

Ethan told his brother he had missed his calling as a comedian or talk show host. Jack used to do hysterical bits poking fun of the LA lifestyle, from the predictable clichés about phony people and fake breasts to the coffee bars that had the nerve to charge nine dollars for a cup of joe loaded with butter and coconut oil, promising to upgrade brain and sexual prowess. Or his rants about the yoga studio next to a family planning center where a former rock-and-roll guru cranked seventies rock while barking orders over the din in a hundred-degree room packed with sweaty opportunists trying to out-yoga each other in a likeminded community of shallow, entitled wannabes and has-beens angling to feel superior.

"Some things in LA don't need a punch line," Jack used to say. "Kale, quinoa, and Arctic char don't belong on a menu at a burger shack!"

Ethan knew that his brother used humor as a defense mechanism because he had so often felt like a fish out of water, but he started to wonder if his brother's witticism was just his reflection of the truth and if he was just being honest. Ethan always laughed, but maybe he should have taken Jack's cynicism at face value; maybe Jack had been trying to tell him that he really didn't like it there.

Maybe Brooke didn't really like it either.

She came down to Santa Monica only because Ethan couldn't go up north to Big Sur every weekend. She was more flexible. And she had her own funny jabs about the life and lifestyles of the Westside.

"All you need is a few million, just for admission," she would joke whenever they talked about raising a family like the couples pushing strollers past Cafe Montana.

And she wasn't wrong. Living in the natural beauty that reminded her of the coasts of Spain and Italy didn't come cheap. Teardowns north of Montana Avenue started at $2.5 million. A decent education for children meant private school, about $40,000 a year, per kid; $600,000 from preschool through twelfth; a million per kid when you factor in college and grad school. Then there was the cost of nannies, drivers, camps, sports, clubs, trainers, and tutors. And that didn't cover the cost of eating organic, shopping at Whole Foods (aka "Whole Paycheck"), frequenting trendy restaurants, vogue vacation destinations, and all the social expectations of the limousine liberals.

Ethan considered another possibility: What if Brooke didn't think Ethan would ever be able to afford a lifestyle on the Westside with the natural beauty of the coast of Spain and Italy? What if she didn't believe that Stalker would make it and that's why she was so concerned about the face recognition feature going up prematurely when he told her that Jack was leaving? She was also practical and well aware of the risks and uncertainties of building a tech company.

But Brooke never demanded such a lifestyle. And Ethan never made any false promises. She strived for a simpler life and was the least materialistic girl he knew. She was generous with others, frugal with herself, always appreciative, never wasteful. She avoided leaving a carbon footprint and didn't even have a driver's license, which was quite the challenge when she moved down to Los Angeles. She once said that if his success didn't manifest the way he had hoped, she'd admire him for trying, and he'd still be the same person she loved.

Who says things like that?

Brooke did.

Girls he had dated in the past were like treasure hunters assessing his potential, digging for loot or baggage. He would always be on guard, often resentful.

But not with Brooke. Never with Brooke. She had heart. She had soul. She would never tell him that she didn't want him to pursue his dreams because she wanted security. But she did want to have kids, and if her childhood had truly been "a knotty affair," as she had described it, then perhaps she didn't want to go through such heartache again.

Ethan never had any doubts about Brooke before, never wondered if her intentions were pure, but then again, he also didn't know all that much about her. She'd avoided talking about her past from the onset and they'd both agreed that all that mattered was the people they had become; everything before had just been preparation.

Sure, Ethan believed in doing some due diligence before jumping into any venture, but Brooke never gave him a reason to be cautious.

And when Jack once suggested that Ethan should slow things down and get to know her better, he told his commitment-challenged brother, "If you search for flaws, you'll probably find some, and that only leads to analysis paralysis—like you."

Jack had countered, "What you don't know might bite you in the ass one day."

Ethan disagreed. "What matters is what you feel in your gut. Brooke and I compliment each other. We're better together, like all the great mergers. Where would J. P. Morgan be without Chase, Disney without Pixar, Exxon without Mobile?"

Jack had had a field day with that one.

Now Ethan was wondering if his brother had a good reason for warning him. What if the first girl he chose to trust implicitly had the deepest darkest secret of all?

And what if it had something to do with why they both left on the same day, without warning?

———

ETHAN ARRIVED AT STALKER and parked besides Bailey's old Jag. They were both always the first to arrive at the office and Ethan was glad that they had time alone. He told Bailey everything and showed him Brooke's note. Bailey was bad with good news, always overreacting, but good with bad news, usually focusing on the bright side.

This time, however, he acted like he had been expecting Brooke's flight, and even responded a lot like Jack.

"You're better off knowing now," Bailey told Ethan.

"Knowing what?"

"Knowing that she's not right for you."

"She's perfect for me," Ethan objected.

"Apparently, she didn't think so."

Bailey could also be blunt.

"Maybe something happened to her?"

"Like what?"

"I don't know. Something."

Bailey cringed at Ethan's lingering hope. "You're a big-picture guy. You should know better. Doesn't matter why. She's gone."

Harsh.

Ethan glanced at the entrance and saw their two Stalker designers arriving, and he wasn't quite ready to field questions or be subject to a pity party. Since Jack's dramatic exit, which everyone had witnessed, there would be lots of questions about why he left and what his departure meant for the company. Ethan needed some distance, especially before news of Brooke's surreptitious exodus leaked.

"I'll be in my office," he told Bailey. "I need some time."

"You don't have time," Bailey said as Ethan walked away. "You have a job to do, to get the site working right, to grow this company."

Bailey, Jack, and Ethan were the only Stalkers with private offices but they rarely used them since everyone else was always visible in the open pen—like most tech companies, prisons, or preschools—and while locking himself inside his office may have given Ethan some time to process his loss, it also gave the rumor mill time to stir.

Over the next few days, no one approached Ethan. He slipped into his office before the staff arrived, and left long after they all went home. He immersed himself in the face recognition issues, everything from managing the press to dealing with complaints when some of the bugs Jack had warned them about manifested, but he also spent time tracing back through every recent interaction he'd had with Brooke and his brother, looking for inconsistencies in behavior, searching for a sign or clue about why his brother wanted to leave Stalker and why Brooke wanted to leave him.

Jack had been making mysterious plans nearly every weekend in the past few months and his secrecy had been making Ethan uneasy. Now he knew that Jack had likely been going up to the Bay Area to meet with Hounddog. That made sense. But Brooke hadn't behaved any differently. Ethan retraced the last intimate moments they shared, wondering if he had been paying close enough attention.

—

JUST THAT PRIOR SATURDAY, Ethan and Brooke had taken a walk along Abbot Kinney—a hipster street in Venice brimming with trendy shops and restaurants. He had noticed her admiring an antique pendant necklace in the window of a quaint jewelry store. He told her that he had to go inside to use their bathroom, and when he came out with a little box and presented her with the pendant, she literally burst into tears.

He'd assumed they were tears of joy.

Brooke was an avid painter, preferred watercolors to oil, and always had an easel set up somewhere. That evening, she had been out on the screened-in porch painting the blood-orange sunset. It was chilly and cozy and Ethan wanted to make a romantic evening that Brooke would never forget. He set up a four-log fire, played a John Legend album, and lit dozens of candles amongst sprawled floor pillows. He lured her inside with the fragrant smell of his special cioppino. He poured her favorite Pinot Noir from Sonoma—*Casa Carneros* 1998—and told her how much he loved her.

She seemed overly emotional. She touched the pendant necklace and burst into tears again, this time even more so.

Maybe they weren't tears of joy.

He couldn't have known then because that moment was interrupted by a booming thud from the adjacent room. Jack shouted, "Dude, you're a country bumpkin!"

They both laughed and Brooke asked, "Who is he talking to?"

Jack shouted again, "Don't pick Adam over Blake!"

"I think he's watching *The Voice*," Ethan said. "He actually DVRs it."

Ethan brought out the seafood medley stew and turned down the lights to complete the perfect mood. He'd been preparing to present some ideas he had for their future together and had butterflies in his stomach. The good kind. When Ethan peeked in the den to see if they had sufficient privacy, Jack was heading out the door carrying an overnight bag.

"Where are you going?" Ethan asked.

"Told you, I made plans."

The door slammed.

Brooke came around the corner. "Did Jack just leave?"

"Gone again," Ethan said with a mischievous grin. "We have the house all to ourselves."

She composed herself and brought him his glass of wine. "How can anyone be so happy all the time?"

"My mother said I came out that way," Ethan told her, as if it were agreed-upon family lore. "My brother got the grumpy gene."

Her smile faded and she said in his defense, "He's just misunderstood."

"You have to admit, he is moody, especially lately."

"Cut him some slack." She turned angry. "You have no idea what's going on in his life."

Ethan had decided then that it wasn't a good time to discuss how they should tell Jack that they wanted a place of their own or inquire about what kind of ring shape she fancied. The mood wasn't right. Something else was on her mind.

—

WAS SHE AWARE OF Jack's plans? Ethan now wondered. *Was she already planning on leaving herself?*

And then he had the worst thought of all: *Could they have run off together?*

CHAPTER 6

BAILEY WAITED UNTIL LUNCHTIME on Friday before he broke the code of silence.

"You have to say something to the team," he said, barging into Ethan's office.

"Come right on in," Ethan said. "You don't have to knock."

"I didn't."

"Exactly."

Bailey sighed. "Sarcasm suits your brother, but for some reason it just makes you sound bitter."

"Thanks for that insight."

"Did you hear what I just said?" Bailey pressed. "You have to say something. They want to know why Jack left. He was a partner. We owe them an explanation."

"What can I say?" Ethan threw his hands up. "He wanted to get away from me so he went to our biggest competitor?"

"Sugarcoat it any way you want. Just tell them something. They're getting anxious, which makes me anxious, and I don't like feeling anxious. Maybe say something about your girlfriend leaving so they realize you're an emotional wreck, but it has nothing to do with the health of our company."

"You can tell them."

"I already did," Bailey admitted, "but it would be nice if you acknowledged it. Tell them that everything will be okay."

Ethan groaned. "Will it?"

"I don't know, frankly, but we have to keep up appearances."

"You want me to make up something?"

"For the love of God, I don't care what you tell them. Tell them that you can't tie your shoes without your brother, that he was the brains and you're the brawn, and once your girlfriend realized, she ran off with your barber. At least they'll feel empathy for you instead of wondering why you've locked yourself away all week."

"If you're trying to cheer me up, it's not working."

Bailey sat down on the edge of Ethan's desk and cleared his throat. "Know what happens when you play a country music album backward?"

Ethan stared back blankly.

"You lose your girl. You lose your brother. You lose your home. You lose your mind. Get it?"

Ethan couldn't even muster a courtesy laugh. "I haven't lost my home."

"Just your sense of humor. Which brings up another thorny issue. The software fixes. With Jack gone, we need to put someone in charge, ASAP. You and I need to focus on other matters—"

"Who's our best programmer right now?"

Bailey didn't hesitate. "Emily."

"Then she's our man."

"Right. Just wanted your blessing." Bailey waved for Emily who was waiting right outside his door.

"Congratulations," Bailey said as she entered. "You are now our lead programmer."

"Wonderful," she mused. "And I'm sure this comes with all the perks of longer hours and no raise."

"I knew she was perfect for the job," Bailey joked. Then he turned back to Emily and asked, "Do you have the other thing?"

Emily held up a green folder. "Right here."

Bailey's beady eyes turned to Ethan, now somber. "Emily has something else to tell you."

Ethan feigned a smile. "What is it, Emily?"

Emily gave Bailey a maddened look, as if he were forcing her to do his dirty work (which he was).

"Go on," Bailey urged.

"Sorry to hear about your life imploding and all," she said with a shaky voice. "It must suck for you—"

"Thanks," Ethan said through clenched teeth, "don't let the door hit you on the way out."

Bailey burst out laughing and repeated, "Don't let it hit you on the—"

"Both of you," Ethan added.

Bailey ignored the request once again and slapped Emily on her ass. "Show him what we found."

"There's this thing in America called sexual harassment," she said calmly, as if talking to a petulant child, "I could sue you for doing that."

"Sue me on your own time, love. This is important. Show him."

"Incorrigible," Emily hissed as she approached Ethan's desk and pulled Brooke's letter from the folder. "I ran this through a Stalker search—"

Ethan grabbed the letter and waved it at Bailey. "You took this off my desk!"

"When you ran off to the loo, yesterday, yes." Bailey pulled a cigarette from his shirt pocket, put it between his lips, and mumbled, "Isn't that why you showed it to me?"

"I showed you in confidence, as in, don't share it with anyone, and don't even think about smoking in here."

"You know I'm trying to quit, Gov," Bailey said as he got up, opened a window, and lit up anyway. He sucked in a big drag and turned to Emily, as if Ethan weren't there. "You'd think a guy who works here would do a background check on a girl before asking her to move in. He never even Googled her."

Emily nodded in agreement. "We look into everyone except the people closest to us. Ironic."

"It's not ironic," Ethan said. "She asked me not to. It's called respect."

"Well, she never asked us," Bailey said. "Go on, Emily."

"So I got her social security number off her credit card," Emily continued. "She only had one. Didn't even have a driver's license—"

"She didn't want to drive," Ethan said defensively. "She cared too much about the environment. Remember her lecture in Big Sur about hydrocarbons? And by the way, that corporate retreat was your idea, to make our staff more conscientious—"

"I remember all that *eco-babble* crap," Bailey said as he coughed up smoke. "Brooke had solicited me for months, offering a significant discount and a hard sell coquettish phone plea to sell me that this company needed this rustic retreat to be relevant, that all the tech start-ups in the know were doing it. Bloody hell, do you think I—the most unlikely outdoorsman on the planet—wanted to hike and watch the sunrise and chant? Being the horny, gullible Englishman that I am, I took her bait even before you fell head over heels. And apparently, so did the entire office. Her Brit brogue gave her a lot of clout with all our prepubescent Angelenos who tend to be impressed with anyone feigning authority, or using the English language properly, for that matter. The fact that she had a thing for tech entrepreneurs didn't hurt either. She went on about how she understood the pressures we suffered from as a new and growing business in a fiercely competitive landscape and assured us she would help us find balance. Think about it. She was selling water to farmers in a drought. Anyone working for a start-up lives a life of sheer imbalance and stress. Most of us are young, ambitious, and competitive."

"Except you," Emily chimed in. "You're not so young."

"Right. I'm old as fuck. But I am ambitious. And when I'm not working, I'm thinking about work, or sex, because I'm competitive "

"I get it," Ethan cut him off. "She was preaching to the choir."

"She was persuasive," Bailey said. "She gave us the full court press. She obviously charmed your pants off, Mr. CEO. Why do you think she wanted to get close to Stalker?"

"It's just the way she is—"

"Wrong. You have no idea who she is. Now shut up and listen to Emily."

"Gentle as a jackhammer," Emily said as she turned to Ethan. "Are you sure you're ready to hear this?"

"He needs to hear this," Bailey huffed.

Ethan tossed a Nerf basketball across the room. It bounced off the rim and the backboard booed. "Go on."

Emily cleared her throat and began, "Brooke Shaw was born in Fresno, California, on September third, 1990. She had been arrested for a laundry list of petty crimes and spent years in a juvenile correctional facility. She became a heroine addict by age twenty—"

"Did you hear that?" Bailey cut her off. "Brooke Shaw lives on the street. She's a homeless woman who eats in soup kitchens and sleeps in cardboard boxes!"

"That's ridiculous," Ethan protested.

"Of course it is," Bailey agreed. "Your Brooke Shaw is from London. Couldn't fake that Kensington accent. She eats quinoa at Real Food Daily, sips espresso from Primo Passo, sleeps on three-hundred-thread-count Egyptian cotton sheets, and most likely has never even been to Fresno—"

"Are you finished?" Emily interrupted Bailey.

"I am."

"So I ran her letter through a fiber and fingerprint analysis," Emily explained, "and look: different signatures. Different thumbprints."

"Different girl," Bailey concluded as he grabbed the green folder, pulled out the police report of the homeless Brooke Shaw, and placed it next to Brooke's letter. "Your girlfriend started using this homeless woman's identity about two years ago—"

"Or bought it," Emily insinuated. "Heroin is expensive."

"The real question is why," Bailey said. "She must have told you something about her past."

"Of course she did," Ethan said, unconvincingly.

Bailey and Emily both waited for him to elaborate, but he didn't because he couldn't. Ethan felt like a complete fool, and it showed.

Bailey asked, "Any idea where she's from?"

"London."

Bailey sneered. "Where in London? It's a big place."

"You just said that she had a Kensington accent. I guess she's from Kensington."

Bailey looked at the floor and shook his head. "She didn't tell him where."

Emily agreed. "Clearly."

"You two are precious," Ethan said. "I feel like I'm being interrogated by Mr. Blue and Ms. Blonde."

"What's that supposed to mean?" Emily asked.

"He's making a *Reservoir Dogs* reference," Bailey explained.

"Never heard of it," Emily said.

"Never heard of *Reservoir Dogs*, Gov. Too young." He winked at Ethan and made a fist pump. "Try another movie from this century, so she gets your point—"

"What I'm trying to say," Ethan fumed, "is that our relationship was based on mutual respect. Have either one of you been in a relationship where the other person wants to know every-fucking-personal-thing?"

They glanced at each other, both blushing, and neither answered.

"Most people need to purge every detail about their past just to be understood," Ethan continued. "We didn't do that because someone always overreacts or dwells about things that you can't change. I loved that Brooke didn't need to know everything and judge me for it. She had the ability to focus on the present. It was refreshing."

"It was also naïve." Bailey sputtered smoke. "Your lack of knowledge about her past made you blind and has turned this into a sordid affair."

"You don't understand—"

"That ignorance is bliss?"

"She must have told you something that could help us," Emily said. "Did she talk about her work?"

"She developed corporate retreats at Dancing Rabbit to help entrepreneurs find more balance. She wasn't as you say—feigning authority."

"What about before you met her?"

"She got her business degree at Oxford and worked for a few socially conscious start-ups—"

"Give me a name of one of them."

"She never told me."

"Did she ever talk about her mom or dad?" Emily pressed. "Does she have any brothers or sisters?"

"What was her family like?" Bailey jumped in.

Ethan wanted to prove them wrong but part of him knew that they had a good point. He had been satisfied with the amount of information Brooke had shared, but maybe he shouldn't have been, so he conjured up what she had told him and acted like the weight of it justified his lack of details. "Her parents are both gone," he told them. "As you know, so are mine. We both related to losing parents so early, and we also both understood why we wouldn't want to rehash that pain. She moved to Big Sur for a fresh start."

"How did her parents die?" Emily asked.

Ethan shrugged.

Bailey looked away and mumbled, "To lose one parent might be regarded as a misfortune, to lose both looks like carelessness."

Ethan let that sink in. "That's kind of profoundly said, Bailey."

"Don't be so impressed," Emily said. "His best lines are stolen from Shakespeare."

"Close," Bailey laughed. "That one is courtesy of Oscar Wilde. They really ought to consider teaching you bloats some classics in your sorry schools—"

"He's just trying to say that it sounds like too many coincidences," Emily said. "Can we—?"

"Right, let's stay on point," Bailey agreed. "Tell us what else you know about her family. Anything, Gov. Names, numbers, old mail, odd references, siblings…something. This is what we do. If we can use our resources to solve this puzzle, it could prove that Stalker can do some good. Think of the ad campaign possibilities."

Ethan shook his head.

Bailey sneered. "I can't believe you were going to propose to this girl."

"Awww," Emily hummed. "You were?"

Ethan shot Bailey a look of disdain. "I also told you that in confidence."

As if he didn't hear him, Bailey told Emily, "He had been ring shopping."

"Awww," Emily hummed again.

"Sorry, mate," Bailey said, "but you don't know *diddly* about this woman. How could you have even considered marrying her?"

"Maybe she was already married?" Emily suggested.

Ethan scowled. "She wasn't married."

"You don't know that," Bailey said. "People don't change their identities unless they're running from something—"

"Or someone," Emily added.

"That's ridiculous," Ethan protested.

"It's also ridiculous that she moved out of your house the same day as your brother," Bailey said, turning serious. "We don't believe in coincidences. We believe in facts and analytics. The odds that they both left you on the same day are one in a million."

"Billion," Emily corrected.

Please, God, no!

Bailey and Emily had had the same nasty thought, Ethan's worst fear—a love triangle revealed. Could the two people he trusted most in the world have fallen in love and run off together? Was it remotely possible? Was it obvious to everyone else? His head was spinning and he couldn't catch his breath.

Bailey asked, "Have you tried calling?"

"She was very clear—"

"I meant your brother," Bailey clarified. "Have you tried calling Jack?"

"I thought it would be best to give him time to cool off and settle into his new life." Ethan realized how that sounded—his new life—and his eyes shifted, somber and doleful.

"Sorry, Gov," Bailey said. "I know how hard this must be, but you have to look at the bright side..."

Ethan looked up, hopeful for the first time.

Bailey smirked. "Things couldn't get any worse."

"Funny as a crutch," Emily mumbled as she walked out.

"Just trying to give him some perspective," Bailey said as he followed after.

The door shut behind them.

And Ethan never felt more alone.

CHAPTER 7

Ethan spent that Saturday searching the bungalow from top to bottom— every closet, drawer, nook and cranny—hoping to find a trace of something left behind, a crumb of a clue, something he might have missed. He tried to go to bed early but despair engulfed him, and he just stared at the ceiling, mind racing. He reread Brooke's letter and examined the canvases she had left piled neatly in the corner, really seeing them for the first time. Ethan appreciated art, but not in the way an artist appreciates people. He had considered himself a big-picture guy, one who saw things from a bird's eye view, but as they say, the devil is in the details, and he still couldn't help wondering if he could have prevented Brooke from leaving if he had paid more attention.

Brooke's specialties were portraits and landscapes. The faces she painted were of people she found interesting or familiar. Her landscapes were scenic views of places she loved, most often a particular area in Napa Valley with an enormous country house beset on a sprawling vineyard and a church in the background. Ethan once asked her about the location, and she told him that it was where her family had spent summers when she was young. She also told him that she hoped to get married there one day, as if she wanted Ethan to make a mental note. At the time, he had assumed it was because that's where she wanted to marry him.

As Ethan sorted through the paintings she left behind, he noticed that some of the portraits shared a resemblance to her and wondered if they were her family members. Then he noticed that mixed in with the landscapes of Napa were some scenes of Dancing Rabbit in Big Sur, where he met her, and he wondered if it was a way to let him know where she had fled. But why? Why wouldn't she just tell him or let him know in her note? He decided that he was grasping irrationally, full of self-abnegation.

And isn't denial the first phase of grief? Or is it anger...?

He couldn't remember, and it didn't matter; he had plenty of both, as well as a shortage of answers, evidence, and consolation.

He called Bailey, his loquacious confidant.

Bailey answered as if he were expecting the call. "Can't sleep, Gov?"

"Can't sleep," Ethan admitted. "Any chance you'd take a drive up north with me?"

"What for?"

"Maybe she's back there, at that place in Big Sur—"

"What if she is?"

Ethan didn't have an answer.

"You'll make an ass of yourself if you barge in on them," Bailey said, "like a...for lack of a better word, stalker."

"You really think it's true," Ethan swallowed, "that they ran off together?"

"I really don't know, but there's nothing you can do about it if they did."

"I could find out why."

"I think you know the reason, Gov."

"Ouch."

"Sorry to be blunt."

"That's what you call it?"

Bailey chuckled. "Despite knowing how much you hate being alone, that's exactly how they left you."

Ethan went silent, now fully aware of the difference between alone and lonely.

"You're a big personality, and you're big, like seven feet tall, I figure you can handle it."

Ethan said, "I'm six five," as if it made a difference.

"A handsome giant who expects everyone to do things his way, on his terms, works well in business. You're a great boss. But people have free choice when it comes to matters of the heart. Some things you can't force, change, or control."

"I'm not controlling."

"I didn't say that you were. But you are a force. Don't let it go to your head."

Something must have gone to Ethan's head because it ached. He wondered if the two people closest to him were so afraid to tell him that he was too controlling and they were unhappy. "Are you saying that I'm more cult than innovation? More David Koresh than Jeff Bezos?"

Bailey laughed. "If you want to grab a drink, I'll indulge you. Drinking is the appropriate response to your situation. No one will blame you if you go on a binge all weekend and stumble into work Monday morning with a horrendous hangover, but they may question your decision-making ability if Brooke has to get a restraining order against you. Uber over to Father's Office. First six rounds are on me."

"That's okay," Ethan said. "I should keep a clear head."

"That's probably good form," Bailey said, sounding relieved that he didn't have to wake up on Sunday morning with a hangover himself. "Call me if you just want to chat, or if you're about to do something stupid, okay?"

After they hung up, Ethan dosed off and awoke ten minutes later. It was futile to try to sleep. It was quiet, unusually so, which made the thoughts in his head grow louder. It wasn't only that Brooke had left, but also the way she left, that she didn't tell him in person.

Seriously, who leaves a Dear John letter on the bed when they move out? Was it an English thing? Was she too polite to utter such words to my face?

It made perfect sense to Ethan why Bailey and Emily assumed that Brooke and Jack ran off together—bad timing and all—but he still maintained that Brooke's departure was completely out of character; it wasn't the girl he knew, or thought he knew, and he couldn't accept that his compass was that far off.

Ethan thought of something Jack used to say in all his glum wisdom: *Imagination is responsible for love, not the other person.*

Could that be the reason it was so different with Brooke? Had he invented who he wanted her to be? Had he confused good manners for respect, great sex for love, a free spirit for his kindred soul?

Were his delusions responsible for this mess?

CHAPTER 8

ETHAN WENT DOWNSTAIRS TO the porch and looked out at the ocean. It was a murky night; the gibbous moon was pushing its edges, now glowing behind a dense marine layer, distilling a purple haze.

He stared at the corner of the porch where Brooke had painted a blood-orange sky, just one week ago, and he couldn't believe that he was now standing there without her, all alone. Everything had seemed so perfect last Saturday night.

But it couldn't have been.

He tried to replay that evening back in his mind, every detail, looking for something he may have missed.

—

AFTER JACK STORMED OUT, after the romantic dinner, after he and Brooke had finished every drop of the *Casa Carneros* 1998—they headed upstairs, made love, and she had fallen asleep in his arms. He caressed her soft raven-black hair for a while. It wasn't even ten yet, and he wasn't remotely tired. He decided to catch up on his email and social media accounts. He gently set her head on the pillow and accidentally knocked over Henry Miller's *Tropic of Cancer*, one of the books she had brought from Big Sur—American authors she wanted to learn about. Luckily Mr. Miller didn't wake her. Ethan opened his laptop and pored over his daily Facebook newsfeed. (He had over ten thousand "friends," so there were always a lot of posts, tidbits, and news updates.)

He noticed one blurb about dating sites from one of his brother's connections. This is when Ethan first wondered if Jack's mysterious weekends might have been all about looking for love, or as Jack put it when he left—wanting to have a life.

Ethan logged into Stalker and ran a simple search on Jack, just a quick scan of common friends and interests. That didn't do much so he stepped it up to Linkability Mode, which allowed him to pick up recent credit card transactions.

He learned that Jack had made two stops that evening: a restaurant and a service station. He marked the locations on a map. Ventura and San Simeon. It was clear that Jack was heading north.

Ethan's screen pinged, which meant that Jack was making a third purchase just then. Before he could see where it was, he saw that Brooke's eyes were wide open, and angry; she had been watching him.

"What's Linkability Mode?"

"It uses metadata to find someone," Ethan explained.

"Like how?"

"Like what they purchase or when they make a phone call or—"

"Why?"

Ethan knew she was already weary of what Stalker did and how invasive its features could be, if used for the wrong reasons. Now he was proving her right. "Where they've been can give clues to where they're going," he told her.

Brooke had expressed concern about Stalker ever since they met. And who could blame her? Anyone would worry about a love interest with a history of stalking, let alone someone who owned a company that offered services to stalk. She had always been so protective of her own privacy, insisted on keeping their prior lives private, and talked a lot about protecting the privacy of the people that came to Dancing Rabbit.

There was a clip in her voice. "You're stalking your brother, aren't you?"

"I'm concerned about him."

"Why?"

Ethan hadn't considered why he was doing it, but the first thing that popped into his head was the consequences of last time Jack kept things from him. "Last time he distanced himself from me and clammed up like this, something really bad happened."

She sat up as if she weren't expecting such a penance. Her voice softened. "Tell me what happened."

"I really don't want to get into it."

"I know you had a friend that killed himself," she said. "Is that what you're referring to?"

Ethan was taken aback. "My brother told you?"

"He did, yeah," she said, matter-of-factly. "It had a tremendous effect on him."

"On him?" Ethan felt the muscles in his shoulders tighten. "Don't get me started."

"I think you should get started. You obviously have feelings about it. Talk to me."

"I thought we weren't going to regurgitate everything that happened before we met."

"You don't have to," she said. "I just thought you might want to—"

"Well, I don't."

"Okay, love," she said as she scooted closer and rubbed his chest. "Let's talk about something else."

Which made him want to talk about it. "Barry. His name was Barry. Our friend."

"You were all quite close."

"Barry, Jack, and I were best friends in school. But I spent a lot of time with someone else that summer—"

"With a girl, no doubt," she teased. "Go on."

"I wasn't around much," he admitted, "so I had no idea Barry was in so much pain. Jack must've known and never said anything."

"When people commit suicide, they usually don't tell anyone that they're going to do it," Brooke said. "Not if they really want to do it."

"Jack had been with Barry every day. He should have picked up on something."

"Not necessarily. And that's a silly thing to hold on to. Blaming your brother for something that someone else did to themselves is nuts."

"You don't understand—"

"I think I do. Your brother distanced himself from you back then and something horrible happened and you blame him. But why do you think he shut you out then...and now?"

"It's just the way he is."

"Go deeper," she said, seemingly impatient with his lack of pathos. "You had a serious girlfriend then, and you do now. Maybe it's hard for your brother to share you. Did that ever occur to you?"

Ethan felt his face turn red.

Brooke asked him, "Do you think you could have talked your friend out of going into the woods and shooting himself?"

"I never got the chance to try."

"Just because you and your brother share the same genetic profile, doesn't mean you're the same. It's those genes that are randomly switched on, or off, that make you different. And those differences are often hidden from the world. "

"You're saying that I don't really know him."

"Nobody knows anybody completely."

—

Is THAT WHY THEY *say love is blind, because you lose lucidity and can't gauge reality? Was our love one-sided? And if she left with Jack—did she know something about my brother that I didn't know?*

Ethan looked out at the view of the ocean from the abandoned bungalow porch considering the possibilities. What other intimacies had Jack shared with her? Did she encourage him to be the man he always wanted to be and to move on? Did he expose a different side of himself to her? Jack had always behaved more uplifting and confident around her. And she treated Jack without censure or condemnation or expectations. Ethan, on the other hand, had always projected expectations onto Jack, or at least that's what Jack had told him. Maybe Jack resented it. Resented him.

Could this be his way of getting retribution? Ethan wondered. *Was Jack capable of such a betrayal?*

Ethan remembered the dreaded look on Brooke's face that night when she caught him stalking Jack. She said something else that night that he never forgot:

—

"Promise you'll never stalk me if we don't end up together."

"I can't do that," he had told her, "because we will end up together. I love you—"

"I love you too," she cut him off, "but you never know how things turn out."

"—Unconditionally," he'd added, as if that were all that mattered. "I love you unconditionally."

—

But she clearly didn't agree, as she had pointed out in her goodbye letter: "Unconditional love is, unfortunately, always conditional."

Ethan couldn't accept that her feelings weren't true, though; he was so sure that the way he felt when he was with her was real, and mutual. He would know if she didn't feel the same. That couldn't have been faked. There had to be something else going on in her life, something she couldn't share with him for some reason. She went so far as to change her name. Either she was hiding something or running from someone. Maybe she was in trouble. Maybe she needed help.

He needed to know.

The marine layer completely obscured the moon now and there was a sudden chill in the air. Ethan went back inside. The bungalow was tenebrous and still; its emptiness growing more sullen each time he reentered the empty home.

He sat on the couch, in the darkness, and fired up his laptop. The Stalker screen projected on his face and he contemplated entering the site as her voice played in his mind.

Please do not search for me or contact me.

Ethan had created Stalker to be a portal of full exposure, a beacon of truth, where technology could explain deceptions and explain betrayals—for anyone who has been bamboozled, double-crossed, or inexplicably dumped. Now he was one of those people, desperate and dolorous, achingly in the dark.

I have to find her.

Ethan reconsidered the pact he had made with Brooke to keep the details of their pasts in check because all that mattered was the present and the people they had become. Now he knew that she'd likely pushed for that agreement to keep something from him. She had only told him that she was a well-bred English girl who came to America after both of her parents passed away, looking for a fresh start, but she never said anything about changing her name, which had to mean that she was hiding or running. If that were the case, she may be in trouble.

Considering her odd behavior—the way she left, the Dear John note, the paintings left behind—it was likely she was in danger, he rationalized, deciding he would just find out if she was safe. If she was, he promised himself, he would back off and accept her decision.

He grabbed his phone, took a deep breath, and called her. He got one ring before her voicemail picked up. He hung up, and without hesitation, he phoned Jack. Got his voicemail, too.

Ethan felt a deeper twinge in his gut. He looked down at his glowing computer screen. It was already cued up to the Likability Mode. He gave himself final permission, and said out loud, "Just show me that you're okay and I'll leave you alone."

He plugged in Brooke's details and ran the search. The pop-ups showed no credit card activity.

He ran Jack's and it showed a gas station purchase near San Simeon a week ago, last Friday, the day he left.

Then nothing.

San Simeon was just south of Big Sur. Jack had charged thirty-five dollars at the station and hadn't used his credit card since. If that was the last place Jack used his credit card, over a week ago, then he had to still be in the area, and if he was, then he had to be at Dancing Rabbit.

Brooke had made such a big deal about how the resort protected privacy. It would make a perfect hideaway. What if Brooke realized that she had chosen the wrong twin, preferred the one who was more "sensitive," and ran away?

Ethan swallowed hard. He felt feverish. He had only been thinking about how both of them leaving had affected him. But what if something had happened to them? No one had heard from either one of them all week. Neither had used a credit card. Neither answered their phone. He had no way of getting in touch with them even if he wanted to. He had to find out if they were safe, and he couldn't wait until morning.

It was starting to rain. And it was getting late. If he left just then, he wouldn't get to Big Sur until around midnight. But it didn't matter.

He grabbed a bag, uncertain if his search would take a few days or a few hours, and packed a few changes of clothes, his Dopp kit, laptop, and some energy bars. He set the Stalker app on his iPhone to All Out Search Mode and locked up the house.

His Tesla Model X was fully charged, which meant he could easily make it to Big Sur before needing to plug in.

So he took off.

Never in his wildest dreams would he have believed he would never be coming back to the cozy beach bungalow.

But he never would.

CHAPTER 9

Ethan ventured the three-hour jaunt up the coast, all alone, in heavy rain, at night, on slick, serpentine roads—held captive by his flailing thoughts—recalling people and places Brooke had talked about, anyone or anything that might shed some light. His mind tracked back to the last night of their corporate retreat, when the Rabbits threw a party for the Stalkers at the inshore pavilion.

—

It was a brisk autumn night. The stars were brilliant and everyone was buzzing from blooming Pink Jasmine, salty ocean breeze, and house wine. Brooke was in the corner talking to her roommate, Anna Gopnik, a bohemian poet wearing an African Dashiki, and Elvis, a diehard hippie who looked like he had stepped out of a Grateful Dead time machine.

Ethan approached as Elvis was delivering a stoned lecture on counterculture movements. "The Beat Generation rejected stifling values and materialism, brought on spiritual quests, the exploration of Native American religions is why we now open our minds—"

"If you ask me, there aren't enough Native American influences around here," Ethan chimed in, hoping to charm Brooke. "If this place had a pig roast and blackjack tables, it would really rock."

Elvis and Anna looked at each other, horrified.

"You're disappointed?" Brooke mock-frowned.

"Hardly," Ethan smiled. "It was a great weekend. My employees needed to forge a new understanding of self and society, so they can pioneer new paths for change."

She beamed. "You were paying attention."

"I'm a good listener," he said, raising his glass. "And you had me at 'organically infused wine.'"

"Organic fruit-infused wine," she corrected him and held up her glass. "I'm glad you like it."

Anna fidgeted, annoyed, and tugged on Elvis's arm. "Come on, I need a refill." She sneered at Ethan and told Brooke, "We'll be at the bar."

Ethan watched them walk away. "The disapproving BFF and Andy Garcia don't like me very much."

"We're not supposed to get too close to the guests. I'm setting a bad example by flirting with you."

Ethan blushed and noticed Bailey staring at Anna's ass from across the room as she approached the bar. "Let's see how she handles herself when Bailey starts up with her," Ethan said. "He can be relentless."

"Anna's his type?"

"Any girl that will have him is his type," Ethan joked. "Is she single?"

"I don't know."

"Didn't you tell me that she was your roommate?"

"Yes, but most of the staff actually do want to disengage and don't like to share their personal stories. Dancing Rabbit protects privacy."

"There should be an app for that," Ethan said, texting himself a note so he would remember to look into it.

Brooke waited until he finished before asking, "So the Stalker thing was your idea?"

"Yep."

"For people to stalk their exes?"

"That's how we're marketing it, but it can do so much more. We use biometrics: palm prints, hand geometry, retina and voice recognition, tracking tools even law enforcement can't use most of the time."

"Why?"

"Privacy laws."

"No," Brooke clarified, "I mean, if it's not only for people that are curious about old lovers, then it's to find people that don't want to be found—"

"It's for full transparency," Ethan said, turning serious. "Sometimes people can't move on. We help them get closure."

"Because jealousy makes people do terrible things?"

"Exactly."

"But greed is the real killer. Am I right?"

He smiled again and put it all together: "'Jealousy makes people do terrible things, but greed is the real killer.' I like that. That's good. Better than our current ad campaign, actually."

"I'll let you use it," she said as she leaned in close, and whispered, "if you tell me the truth. What made you come up with such an invasive business model? Are you running from something? Or trying to—?"

"My intentions are completely honorable," he said, revealing his pirate's grin. "To take the company public so that I can make Fast Company's top thirty under thirty and become more powerful than God, or Bill Gates."

Brooke shrieked louder than she meant to.

"Are you shocked by my shallow ambitions or impressed with my naked honesty?" he asked.

"Neither. I just find it hard to believe you're not yet thirty."

"My birthday's in a few months, but don't tell anybody. Thirty is the new sixty in the tech world."

They laughed and shared stories and Ethan didn't want it to end. He took her hand and they walked toward the moonlit archipelago. Angry waves slammed against the jutting canyon walls. Ethan told her, "I'd really like to see you again."

She stopped and turned to him.

Off her aporia, he asked, "Is this where I need to say something so transcendent that it completes my transformation?"

"Or mine," she said. "Give it your best shot."

He intensified his gaze. "I knew the second I laid eyes on you that you were my missing piece. Let's start making some memories."

She shrieked so hard she spilled her wine.

Ethan got so flustered he stuttered, "That was, ugh, I know... gimme another try—"

"No. Don't! Please." She moved inches from his lips and told him, "It was perfect."

Their first kiss was a deep one. Ethan felt it throughout his body and knew his life would never be the same. And apparently so did she. "I just broke the one promise I made to my father," she told him.

"Never kiss a guy until he takes you on a proper date?"

"Never fall for the most charming guy in the room."

"Why would you promise such a thing?" Ethan mused, looking down at the raging waters crashing against the jagged rocky formation they were standing on. "It's as natural as this spectacular phenomenon."

"And just as dangerous," she giggled. "My father was French, so he would know. *L'amour nous fait faire des choses folles.*"

Ethan waited for her to explain.

"Love makes us do crazy things."

—

ETHAN STOPPED AT THE gas station in San Simeon where Jack had used his credit card last. He showed a recent picture of his brother on his iPhone to an attendant.

"Do you remember this guy?"

The attendant reeked of musky hemp and looked like he couldn't remember his own name. "Should I?"

"He purchased gas here a week ago last Friday, around this time."

The attendant snickered and looked down at his Android game. "A lot of people come through here."

"Were you working last Friday?"

"I would have been here, yeah. You a cop?"

"No. I'm not a cop."

"Why are you asking?"

"He's my brother. I'm looking for him."

"Shit!" The attendant looked up from his game of Heist, annoyed, as if Ethan had made him lose, and took another glance at the picture of Jack. "That's you without the beard, dude—"

"No, it's my brother. We're twins."

"Oh, man, that freaked me out for a second. I think I do remember him, actually. He filled his tank, bought a few sandwiches and sodas."

Jack might eat a few sandwiches but he would never order two sodas, so Ethan asked, "One or two sodas?"

"Oh, man, I don't remember."

Ethan asked, "Was he alone?"

"I think so. Yeah."

"Would you have noticed if someone was in the car when he came up here to pay?"

"If she was hot, blonde, and stacked, I'd notice." The attendant laughed as if it were the funniest thing in the world, and then reset his game. "Good luck finding your bro, dude."

Ethan noticed a poster over the attendant's head and read: *The illusion of control is as elusive as the illusion of love.* Ethan smiled as he headed back to his car. Just a week ago, everything in his life was on track. He had meticulously plotted and planned every detail of his life. The start-up he had built with his brother was taking off and he was preparing to propose to the love of his life. Now his brother and his girl were both gone and he just wanted to make sure they were both safe.

Beyond that, come what may, as Brooke would say.

He drove the final stretch into Big Sur, where the winding cliff roads overlooked a magnificent ocean view that made everything seem possible, especially to an optimist, and remembered his own father's favorite expression: *Der mentsh trakht un got lakht.*

It was Yiddish and it was never more appropriate.

Man plans and God laughs.

Ethan white-knuckled his steering wheel as he came around a sharp curve, never more uncertain about what his future would be, and prepared for the worst.

CHAPTER 10

J UST BEFORE MIDNIGHT, ETHAN turned onto a narrow path leading up to Dancing Rabbit. There was a glow from the reception. He parked and headed inside, setting off door chimes as he entered.

Elvis, the elder Andy Garcia doppelgänger, looked up from a worn copy of *The Power of Now* and greeted Ethan as though they had never met before, "Evening, sir. Still raining out there?"

"Sure is." Ethan extended his hand. "How have you been, Elvis?"

Elvis's shake was limp and cold. "I was just about to close the office. Do you have a reservation?"

"Ethan Stone," he reminded the aging hippie, who he assumed was stoned. "Brooke's boyfriend."

Elvis stared back dimly.

"I met her here at our corporate retreat last year. My company is called Stalker. I have a twin brother."

If Elvis had remembered, he revealed nothing. "We're completely booked this weekend," he said, shaking his head at his reservation book.

"I'm not here for a cabin," Ethan tried again. "I'm here to see Brooke. Brooke Shaw."

Elvis's eyes glazed over.

Definitely stoned.

Ethan glanced at the reservations. "Is she here?"

Elvis shut the book. "I can't tell you that."

"Why not?"

"We protect our guests' privacy."

"Then she is here."

"Didn't say that," Elvis slurred.

"I know, but…" Ethan stood tall, his imposing frame letting Elvis know he was serious. "You know me, and you know that Brooke is my girlfriend. She worked here until a year ago when she moved down to Santa Monica to be with me—"

"If she wanted you to know where she was, she would have told you, wouldn't she?" Elvis pulled a set of keys from his pocket. "I'm sorry but I have to lock up. You'll have to leave."

Ethan barged through the door leading out to the property.

Elvis reached under the counter, grabbed an X26 Taser gun, and ran after him.

The retreat was pitch black. It took a few moments for Ethan's eyes to adjust. The steady rainfall made the resort look completely abandoned.

Ethan made a beeline toward Brooke's former cabin. There was a soft glow coming from the window.

"Stop right now or I'll shoot," Elvis hissed, a throaty out-of-breath plea as he pointed the Taser, which looked like a blunt toy gun. "You can't go in there!"

Ethan turned back and saw the wire-thin gray-haired flower child shaking. "No, you won't, you're a pacifist who doesn't believe in violence."

Elvis was hard to see through the dark haze, but Ethan could hear him perfectly clear, "Hell, I won't. You're trespassing, and I know my rights!"

Ethan made a quick decision. Assuming that the old hippie was wasted and couldn't hit the backside of a barn, he continued on. If he should get zapped, it seemed less painful than finding his brother in bed with Brooke.

He burst inside the cabin like a bull in a China shop, knocking over an end table and a stack of books, and tripping over two chairs. Two people screamed, then fumbled with the blankets to cover their naked bodies. Ethan didn't need to see them to know that it wasn't his brother or Brooke. "Sorry," he said, as though that excused him barging in on them, and headed for the door leading to the adjoining cabin. "Is Anna still living in there?"

"Who's Anna?" the naked lady asked.

Ethan said, "A bohemian-looking girl, writes poetry, works in the mess hall—"

Ethan glanced back and saw Elvis's dark shadow stealthily approaching through the downpour.

"There's no one in that room," the naked man said.

Ethan went inside. The bed was made and the shelves were empty. No Anna.

When Ethan passed back through, Elvis actually fired the Taser!

Two dart-like electrodes shot out and delivered an electric current that not only stung like hell, but also caused complete neuromuscular incapacitation. And because the force applied is proportional to the strength of the person receiving the shock, Ethan received a huge sensory overload and he collapsed to the ground.

"Come on out," Elvis ordered. "I warned you."

Ethan felt a series of muscle contractions, but the pain faded quickly. It took him a minute to shake it off and get back on his feet, and when he did, he saw the naked couple staring at him, looking more stunned than he had been when he was zapped.

"Apologies for the intrusion," Ethan said to them as he walked out and shut the door behind him.

Elvis met him outside, still pointing the Taser. "Time to leave, fella."

Ethan nodded and headed for the exit. Elvis followed him out, staying close, and just before they got to the door, Ethan swatted his arm down, yanked the stun gun out of Elvis's hands, and turned it on him.

"Where's Brooke?" Ethan tried once more, knowing one of the Rabbits likely heard the commotion, called the cops, and that he didn't have much time to get out. "I need to see her."

"She's not here."

"Was she?"

"I can't help you."

Ethan tried a different tact, to appeal to Elvis's loyalty to his community. "She may be in some kind of trouble. I just want to know that she's safe."

Off Ethan's look of desperation, Elvis said, "I really don't know where she is."

"Then let me see whatever employment file you have. Anything will help. I need an address, a family member's name, a number, something to go on. Please."

"We don't keep files. People come. People go. We don't ask, they don't tell."

"I know you protect privacy—"

"We respect privacy," Elvis corrected him. "That's how we roll."

Some dogs barked and a few cabin lights went on.

Ethan remembered the promise he made to Brooke, to never stalk her, never look for her should they part. "Please don't say anything," Ethan said as he handed the Taser back. "Sorry I barged in like I did."

Elvis watched Ethan walk away under the blanket of rain.

—

ETHAN GOT BACK INTO his car and contemplated his next move. Brooke was MIA and decidedly unreachable. Jack would be easier to find, assuming he had told the truth about his job at Hounddog. Ethan checked the Stalker app to see if there was any progress but his search hadn't found any leases in the area under Jack's name. There were, however, several under Hounddog. It was possible, even likely, that the company leased a place for his brother; the Wizard of Silicon Valley was known to treat his people well.

The rain started to come down heavier. Ethan headed north onto Highway 1, his adrenaline pumping, mind racing. He had to get a hold of his brother. Worst-case scenario, he would show up at the Hounddog offices on Monday morning. But until then, he would keep calling. He hit the speed dial.

On the fifth ring, Jack's voice message played. Jack usually shut his phone off when he went to bed, never using the silence mode, and it was well after midnight. Ethan hoped that was the reason his brother wasn't answering. After the beep, Ethan spoke, his voice shaking, unaware of how angry he sounded, "In case you don't know, Brooke left me—"

Ethan veered around a sleek curve and his car skidded. He dropped his phone, grabbing the wheel with both hands. Another car was approaching fast, blasting its horn, making it worse as Ethan countered, barely missing a head on collision.

Barely.

He regained control and fumbled for the iPhone. His voice was more frantic as he continued, "Everyone at Stalker seems to think you ran off with her. Everyone except me, of course. I know you wouldn't do something so low." He paused as if he were expecting him to respond. "Then again," he added, "I never thought you could walk out on a company that we built from the ground up, without any real explanation, without discussing it with me first, and I haven't heard from you all week..." He paused again, aware that he sounded too harsh. He really wanted his brother to return the call, guilty or not. He continued, "We really need to talk. Call me. It's late, but I'll be awake. I'm in my car, heading up north to see you. Call me. Call me. Call me."

Ethan hung up and tried to imagine what could be going through his brother's head. They could usually sense when the other was in crisis, uncannily so, and he didn't feel anything, as if he had been released from their bond.

As Ethan navigated the slippery, snaky road, he thought about example after example of when he and his brother had shocked people with their intuition, sometimes even surprising each other. There were little things like knowing what the other was going to order at a restaurant or when the other had a bad day. Once Ethan had dreamed that Jack fell off a horse, and sure enough, the next day he learned that his brother did in fact get hurt horseback riding at camp. And there were big things, too, like when their mother was going to die and Jack drove to the hospital, not knowing why, even before Ethan called him with the news. Jack was not only his geminate brother, he was his closest ally in life. Sure Jack had shut down from time to time, on purpose, just like his iPhone, so he could recharge, but Ethan had never before felt this kind of disconnect. He wracked his brain to figure out why. Maybe the stress of building a start-up had just gotten to Jack. He didn't deal with pressure well and there was a lot on the line. Their employees depended on them. If Stalker failed, getting financing to start another venture would be twice as hard, maybe impossible. And since Ethan had been spending most of his free time with Brooke, maybe Jack didn't have anyone to talk to. Ethan wondered if he had been there for his brother.

It was more in his brother's nature to shut him out than to play Judas, but not Brutus. The more Ethan thought about it, the idea of Jack running away with Brooke seemed more and more unlikely. It wasn't in his DNA, and it was out of character for Brooke, too.

She had always frowned upon cheaters. Her father had been unfaithful to her mother, which she referred to as his one tragic flaw— one of the few details she shared with Ethan about her family. She would joke about it and say that she forgave her father because he was French, but his infidelities definitely bothered her. She once asked Ethan why he thought men cheat. He knew at the time that it was a test, her probing him to see how he answered. He told her that he once heard that it was because they feared death.

"Women fear death just as much," she countered.

"But men are mostly hunters," he tried, regretting immediately that he was defending an undefendable gender. "Their competitive nature and all—"

"That's horrible," she said, tears welling up. "You will surely cheat on me then."

"I could never cheat on you for two reasons," he told her. "One, you'd know immediately, and two, I would never risk losing you."

She'd seemed pleased with his answer, or so he had thought.

She'd seemed pleased with their life together, too, but now she was gone.

Just then, Ethan saw lights flashing ahead. Several emergency vehicles were stacked on the side of the road. As he drew closer, he could see a crane fishing for a car that had crashed through the barrier and plummeted over the hard-edged, jagged cliffs, and down to the ink-black sea.

He pulled over and glanced at the deadly drop over the ledge. It was too dark to make out any details. His stomach tightened in the way it did when he knew something bad had happened to his brother, and the worst possible thoughts ran through his head, thoughts that suddenly made an affair seem trite.

An officer was positioned on the road, guarding the taped-off area and waving on slowing lookie-loos. The moment Ethan got out of his car, the officer shouted, "Get back in your vehicle, sir."

"Can you just tell me what kind of car went over, Officer?" Ethan shouted back, imagining Jack and Brooke floating away in the rough sea, together, their unfathomable betrayal and secrets drifting away.

"No. Back in your vehicle. Keep moving on."

"I'm looking for some people who might be heading up this way and I haven't been able to get through."

"You're looking for what?"

Their voices were muted by the rain. Ethan took a few steps forward and tried to explain, "I haven't been able to get through to them on the phone and I just want to make sure—"

"This is an investigation, sir. I need you to get back to your vehicle."

The officer didn't want to leave his post but was getting irritated. Ethan knew the officer wouldn't let him through, so he waved, as if thanking the officer for permission, and headed for the crushed metal barrier opening.

The officer shouted, "Don't even think about it!"

By the time the officer waited for a passing car, Ethan had already disappeared into the pitch-black muddy slope. The officer grabbed his walkie-talkie and warned the officers below. "Civilian approaching!"

Another voice echoed a complaint, but it was too late. Ethan was already upon them.

CHAPTER 11

D ETECTIVE GREGORY RAMSEY MET Ethan on the egress, his stalwart disposition under sanctioned rain gear, one hand on his firearm. People who stopped were usually well-meaning civilians, but you never know.

Ethan showed his hands with a peacemaking wave. "Good evening, sir…I tried telling the officer up there…I'm looking for…My brother is moving from Los Angeles to San Francisco and I haven't been able to get a hold of him. I saw the emergency vehicles…"

"You're not supposed to be down here," Ramsey told him.

"I know, but—"

"What's your name?"

"Ethan. Ethan Stone. My brother's name is Jack—"

"We haven't recovered any bodies yet," Ramsey told him. "The tides are strong and it's dark. Maybe we'll know more when the sun comes up."

"Was there anything of theirs in the trunk?"

Ramsey looked at Ethan curiously. "You said you were looking for your brother, what makes you think there's more than one person?"

"My girlfriend might be with him," Ethan tried to explain. "They both left unexpectedly last week—"

"Last week?" Ramsey cut him off. "This car went over tonight."

"But there's a possibility that they had been staying at Dancing Rabbit, down the road, and I just thought the worst, as you can imagine—"

Ramsey's face tensed. "Did you go there, to Dancing Rabbit?"

"Yeah."

"And?"

"And they wouldn't tell me if they were there or not. They have a privacy policy."

Ramsey shook his head as if he already knew.

Big Sur had very few intentional crimes. Most residents were wealthy owners of second homes. The occasional need for detective work usually came from transients or tourists or the rare suicide. Accidents like this were common, given the many hairpin turns on Highway 1, the only road that traverses through the five-mile stretch. Whenever it rained heavily, like it had that night, Ramsey was never surprised to be awakened and sent out to investigate. It was always tragic, and he rarely suspected foul play.

Until lately.

The area had had an unusual amount of missing persons and it was getting national attention, not the kind Ramsey wanted to end his career with.

"We've recovered two suitcases," Ramsey told Ethan. "We're going through the contents now. Might as well take a look, since you're here...Follow me."

Ramsey had been on the Big Sur force for eighteen years, and hoped that this would be his last. His dark, leathery skin was a reminder of his youth growing up on the beaches near San Diego; his thick skin was a memento of his early career at the Los Angeles Police Department where he was assigned to drug trafficking, robbery, homicide, burglary, prostitution, and theft extortion in South Central. With two stab wounds and three bullet removals to show for those eleven years of survival, he was transferred to Big Sur partly for his exemplary service, but mostly to prevent him from getting popped by relatives of the dozen Bloods and Crips he'd put away in the nineties.

Ramsey led Ethan toward a tarp around the bend where they were shielding the evidence from the downpour.

Detective Johnson, a weathered, balding, stocky fireplug, wearing the same commissioned rain gear, glanced up at Ethan.

"This is Ethan Stone," Ramsey explained. "Says his brother and girlfriend might have been heading up north. Let's see if he can ID the cases."

Johnson sneered, one hand on top of a dark blue suitcase, the other over a red one. "A bit early in our investigation for that, don't you think?"

"He says his brother and girlfriend may have been staying at Dancing Rabbit," Ramsey said, his head dipped with a telling nod.

Johnson's face soured the way Ramsey's had when Ethan first mentioned Dancing Rabbit.

Ramsey and Johnson had been partners for five years at the Los Angeles Police Department, and their entire stretch in Big Sur. Whereas Ramsey was worried about finishing his decorated career on a high note, Johnson was more focused on staying safe and protecting his pension, always cautious about every protocol. Johnson begrudgingly opened the dark blue suitcase. It was packed with men's clothes.

Ethan sifted through a stack of neatly folded shirts and shook his head.

Ramsey said, "By the look on your face, those are not your brother's clothes."

"Definitely not," Ethan said, relieved.

"Open the other one," Ramsey told Johnson.

Johnson glared up at his partner, quizzically.

"Just to rule it out," Ramsey said.

Johnson opened the red suitcase. It was stuffed with a woman's belongings. Ethan reached inside and pulled out an African Dashiki. "This is Anna's."

"Is Anna your girlfriend?" Ramsey asked.

"No, Anna Gopnik is a lady I met at Dancing Rabbit last year, and I remember this Dashiki thing—"

"Because it's unforgettable," Johnson said as he snatched the funky garment and put it back in the red suitcase. "Another rabbit hole," he snapped at Ramsey.

Ramsey put his hand up to quiet his partner.

"Am I missing something here?" Ethan asked.

"We've had more than our share of missing persons in this area lately," Ramsey explained. "And they all seem to have some connection to Dancing Rabbit."

"Ergo, 'the rabbit hole,'" Johnson said. "Notice anything strange when you stayed there?"

"Other than denying people processed foods," Ethan said, "I don't think they do anything suspect."

"This is a virgin investigation site and he shouldn't be down here," Johnson reminded his partner.

Ramsey nodded in agreement and said dismissively, "Careful on your way out, Mr. Stone."

Ethan started up the slope, and then turned back, "If it helps your virgin investigation, Anna Gopnik was in that car with a guy named Rufus Wall and they were on their way to Palo Alto."

Ramsey stepped forward. "How do you know that?"

"Says so, under the blue suitcase, Detective."

Ramsey lifted the dark blue suitcase and there was a red nametag attached, bright as a neon light. It read: *Rufus Wall. 1641 Chestnut Street, Palo Alta, CA.*

Ramsey pat Johnson on the back. "Nice work, Detective."

Johnson adjusted his thick geriatric glasses. "I didn't see that—"

"No you didn't." Ramsey laughed at his old partner and then shouted up at Ethan as he climbed back up the hillside, "Drive safe. Roads are a mess tonight."

———

ETHAN CONTINUED NORTH ON Highway 1. He pulled out his phone, and considered calling Brooke again, this time without a caller ID so she wouldn't know it was him and might pick up.

The detectives' suspicion of Dancing Rabbit's involvement in recent disappearances made Ethan even more concerned about Brooke. Checking on her well-being seemed more than justified now;

her safety was more important than a broken promise, especially such a precarious one, a goodbye without an explanation, discussion, or at the very least, a warning.

Just a Dear John note.

Please respect my decision. There's nothing you could do to change my mind. Please do not search for me, or contact me. I love you and always will. I am truly sorry...

Ethan went ahead, blocked his caller ID, and made the call. It rang once, and he was hopeful; twice, and...he thought he heard her pick up as approaching headlights flashed in his eyes. It was a delivery truck taking the curve too fast and scraping the guardrail. Ethan swerved in time, but before he could counter his skid, another car came around the bend, also losing control, and forcing Ethan to avoid collision by turning off the shoulder of the road.

His car bumped, dipped, tipped, and skidded down a steep weedy gradient. His head slammed into the steering wheel and he went unconscious. Luckily, the car had stopped just before it slammed into a huge oak tree. Unluckily, the ditch he had landed in was covered in overgrown shrubs, so that no one would see him when they drove by.

The next thing Ethan saw was morning.

CHAPTER 12

NINE HOURS AHEAD IN London, Clinton Godeaux was at a breakfast meeting in the Crowne Plaza Hotel. He was wearing a dark debonair Armani suit, Barker Black Ostrich shoes, and a Gucci tie. He always wore a Gucci tie and he didn't want to get it soiled when the waiter served his plate of pan-fried pheasant with gooseberry sauce. He tucked the tie into his shirt and his phone pinged. At first he thought it was his office reminding him of his next meeting. But when he took a look, he realized it was much more significant, a message he had long been waiting for: an alarm from his Stalker account.

The new Face Match Mode filled his request.

His chest went aflutter, but he barely showed any physical reaction whatsoever. He just excused himself from the two executives he was sitting with, explained that he had a family emergency, and ordered his driver, who was waiting by the exit, to take him to Heathrow.

Immediately.

Two days of relentless rain amidst pea soup made his commute from the city a nightmare. It had also delayed many flights, which he learned when he searched for the first flight to Northern California on his Skyscanner app. The next flight to San Francisco would be late in the evening, so he decided he would take an earlier flight to Los Angeles instead. He'd be able to take care of a problem with his company in Santa Monica first, and then head up the coast to deal with his Stalker match. Kill two birds with one stone, as they say.

His driver dropped him off at the International terminal and he headed for the gate. He laid down his Passport on the counter like he were displaying a royal flush, and told the attendant his seat preference, as if he were ordering a Chateaubriand dinner from a waiter. "I'll have a window seat. Close to the front. Next to no one. Happy to pay for the empty seat."

"We're completely full in first class," the attendant told him. "I'm sorry, sir."

He cracked open his passport to show three £100 bills dangling out, and added, "Any window will do."

The attendant took the bait and searched her computer. "Let me double-check, just to be certain."

"Of course." He leaned in closer and lowered his voice, "If you don't mind my saying so, that's a beautiful *écharpe* you're wearing," always the *mot juste*.

The attendant blushed. "I think something just opened up."

On his way to the gate, he phoned the bounty hunter he had on payroll in the Bay Area named Ace and gave him specific instructions.

The day of reckoning had finally come.

CHAPTER 13

E THAN'S AWOKE TO THE sound of his Marimba ringtone. Ethan knew it was very early in the morning because he could see the ginger blush of sun making its way over the horizon. He rubbed his aching head and felt a swelling bump that wouldn't go away anytime soon, and spied his phone on the passenger's side floor. He reached for it, remembering the moment before the accident when he had been calling Brooke, and answered with a raspy, but hopeful, "H'llo?"

"You want the good news or the bad, Gov?"

Ethan sat up and grunted. It was Bailey and he sounded cheerful. Then again, Ethan thought, he always did.

"Okay," Bailey began, first the good: "Our Face Match Mode seems to be working just fine—"

"You got a match on Brooke?"

"Two, actually."

Ethan sat up and rubbed his temples. "Tell me."

"The first one came from the DMV. She got a driver's license at Vallejo DMV office yesterday. Didn't you say that she couldn't drive?"

"I said she didn't want to drive. Where's Vallejo?"

"Near Napa."

"What's the bad news?"

Bailey took a long deep breath before he told him: "The second match came from the picture she filed at the Recorder County Clerk in Napa yesterday, late afternoon."

"'The picture she filed'?"

"For a marriage license."

Ethan grunted again, this time like he was in real agony. "She's not wasting any time."

"Sorry, Gov."

"Is she marrying my brother?"

"Don't know…maybe."

"Either she is or she isn't—"

"She's marrying a guy named Benjamin Carver," Bailey told him. Ethan took a moment. "I don't know who that is."

"Neither do I and I think that's on purpose," Bailey explained. "Just like Brooke, this Benjamin Carver has a questionable digital footprint. I found his birth certificate. He was born in Simi Valley, California, and would be twenty-nine years old now. He hasn't filed a tax return in a dozen years. No home. No job. He's likely a vagrant. A ghost. Get my drift?"

"You think he's also using a stolen identity?"

"Looks that way. That's why I thought that it could be your brother. Same age. No digital trail so he could appear out of nowhere and no one would know anything about him."

There was a long silence while Ethan absorbed the new information.

"Why don't you meet me at Bulletproof Coffee on Main? We can grab a little joe and—"

"Can't," Ethan told him, "I'm up in Big Sur."

Bailey groaned. "You're kidding me. I told you to call me before you did anything stupid."

"I know you did. And you were right. I didn't find them at Dancing Rabbit and that old hippie guy that runs the front office hit zapped with a Taser. Those electric currents really fucking sting."

"You're lucky hippies don't believe in the second amendment. Those bullets really fucking kill—"

"Wait a second," Ethan blurted. "You said they filed for a marriage license, but you didn't say that they actually got married yet, right?"

"I'll check their status again," Bailey said as he logged into the Stalker site, "but does it really matter—?"

"If you use our Marital Link, it will say if a ceremony has been officiated by a rabbi, priest, Justice, Magistrate, Captain—"

"I'm looking." Bailey got the same message as before. "Nothing else here. *Nada.* They just filed for a license."

Ethan said, suddenly relieved, "The license only allows you to be married. Just having the license does not mean that you are married."

"I thought the license means that you are married, and that all the pomp and circumstance—the vows, the dress, the cake—were just for show."

"You need both," Ethan explained, well versed from the research he had done when he and Jack set up the Marital Link feature. "They have ninety days to have it officiated and recorded. Point is, there's still time."

"To stop them? Are you serious?"

Ethan checked his watch. "Weddings are usually in the afternoon, right?"

"Depends. Was she affiliated anywhere?" Bailey asked.

"I'm not sure."

"You didn't even ask her about religion, did you?" Bailey huffed. "Too busy talking about real intimate things to broach that ol' staid acid test, huh?"

"Don't start with me, Bailey. I'm sitting in my car, in a ditch, trying to figure out why she and my brother left on the same day, why she never told me her real name, and why she's running off to marry a guy who is also probably using a false identity. Weddings are usually announced. Just run a search—"

"My point is," Bailey interrupted with a quiet voice, "that most people at least know how their significant others were raised, something about their family, and at the very least their religion. I know that you were raised Jewish, right? Did she spin the dreidel or deck the halls?"

"She celebrated Christmas."

"Bravo," Bailey said. "You know more about her than I gave you credit for. I'm taking a look in the state of California—"

"Narrow it down to Napa Valley," Ethan said.

"Right. That's where she filed."

"It's also where she often escaped to." Ethan's voice softened as he explained. "She left behind several paintings in her closet. A lot of them were of a place she spent summers with her family." He just then remembered, "She once told me that she hoped to get married there one day."

"I'm narrowing it down to local churches."

"The church she painted overlooked a vineyard," Ethan added.

"Doesn't everything in Napa overlook a vineyard?"

"There was a gigantic oak tree right outside the church. And there was a big estate in the distance, like a French château. It was all green, dark blue, almost a navy, with white trims—"

"There are no wedding announcements with their names at any church in Napa Valley," Bailey said.

"There can't be that many churches. If you look on their websites, I'm sure they all have photos. I'll find a picture of one of her paintings in my photo library and text it to you."

"Okay," Bailey agreed. "I'll call you back if I find something."

———

TEN MINUTES LATER, BAILEY called back.

"St. Francis Church, the north end of the valley. On their website, there's a photograph of a ridiculously happy bride and groom looking out at the vineyard at sunset. It's rather corny, actually."

"Is there a big oak tree?"

"Yes, the couple I'm talking about is standing in front of it with smiles so bright I think I'm going blind. And there's some kind of castle in the distance, looks like what you described: an enormous French château with tall, narrow bushes around it—"

"Cypress Pines," Ethan blurted. "That's it! Thanks, Bailey, I owe you one—"

"Wait!"

"What?"

Bailey sounded frantic. "I'll call the church the second they open and call you back."

"Why? I could be up there in an hour or so."

"There's no point!" Bailey shouted. "What are you going to do?"

"Ruin a wedding. Maybe kill my brother."

"Brilliant, Gov."

Ethan realized how ill-considered and boorish his plan was, and he assured Bailey, as if he were still trying to convince himself, "If this is an awful betrayal, I'll learn to live with it and move on. I'll turn around and come right home. But I need to know."

Ethan turned the key. The engine whined. He sighed, "If I can get my car started."

"Maybe someone up there is trying to tell you something," Bailey said.

Ethan cranked the ignition again. This time it turned right over. "Yeah," Ethan said, "like I better get my ass in gear." His wheels whirled. The Tesla plowed over the dense shrubbery and out of the dip he had landed in on the side of the road.

He was back onto Highway 1. The rain had lifted. Rays of sun splayed through Cimmerian clouds as Ethan raced up the coast—a look of dread in his gaze, a huge dent in the front end of his car, two holes in his heart.

And more time to reflect on the things he had blocked out about his brother and soon-to-be fiancée; so much of his focus had been on his work, he had been so preoccupied with Stalker, so indefatigably driven to succeed at all costs—was he now paying the price?

Or was he a victim of concurrent negligence?

He had always worked longer hours than anyone in the company. Jack led the technical side. His team could only code so fast and he didn't need to be looking over their shoulders. Unless they were under a deadline, Jack kept relative normal hours. Ethan oversaw everything else in the company, and there weren't enough hours in any day. Thus, Brooke and Jack spent a lot of time together, alone. Ethan used to be grateful Brooke hadn't been waiting for him all alone. Now he was wondering if it had been such a good idea. Awkward memories started to appear in his head, moments he hadn't given any credence to before. And then he recalled something that had occurred just a few weeks back.

—

HE HAD COME HOME from work late after a brutally busy day. He was tired. The bungalow was dark and he assumed Jack had already retired to his room with his door shut and Brooke would be upstairs waiting for him in their bed. But when he walked in, he noticed that they were both on the couch in the living room, sitting rather close together in dim light, talking in hushed voices. He drew closer, more intrigued than suspicious, and they both noticed his large frame filling the doorway.

"Speak of the devil," Jack said, separating from Brooke.

"You're home early," Brooke said as she stood up to greet Ethan with a kiss. "I thought you were going to check out the new office space with Bailey."

"The realtor had to bail," Ethan explained.

"I can make you an omelet or something if you're hungry," Brooke said. "We ate already."

"I had a sandwich at the office. I'm okay."

Jack got up and said to Brooke, "We'll finish this conversation another time."

Ethan sensed his irritation and joked, "If I'm interrupting, I can come back later—"

"He always does this," Jack said, as if Ethan wasn't there. "Whenever we're about to have a birthday, he snoops around."

"He is a bloody stalker," Brooke teased. "Maybe your next start-up will be called Snoop Around, for people who just need to know. It'll be huge!"

She had ribbed Ethan about privacy issues from the day he told her what he did, and often asked him to be cognizant about all the negative ways a tracking application could be misused.

Ethan felt tickled by their surreptitious birthday plans and always enjoyed their humor together, even when they ganged up on him. "When you walk in on people and they say, 'Speak of the devil,'" he teased back, "it begs the question: pray tell, what were you two talking about?"

"You're impossible," Brooke swatted him playfully, "and don't give me the third degree. I'm not talking, not until your birthday, *Comprenez vous?*"

Jack chimed in. "She wanted gift ideas so I told her how badly you want the newest Transformer action figures. You could keep it on the mantel next to the Dancing Rabbit statue."

The Dancing Rabbit statue was a running joke with the twins. Brooke had given it to them after their corporate retreat to remind them of the importance of mindfulness and transformation. They both thought it was a kitschy eyesore, but kept it above their fireplace in their living room, so they wouldn't offend her.

Ethan played along, "I see my brother's still asking people to buy gifts for me that he wants. Don't they call those 'squirrel gifts'?" Jack kissed Brooke on the cheek and then headed for his room. "G'night, kids."

Ethan pulled Brooke down to the couch and wrapped his arms around her. "Alone at last."

"Since we're on the subject of the big three-oh, maybe you can weigh in on how you would like to celebrate. I don't want to disappoint you."

"Seriously," Ethan said, "it's not a big deal to me. Don't go overboard."

"Your brother said you would say that."

"Really."

"And that if I don't meet expectations, you'll pout for a week or so."

Ethan laughed, "You just helped me decide what I'm getting him for the big day: a muzzle."

"You're not going to give me any hints about what you want?"

"Surprise me."

"Okay, I will."

Ethan smirked.

She pulled away and smacked his shoulder. "You don't think I can, do you?"

Ethan laughed. "You wear your heart on your sleeve, and so does my brother. One of you will slip."

She headed upstairs with a cunning grin. "We'll see about that."

———

AT THE TIME, ETHAN didn't think it was inappropriate. It seemed like an innocent exchange, but as he stared out at the open road, he wondered if he had walked in on a more insidious conversation that evening, if the discussion about his birthday celebration had just been a cover for what they were really discussing—possibly their feelings for each other, a sordid affair, and their departure. Ethan glanced at his Stalker settings to see if there were any results yet. He hoped the high gear, balls out, by-any-means-necessary mode would help him learn the truth, as he intended the app to do when he created the company. But another question nagged at him now that he was using Stalker as a client:

Will the truth really set me free?

CHAPTER 14

E THAN SEARCHED FOR THE exit off Highway 29, and as he came to the top of the hill, he looked down on his first glimpse of Napa Valley, a panoramic view of the exquisite countryside; filtered light through coral and carmine fall frondescence streamed across the land like gentle brushstrokes—visual eye candy that explained one of the reasons Brooke likely couldn't get Napa out of her head.

He drove past rolling wineries, Trunbull, Peju, Grgich Hills and through Yountville, a gorgeous town peppered with artisan shops, Michelin-starred restaurants, wine-tasting inns, farmers' markets— every angle a spectacular vantage. He wished that he could have experienced it with Brooke, at least for a visit. She had wanted to. He'd kept putting it off, too busy with Stalker, always afraid he would miss out on something if he didn't keep his eye on the ball, and ironically, he seemed to have missed the most important thing of all.

A winding road led up to St. Francis Church. The parking lot was nearly full. Ethan found a space in the last row and headed for the large glass doors that led into the chapel. Butterflies in his belly fluttered, anticipating the train wreck he was about to walk into. He imagined seeing Brooke at the altar with his brother, both preparing to say "I do" to a lifetime of love, looking up as he pounded on the glass windows, like Dustin Hoffman did at the end of *The Graduate*. He and Brooke would escape together on a yellow bus, leaving everyone behind as they headed into the unknown.

Then he slapped his face to prepare for reality; "Come what may," as Brooke would so often say.

He went inside the church and followed a long hallway leading to the sanctuary. He could see through the large glass doors that it was a full house. He took a deep breath and went inside. Several people glanced back at him. The morning light through stained glass windows above the altar beamed colorful rays over Father Oliver, an impassioned priest with an arresting shock of white hair, expressive hands, and a heavy Parisian accent; a master French showman performing.

But he was not performing a wedding.

It was a Sunday morning service and the priest was in the midst of a fiery sermon. "'And the Lord said, two nations are in thy womb; two people from within you shall be separated; and the one people shall be stronger than the other; and the elder shall serve the younger…'"

Ethan moved down the aisle and spotted a seat near the front. The priest paused as Ethan slid into a pew, then continued, "The passage in Genesis twenty-five: twenty-six begins with Jacob seemingly trying to pull Esau back into their mother's womb. The grasping of the heel is a reference to deceptive behavior. Esau was the first to be born with Jacob following, holding his heel, pulling him down. Jacob was the second son, and we think of him as a headstrong person who acts impulsively without sufficient thought…"

Ethan's mind drifted. Hearing Father Oliver run on about biblical twins only made Ethan feel bad about assuming the worst about his brother before knowing the truth. He felt guilty about living with blinders, letting so much resentment build up. He missed Jack terribly just then.

When the service was over, Ethan waited near the back door until Father Oliver finished greeting his congregation. Then he approached.

"I'm in from out of town, and I came as soon as I could. What time will the wedding start?"

"What wedding is that, son?"

"Brooke Shaw's wedding. She didn't give me a time."

"Brooke Shaw?" The priest's ruddy skin blushed a redder hue. Ethan thought it was because the man did not have a poker face, didn't want to lie, or he was afraid of something, perhaps being unable to keep a secret, or worse. Ethan noticed him glance at the exit. There was a large man with a shaved head and tattoos running down his arms standing in the doorway watching them, and it made the priest even more uneasy. "I'm sorry," the priest told Ethan, "but you're a day late. She got married last evening."

Disappointment engulfed him, and it must have shown on his face.

"Come with me," the priest said. "Let us have a little chat in private."

Ethan followed him back down the long hallway. Neither said a word until they entered a large study with overstuffed bookshelves on two walls, and floor-to-ceiling windows behind a cluttered desk.

"Have a seat." Father Oliver gestured to two French leather club chairs.

Ethan's eyes were drawn to the windows behind the desk, and he was awestruck. It was unmistakably the view that Brooke so often painted beyond the cathedral: the castle-like estate surrounded by tall Cypress Pines, an equestrian ranch and vineyard in the distance. Brooke must have wanted him to come there, the reason she had left her paintings in his bedroom.

But why?

"Is this where they got married?" Ethan asked the priest, his voice unable to hide his reverence.

"Out there, under the big oak tree," Father Oliver confirmed. "It was a lovely sunset, just beautiful."

At least her fairytale came true.

"I must have misinterpreted the invitation," Ethan said as his imagination ran wild again, envisioning everyone he knew being there, the entire Stalker staff cheering them on, throwing rice, as Brooke and Jack tucked into a Bentley chauffeured by Bailey. "Were there a lot of guests?"

"It was a private ceremony," the priest told him.

"How private?"

The priest peeked over his bifocals with a curious grin. "How did you say you knew her?"

"I didn't."

Father Oliver waited for him to elaborate.

"She was my girlfriend," Ethan finally confessed.

"I thought as much," the priest said. "She made her choice, son. Sometimes acceptance is our only option."

"I realize that. I just...I need to know who the groom is. Just tell me, please...did he look like me?"

"That's a strange question."

"I'm a twin," Ethan explained. "An identical twin."

"The betrayal you are imagining..." the priest shook his head wittingly. "She didn't marry your brother."

Ethan stared back, unconvinced.

"I can see that you won't be at peace until you know for certain," the priest said, "so hopefully this will put your mind at ease." The priest pulled a Samsung Galaxy from his pocket, opened up a photo, and turned it to show Ethan. The groom, Benjamin Carver, or whoever the man in the picture really was, was a thirty-five-year-old clean-cut man wearing a navy suit and an awkward grimace, a smile for the camera almost as forced as Brooke's.

The blood rushed back to Ethan's face. At least the groom was not Jack.

"I can understand the betrayal you must have imagined," Father Oliver said. "I know a little something about twins. If you were listening, my sermon was about the most famous twins..." He looked up and pointed at a painting above Ethan's head, of Jacob's dream, a ladder ascending to heaven, and he smiled. "You can now heal the wounds between you and your brother, perhaps?"

"I really started to believe he ran off with her..." Ethan grabbed the priest's phone as if it were part of his exuberance. "But it was this guy, huh?"

Ethan expanded the photo so he could get a better look at the bride and groom. Their arms were all pointing straight at the ground, stiff—body language that told Ethan they weren't really together, definitely not in the way he and Brooke had been. He and Brooke would be touching, connected somehow. This picture showed no affection. No connection. Brooke looked stunning, as always, but she was wearing a simple white dress that Ethan had seen her wear at least twice before. And she wouldn't have worn an old dress for a new marriage. Ethan concluded that she rushed to marry this guy like her life depended on it.

"I hope this settles your mind, son," Father Oliver said as he held out his hand so Ethan would give his phone back.

Ethan dipped the phone under the desk, as if he were taking one last look, and swiftly texted the picture to himself, without the priest noticing. Then he rendered a hollow smile and handed the phone back. "Thank you for showing me. I'm truly relieved."

"But not completely," the priest said.

"It shows, huh?"

"You loved her."

"I still do," Ethan admitted. "And since you've known her since she was a child, you could understand why."

There was an awkward silence. Ethan knew the priest was his best window into her past. He also knew that the man wasn't going to betray Brooke's trust.

"I know that her family came up here for many years," Ethan said, hoping to get him talking. "She told me she hoped to get married here one day."

The priest just nodded.

"She never told me, though, why she had changed her name to Brooke Shaw—"

The priest looked away, and his ruddy skin glowed as red as it did when he first mentioned her name.

"Please, for her sake," Ethan pleaded, "tell me who she was."

The priest's voice dipped. "I can tell you this: She's had a lot of loss in her life. She deserves this chance to start over. To be happy."

"I know that she lost both of her parents in a short time. She told me that she wanted a fresh start, but that couldn't be the reason she changed her name."

"I'm sure she had good reason and we do need to respect her decision."

"The way she left makes me think that she's running from something, or someone...that maybe she's in some kind of trouble."

Ethan could see that Father Oliver didn't like being in this position. He was hiding something. He likely knew that Brooke was in some kind of danger, too, but he wasn't going to breach her trust.

Ethan tried one more angle. "Can you tell me anything about the guy she married?"

"I just met him yesterday."

Ethan shook his head, showing his concern. "That's what I was afraid of."

"He seemed like a nice fellow."

"They always do," Ethan said as he stood up and started to walk out. "Thank you for your time." Ethan stopped in the doorway and turned back. "Who was the man with tattoos, in the sanctuary?"

The priest didn't answer.

Ethan tried again. "There was a big guy with a shaved head and tattoos running down his arms standing in the doorway watching us. When he looked at us, you suggested that we talk in private."

"I don't know..." the priest hesitated, and then continued, "He approached me before the service and also asked questions about her—"

"What kind of questions?"

"He wanted to know where she went after the wedding, where he could find her."

"What did you tell him?"

"I told him that I didn't know, because I don't."

Ethan thanked him and walked out of the church, now more certain that she was running from something terrible, something she couldn't tell anyone about, even her priest.

Ethan needed to find her.

He walked into the blaring late-morning sunshine and headed back to his car. On one level, he was relieved that Jack had not run off with Brooke. But he also felt more ashamed for even considering such a betrayal. He needed to apologize, and more than ever, he really wanted his brother's help. He got into his Tesla, drove out of the parking lot, and grabbed his phone to call Jack again.

In his rearview mirror, he noticed the tattooed man with the shaved head climbing into a banged-up Dodge Grand Caravan and possibly following after him.

CHAPTER 15

Jack sat up in bed feeling like he'd descended into hell; disheveled, disoriented, surrounded by scattered clothes, two empty bottles of Far Niente Oakville Napa (a vibrant Cabernet), leftovers from a romantic La Fusion dinner (a Latin American restaurant in the Financial District he'd had delivered via GrubHub app), and a few indiscretions carelessly left behind in the throes of passion.

He took it all in with a smile. His new life had promise. Then his iPhone lit up and his brother's cheerful photo popped up with caller ID. Jack was in no mood and considered letting his voicemail pick up. Then he heard his shower go on. His lovely houseguest would be awhile. A perfect time to tell Ethan that he needed space. He picked up and sounded annoyed, "Kind of early for a Sunday morning—"

"Where the hell have you been?" Ethan started.

"Are you my parole officer?" Jack hissed. "I'm in bed and I'm hung way over. Where are you?"

"Church."

Jack laughed. The ice had been broken. He missed his brother, too, and he was tired of feeling angry.

"I tried calling you last night," Ethan said. "I left a detailed message."

Jack glanced his unheard messages count. "I shut my phone off."

"I figured. Want to know why I'm at a church?"

"You converted?"

"Brooke got married—"

"What?" Jack rubbed his throbbing head, realizing his brother was serious, and seriously distraught. He softened. "Tell me what's going on."

Ethan explained everything that had transpired since Jack left Stalker: how he came home to Brooke's Dear John letter, how Bailey and Emily found out that she had been using a fake name, how the Face Match Mode feature found out that she was marrying a man named Benjamin Carver—who was also using a false identity—and about the conversation he'd just had with Father Oliver at the church in Napa Valley.

Jack interrupted as he rubbed his aching temples and sat up. "I need to process all of this."

Ethan waited a beat and then asked, "So you had no idea she was thinking about this…leaving me?"

"Of course not," Jack snapped back. "I called her to say goodbye when my movers came last week. I left her a message but she never called me back."

Ethan merged onto the highway and glanced back at the van in his rearview. The banged up Dodge Grand Caravan was behind him. The big tattooed guy was driving, and there were at least two others with him. Ethan told Jack, "I think I'm being followed."

"You think you're being followed?"

"I noticed this guy at the church watching me," Ethan explained. "He was wearing a wifebeater and his arms were completely covered in tattoos. Not the churchgoing type. The priest told me that this guy had approached him earlier, asking questions about Brooke. Now I'm on the freeway—"

"Slow down," Jack told him. "See if he passes."

Ethan moved over to the right lane. The van followed. "He's still there."

Jack asked, "How's the charge on your Tesla?"

Ethan checked the dashboard. "Low. Maybe I can squeeze fifty miles."

Jack thought his brother was crazy to get a car that needed to be charged, as well as one that he couldn't really afford until Stalker was in the black. "I told you that you were being ridiculous when you got that overpriced toy."

"I wanted to express my commitment to the environment."

"And to Brooke," Jack said.

"I also wanted to show my commitment to Stalker, that I had faith in its success," Ethan said, as if that were the most noble excuse.

"Overly optimistic as always," Jack said, realizing he had a smile on his face. They had been through this rigamarole many times and he'd missed their banter.

"I don't see the van anymore," Ethan said as he checked all his mirrors. "Maybe they took the last exit."

"Okay good."

Ethan said, "Wouldn't it be cool to make an app that would combine GPS tracking with sensors that calculated cars keeping a similar distance for consistent times that would warn you that you're being followed?"

Jack laughed. "The only customers for that feature would be criminals."

"Good point."

Jack could tell that his brother was rattled. He loved to brainstorm new ideas whenever he was on edge, his way of funneling nervous energy. "Tell me about this guy Brooke ran off with," Jack said. "You think he's an old boyfriend?"

"I have no idea...I thought she ran off with you at first—"

"That she ran off with me?" Jack laughed harder. "You're an idiot."

"I know, I know, and I owe you a big apology. I used the Likability Mode, and when I saw that the last time you used your credit card was almost a week ago near Big Sur, I thought you were hiding with her in Dancing Rabbit."

"I haven't used that credit card since then because Hounddog gave me a new one."

"Of course they did," Ethan said. "That's how the Wizard of Silicon lured you—"

"You thought I would betray you like that?"

"I did," Ethan confessed. "I'm sorry. I know you would never—"

"I would," Jack teased. "She's just not my type."

"I'm starting to think you don't have a type."

"What you don't know is a lot." Jack looked around the room at the scattered clothes and remnants of the night. "Still no sign of the van?"

Ethan glanced in his mirrors again. "I don't see them."

"Okay, I'm leaving my phone on. When we hang up, use the Stalker Phone Tracker to get to my new pad. My next-door neighbor has a Tesla. I'll ask him if you could plug into his charger. We'll sort this all out when you get here."

Stalker's Phone Tracker took the GPS signal from the most recent phone call and Siri navigated directions. The feature, however, didn't have the ability to know whether or not you're still being followed by a dark van with three tattooed, contracted thugs.

And neither did Ethan.

After they hung up, a blow dryer went on in Jack's bathroom, which reminded him that he didn't have much time. Ethan would be there in less than an hour. So Jack jumped out of bed and shouted through the bathroom door, "My brother's on his way over. You'll have to get going."

The blow dryer shut off and his houseguest asked, half joking, "You want me to leave through the back door or something?"

"If you don't mind," Jack said, dead serious. "We can't risk anyone seeing us together yet."

CHAPTER 16

Jack got dressed, straightened up, and prepared for his brother's arrival. He could only imagine what Ethan had been going through that past week with him leaving their business, moving away to work for Stalker's biggest competitor, and the love of his life running off and getting married—all without warning.

Jack now felt worse about the way he left. Releasing all his pent up anger toward Ethan was his way to minimize his own guilt; something he was aware of, but not proud of.

Jack hadn't made his decision to leave lightly, and he wished that he could explain all the real reasons he ultimately decided to go, but he also feared that Ethan wasn't ready to hear the truth, nor was he ready to tell him. Ethan always had the same expectations for Jack as he had for himself, as if they were the same person. Jack assumed it was a twin thing, and maybe it was, but it was also wrong.

Stalker was really Ethan's vision—his concept, his baby. Brooke was Ethan's girl—his affection, his love. Santa Monica was Ethan's style—his refuge, his culture. Even the home they lived in— their bungalow—and the office they worked in—the Third Street playhouse—was oozing Ethan.

Jack wasn't jealous of Ethan. He wanted his brother's dreams to be realized. But living under the shadow of an ambitious, charismatic optimist meant that his own dreams were always suppressed.

Jack was primarily a programmer—tech oriented, introverted, and antisocial—and everyone assumed that he was all function and no form. But that wasn't the case. He had another side that cared deeply about design and aesthetics. He wanted to live an honest expression of who he really was and this desire was growing stronger. He felt that he needed to separate from his brother on all levels so he could be seen, so he could be real. If Ethan was Silicon Beach, Jack needed to become Silicon Valley. If Ethan were a Stalker, Jack would become a Hounddog.

Fire and rain; black and white; chalk and cheese.

And the Wizard of Silicon Valley made all that possible. Sean McQueen was so successful in part because he knew how to listen to the needs of the people he brought into his fold. When Jack met McQueen, he was able to be who he wanted to be; he felt heard; he felt known.

The Hounddog Human Resources team used technology to make Jack's transition easy and his home a true expression of who he was. They accumulated information from his search engines and purchase history. An algorithm assessed the data and linked to hundreds of items from around the globe, everything from types of neighborhoods to homes, furniture to clothes, restaurants to types of entertainment. They asked Jack to rate the pictures on a scale from one to ten, and then they analyzed all his preferences and made an environment that would best suit him.

And then they got busy.

They leased a Gothic-style Victorian in The Haight—an iconic eclectic community on a great walking street with exclusive boutiques, high-end vintage shops, hip cafés and restaurants—and decorated the home to Jack's style. There was nothing they put inside that Jack didn't love. They placed every knickknack, based on his Taste app; filled his refrigerator, based on his Table app; set up playlists, based on his iTunes app, filled his bookshelves, based on his Kindle app; lined his closet, based on his BuyVia app; stocked his wet bar with top-shelf vodka, based on him telling them that he loved vodka.

Jack was immediately transported into his new life, just the way he wanted it, and he didn't have to share it with his twin brother like he had with almost everything else in their interdependent lives. Ethan was about to see a different side of him and he hoped his brother would appreciate it. That would be a good start. Jack was the brother who never cared what other people thought of him. But for some reason, he cared very much about his twin brother's opinion.

The irony didn't escape Jack. That's what Brooke would call a "twin paradox."

Brooke taught Jack a lot about being a twin.

Jack wanted his brother to walk into a delicious aromatic feast and truly appreciate the full effect of his new home, and the new him, so he began to prepare a delicious breakfast. He went all out and whipped up his hangover special: broccoli, tomato, and cheddar omelet, hash browns, turkey bacon, fresh-squeezed juice, and fresh-brewed coffee. Cooking had always relaxed Jack, especially when he was hungry or anxious or drifting into his default setting of self-doubt.

As he navigated his new kitchen, his mind wondered back to the recent confrontation he'd had with Ethan, just a few weeks back. He and his brother were enjoying a couple of bottles of Eagle Rock, a local beer, on their small grass-patch backyard. Brooke was in the kitchen and the twins could see her pass back and forth across the window, radiant and graceful even in her domestic duties.

———

ETHAN SAID, "I REALLY love her, you know."

Jack grunted, "Uh-huh."

"She's amazing."

"She is that."

"And you two spend a lot of time together."

"We do," Jack agreed, knowing his brother was prodding him. "What's your point?"

"You know she and I are getting serious, so I want to know your opinion. You have an opinion on everything else, so I'm asking—"

Jack had spent so much time with Brooke and he trusted her implicitly. He told her things he couldn't tell his brother. And Ethan didn't like it. "I think she's a huge improvement from the girls you've dated," Jack snapped, "probably better than you deserve. If you're trying to make a point, make it."

Ethan stayed calm. "You've been telling her a lot of things lately that aren't really appropriate."

Jack felt the blood rise to his face. Ethan was staring at him, as if he were waiting for a confession. "Like what?" Jack asked, hoping, praying that she didn't tell him anything he wasn't prepared for him to know.

Ethan's chest puffed out like he did when he had been holding something in and was about to explode. "She said that you told her about Barry."

Jack was relieved it was just that.

He could trust her. Of course he could.

"I did tell her about Barry," Jack admitted.

"Don't you think that's something I should have told her about?"

"Then why didn't you?"

"We just hadn't gotten to it yet."

"If it was so important to you, then you would have said something."

"Barry was my friend, too," Ethan said.

"I had a different relationship with him."

"It's not a competition."

"I didn't know you owned the rights to that loss," Jack sighed. "Am I supposed to filter what I discuss with her, or do I need your permission—?"

"Just stop telling her all this personal shit. She's my girlfriend."

"You sound jealous."

"I'm not...You're inappropriate."

Their insults overlapped from there, a cacophony of built up rage.

Jack: "You're judgmental. Egocentric. Entitled."

Ethan: "Sneaky. Secretive. Ungrateful..."

"Ungrateful" was his code word for "you would be nothing without me" in Jack's mind, and it made him furious.

But Ethan was first to get physical. He shoved Jack. Jack shoved back. It escalated into a flurry of jabs, and ended in a pointless wrestling bout on the grass-patch, until Brooke opened the kitchen window and shouted at them to stop their nonsense.

They helped each other up, both laughing like twelve-year-olds. But they both knew on some level that they were growing apart, or at the very least, ready to enter a new phase of their twin-hood.

—

THE THOUGHT OF THAT fight weighed heavily on Jack now. He still had a deep secret that he wasn't prepared to tell his brother. He was painfully aware that he couldn't have an honest relationship with that burden. It was the primary reason he had to leave Santa Monica. Now his brother was coming to him, desperate, in the dark, and in need of his help. Jack decided that he would just focus on that.

For now.

He checked the Stalker app. It told him that Ethan was very close. He felt a rush of anxiety, the pit-in-the-stomach kind. He wondered how much longer he could keep the truth from his brother.

And then his doorbell rang.

CHAPTER 17

E THAN WALKED FROM ROOM to room truly impressed. "Looks like you've been living here for years."

"I know, right?" Jack agreed, following behind. "They really know how to take care of their people."

"It helps if you're financed by tech-genius billionaire Sean McQueen," Ethan said.

Jack grinned. "Now, now."

It was immediately obvious to Ethan that Jack was proud of his new life and wanted his approval. He also knew there was no point in making Jack feel bad about his decision to leave Stalker. Ethan remembered feeling relieved when Jack told him he was moving out because he and Brooke could start their lives, alone. Now that Brooke was gone, the tides had shifted for Ethan, but it didn't change the fact that his brother was ready to venture out on his own, and it was for the best. It was time.

After they looped back to the kitchen, Jack made two perfect cappuccinos with his shiny new Keurig coffee machine and they sat down to discuss Brooke. Ethan filled Jack in on the sequence of events since she left: details about the note and paintings she left behind, what the Stalker app had shown so far—the false profiles of Brooke and her new husband, Benjamin Carver—and all his concerns.

Jack got up and paced, the way he did whenever he was revving up to problem solve, stopping only for sips of coffee, and then he began: "The love of your life just left—without any explanation—and married some random guy, right?"

"Right."

"Both of them are using false identities. She told you not to search for her but you think she did that because she's in danger and didn't want to drag you into the fray."

"That about sums it up," Ethan said. "Your assessment, my dear Watson?"

Jack turned to his brother and looked bewildered. "It takes time to really know someone."

"I know," Ethan admitted. "Bailey read me the same riot act, that I didn't know anything about her. And you guys are right. I don't know why she left. I don't know whom she married. I'm completely in the dark. But I don't think I was blind. I know what we had was real—"

"You don't have to convince me," Jack said. "I know how you felt about each other. If you think she's in trouble, then she probably is. What can I do to help?"

Ethan searched his iPhone photo library. "You said that Hounddog's face recognition software works really well, that it's further along than ours."

"They call it their PI function. It's still in beta but it has more range, more databases—"

"Well, I have this picture." Ethan showed Jack the photo of Brooke and the man using Benjamin Carver's alias getting married.

Jack grabbed the phone, pinched the picture to blow it up, and his eyebrows raised. "Wow."

"What?"

"He's a lot better-looking than we are."

Ethan laughed. "You're a dick."

Jack texted the photo to his own phone. "I'll run the picture at Hounddog."

Ethan jumped up. "Awesome, I'll get ready—"

"You can't come with me, though. Authorized personnel only."

"Seriously?"

"Seriously."

"You want me to just wait here?"

Jack tossed him a dishrag and said, "No. I want you to clean up the kitchen. And yourself."

Ethan's car needed to recharge, and so did he.

"Make yourself at home," Jack said as he walked out. "I'll call if I get a match."

———

THE DARK GRAND CARAVAN was parked on the corner of Market Street. The three men inside all had shaved heads and bulky prison weight-lifting bodies. Ace, the driver, was a relentless bounty hunter who rarely needed any help. He brought the other two along because his employer wanted every guarantee that the target, a thirty-year-old English woman using the name Brooke Shaw, was found. Ace didn't know how much ground they would have to cover or how much muscle they'd need to use, so he took the extra precaution. Wade Franks and Dale Norton were cramped in the back where the seats had been removed. They knew each other from the California Department of Corrections and Rehabilitation state prison for men and were used to sharing small spaces.

Ace had wanted to nab the target at the church in Napa and get the job over with, but Brooke was already gone when they arrived earlier that morning. Ace had to find another lead. When Ethan showed up at the church looking for Brooke, he became that lead. Ace called in Ethan's license plate and learned Ethan's home address and place of business in Santa Monica. A few phone inquiries proved that Ethan had been involved with Brooke. And just by observing the way Ethan had rushed in and out of the church, Ace knew that Ethan was desperate to find her. What Ace didn't know was that Ethan had an identical twin. So when Jack—the clean-shaven brother—walked out of the house and headed for a Prius parked on the street, Ace assumed that Ethan had used this place as a second hideaway, shaved, cut his hair, changed into different clothes, and switched cars, all so he wouldn't be identified.

Now Jack was their lead.

"Should we take him now?" Wade asked, gripping the Glock 19 tucked into his pants.

"Not yet," Ace said. "Let's see where he's going. Hopefully, he'll take us right to her."

"What if he doesn't?" Dale asked.

"Then we make him talk."

"What if he doesn't talk?" Wade asked.

"Then we turn to Plan B, which is never easy, always violent, and sometimes deadly."

Wade and Dale smiled at each other.

Ace watched Jack start the Prius and inch out of his parking spot.

"Let the fun begin," Ace said as he pulled out and followed after him.

———

HOUNDDOG WAS BASED IN a nondescript office complex. The parking lot was always busy, even on Sunday, but Jack found a place to park close to the lobby and ventured inside. Even after a week of navigating Hounddog's security protocol, entering the office was nerve-racking, especially knowing that he wasn't there to conduct official Hounddog business. They took their security even more seriously than Stalker, which was probably overkill—biometrics designed by biometric developers. Jack was well aware of the reasons: state-of-the-art surveillance, employee vetting, and extreme caution were a necessity to prevent leaks, fraud, theft, and deception. When he was at Stalker he had to keep his eyes on everyone; now he was being watched.

Jack fumbled for his access code and then put his eye up to the retina display for a scan. If that weren't enough, a robotic voice asked him to place his thumb on the print detector plate that shot out of the wall, inviting Jack to sacrifice his thumb.

Jack put his thumb inside, turned to the guard standing by, and joked, "If I choose to take this mission—"

The guard laughed heartily. The door released, and Jack went inside.

The Hounddog office had an open floor plan just like the Stalker space that Ethan had designed, but twice the size. Many of the employees were there, working away as if they didn't know it was the weekend, or that a world existed outside of their computers. The tech culture seemed to be the same here as in Santa Monica, mostly hardworking grown adults dressed like sixteen-year-olds crunched over their computer keyboards. And if any of these Hounddogs were aware of Jack as he made his way across the room, none bothered to say hello—which was also typical of programmers. Jack wasn't offended. He took this job to get away from managing socially and emotionally challenged techies (like himself), and for love. And he didn't want to draw any unnecessary attention just yet. He was there to help his brother search for a missing person with software that was not yet approved for their site, something Hounddog employees were sworn not to do. Like Ethan, Jack justified the discretion in the name of Brooke's safety.

Jack found an empty terminal toward the back of the room. He fired up the computer and prepared to use the PI Mode, Hounddog's face recognition feature. Sean McQueen had told Jack about it when he was interviewing, but he hadn't yet had the chance to see how it worked for himself. So he input the wedding photo of Brooke and Benjamin and gave it a whirl.

An animated hound dog came on screen and started sniffing around. Right from the start, Jack loved the Hounddog platform. It had basically the same foundation as Stalker's, but it was more user-friendly and fun. It fascinated Jack how people working on the same idea at the same time with the same resources could come up with completely different results.

Just like twins.

Jack watched the numbers and colors blink on the computer screen as it searched hundreds of random data banks throughout the country, even internationally. He figured it could take an hour or so to process, but just when he got up to grab a cup of coffee, the animated hound dog barked at him, and the screen blinked a match.

It took less than a minute.

The first match paired the wedding photo to the pictures they took when they each applied for driver's licenses and then their marriage license. The county databases listed vital statistics of Brooke Shaw and Benjamin Carver.

Jack was impressed.

The hound dog barked again. There was another match. It came in a folder with a Hounddog logo. Jack opened it up and gasped, "Holy shit."

Other programmers looked over, as if Jack were a freak playing a Vegas slot machine spewing coins. It certainly didn't justify any of them to pull away from whatever they were working on and introduce themselves to the new guy.

That was just fine with Jack since he didn't want any of them to see that he just figured out who was using Benjamin Carver's identity, especially since all of them would all know who that man was.

CHAPTER 18

JACK CALLED HIS BROTHER. Ethan didn't pick up until four or five rings, and when he did, he was laughing.

"What's so funny?" Jack asked.

"I was just taking a shower. I had soap in my eyes. When I reached for my phone, I grabbed a pair of racy red underwear with an embroidered S&M logo. Is that the official brand of San Francisco now? Did S&M replace Fruit of the Loom? When did you get so kinky?"

"That might be funny if we were eight," Jack said, annoyed. "Do you want to hear what I found or not?"

"You got a match? Already?" Ethan wrapped a towel around his waist, stepped out of the bathroom, and dropped his voice an octave. "I'm sorry. Go ahead. Tell me."

"Benjamin Carver was an employee here."

"What?!"

"He worked at Hounddog. Until recently. He put in his resignation almost two months ago. His last day was a week ago."

Ethan took a moment to let it sink in. "Brooke married a guy from Hounddog? How is that possible?"

"I don't know. But he was a lead programmer and had been with the company since they opened their doors. There's a good chance they hired me to replace him."

"He was a lead programmer?"

"And a polygamist," Jack said. "He was already married."

"Seriously?"

"I'm reading from his file. His wife's name is Sarah. They live in Palo Alto. No kids."

"He was already married," Ethan repeated. "Do you think he's living a double life?"

"Could be."

"What's his real name?"

"Rufus Wall."

It took Ethan a bit to realize why the name was familiar, and then he blurted, "Rufus Wall is dead."

Jack scrolled down Rufus Wall's file. There was nothing about the former Hounddog employee dying. "Not according to this—"

Ethan cut him off, "Remember when I told you that I stopped at Dancing Rabbit?"

"Yeah. The old hippie zapped you."

"Right. After I left, I headed up north," Ethan explained, "and I saw that a car had gone off the side of Highway 1, where the road winds like a snake and there's a hundred-foot drop down to the ocean below. I had a really bad feeling, so I pulled over. I thought the worst, that it was you or Brooke, or you and Brooke—"

"I get it, your imagination went wild."

"They were bringing up a car," Ethan continued. "I told the police that I was concerned. They showed me two suitcases they had already found. One of the cases had a name tag."

"Rufus Wall?"

"Yep. With a Palo Alta address."

"The second suitcase didn't have a tag but I know whose it was. Remember Brooke's roommate, Anna?"

"Her roommate?"

"Yeah."

"Hang on, I'll check the local news sources...." Jack ran a quick search and found a press release from the *Big Sur News*. "The car they brought up was a red Mini Cooper, belonged to Anna Delaney Gopnik."

"Bingo."

"Says they are still searching for bodies."

"The cops said something really odd," Ethan remembered. "When I told them that I knew Anna from Dancing Rabbit, they seemed rattled, and said there had been a lot of missing people that have some connection to the resort. One of the detectives called it 'the rabbit hole' and asked me if I'd noticed anything strange when I was there."

"'The rabbit hole'?"

"What if the Dancing Rabbit people are all using false identities like Brooke? What if Rufus Wall left Hounddog, faked his death, used Benjamin Carver's name, and then married Brooke—?"

Jack cut his brother off, "Why would they be going to all that trouble?"

"I don't know."

"I think your imagination is going wild again. Sounds like a stretch."

One of the Hounddog programmers came from behind and asked Jack, "Going to be long? I need to print."

Jack quit out of the program using a short keystroke before he spun around. "All yours. I'm through, actually."

Jack walked away and crossed the room. "I shouldn't have this discussion here," he told Ethan. "Call you back when I get outside."

———

ETHAN FINISHED DRYING OFF, got dressed, and ran down to the kitchen to run a search of Rufus Wall on Jack's laptop. He found a short Wikipedia page listing an impressive programmer résumé: educated at MIT, started at Intel, a long stint at Microsoft, helped Amazon develop their analytics, headed up Tinder, and then moved on to Hounddog.

Ethan's phone rang and he picked up quickly. "How would Brooke know a guy from Hounddog?" he asked Jack again. "Don't you think that's really weird?"

Jack waited for his eyes to adjust from the fluorescents to the bright sunlight in the parking lot. "She had a life before you," Jack reminded him.

"I'm not buying that. Too random that she would marry a guy from our competition. And besides, her life before me was in London."

"Wasn't she in Big Sur for about a year before you met her? And didn't she run the retreats for tech companies? Maybe it's not that random."

"She hated the tech business. She was trying to get tech people back down to earth, away from their devices. She once told me that one in ten American adults confess that they check their emails when they're having sex, to make the point. She wanted to simplify our lives. Unplug. She hated what we do—"

"Not true," Jack told him as he moved past the guard in the lobby, "she didn't hate the tech biz at all. She's the reason I moved up here."

"Brooke was the reason you what—?"

"She introduced me to the guy who hired me," Jack confessed.

"Why would she do that?"

"She knew I wasn't happy," Jack explained. "She was trying to help me."

"She was trying to help you?" Ethan repeated.

Jack sensed Ethan's anger growing and added, "But her leaving you had nothing to do with that."

"You sure about that?"

"I promise you," Jack told him. "Look, I like Brooke. A lot. I know that she loved you. God knows why." Jack laughed, without his brother joining in, and then he turned serious again. "She's not the type to run off with an old boyfriend on a whim. I agree with you that she must be in some kind of trouble. I had no idea she was using someone else's name and I can't imagine why she married a guy from Hounddog. None of this behavior is like her. But if she's going through all this trouble to disappear, I just don't know what else we can do—"

"We can start by finding out more about the guy from Hounddog," Ethan said. "Is there someone there you can talk to about him?"

"It's my first week, for Christ's sake—"

Ethan pressed. "Someone who knows what's really going on in that place?"

"Yeah…" Jack hesitated, and then told Ethan, "there's someone I can talk to—"

"Today? On a Sunday?"

"Yeah, yeah. I'll let you know what I find out."

"Great. Thank you. I'm going to take a drive to Palo Alto, visit Rufus Wall's wife, find out what she knows—or thinks—happened to her husband."

Jack said, "The police would have notified her about the possibility of her husband going over a cliff by now, don't you think? She might be a wreck."

Ethan grabbed his car keys and headed for the door. "Unless she's in on it."

———

JACK LEFT HOUNDDOG, GOT into his car, and drove out of the parking lot, still completely unaware of the dark van following him. Once on the road, he called the Hounddog that knew the most, the top dog himself.

Sean McQueen picked up on the first ring. "I was just thinking about you," he said.

"We need to talk," Jack told him. "Are you busy?"

"I don't like the sound of that," Sean chuckled. "Cold feet so soon?"

"Nothing like that," Jack assured him. "I'm coming from Hounddog. I need to ask you about an employee."

"Who?"

"We probably shouldn't have this conversation on the phone. Can I come over?"

"Now you're really scaring me," Sean said. "You think your phone is tapped or something?"

"Or yours...I don't know—"

"I have a phone that can detect a trace," he said. "I'll call you right back on a secured line."

At thirty-five, Sean McQueen was one of the most envied entrepreneurs in the valley, and he had his share of enemies as well. He had a reputation for building companies and selling them off as soon as they were overvalued, moving them around like a master chess player, always a few steps ahead, always unpredictable. He also stayed out of the limelight, kept his personal life private, which all added to his mystery and earned him the title "Wizard of Silicon." Truth was, he had invested in his share of now-bankrupt companies, but because he was always operating from "behind the curtain," few people knew he was involved by the time he dumped those dogs.

Players and pundits in the valley were always skeptical because he didn't run with the wolves, didn't gossip, and didn't keep his companies porous. His absence from big tech events and the fact that he was handsome, flamboyant, and wicked smart made him a target of speculation for everything from his motives to his sexuality.

Jack's phone rang seconds later.

"Talk to me," Sean said. "This line's safe."

"What can you tell me about Rufus Wall?"

"What do you want to know?"

"Why did he leave Hounddog?"

"He had another opportunity he wanted to pursue. He didn't tell me what it was, but he gave notice a few months ago. That's why I had time to find you—"

"I found you," Jack reminded him.

Sean laughed. "You know what I mean. Why are you asking about him?"

Jack told him, "He married Brooke yesterday. Brooke Shaw."

"I thought she was seeing your brother—"

"So did he."

"—Can't be the same Rufus Wall," Sean said, "Our Rufus Wall was already married and you can't get a divorce in California that fast—"

"He used the name and social of some vagrant from the sticks," Jack explained. "A man named Benjamin Carver... Hold on, I'll send you a pic to confirm that it's the same dude."

Jack texted the wedding photo.

"That's him," Sean confirmed. "That's definitely Rufus. I guess he did leave to pursue another interest. How's your brother dealing with this?"

"He's worried about her."

"I get that, it is worrisome," Sean agreed. "I like to think I hire well and I always thought Rufus Wall was a really good guy. He was a model employee. He was smart and people liked him."

Jack asked, "Can you access his Hounddog file from your house?"

"I can access anything from my perch. Why do you think I come to the office so rarely?"

"Because you can," Jack said. "I want to hack into his company phone record and email history."

"What? Why?"

"Because I can," Jack said.

Sean laughed.

Jack explained, "His correspondences will tell me where he's been, who he's talked to, and hopefully where he's going. I have to help my brother find out if Brooke is safe or not."

After a beat, Sean said, "If anyone finds out that I let you into his personal file to do that—"

"They won't."

"Promise me no one will ever know."

"I promise," Jack assured him. "I know how to keep a secret."

Sean smiled and sighed, "I can't argue with that."

CHAPTER 19

WITH THE TESLA FULLY charged, Ethan set his Stalker app to guide him to Rufus Wall's Palo Alto address and headed out to see the wife Rufus had left behind.

Once Ethan was on the freeway, he called Bailey to check in. Bailey picked up before the phone rang, as if he were waiting for the call, "So what happened?" Bailey buzzed. "Did you crash the wedding?"

"I was a day late," Ethan told him. "They've done the deed and are long gone."

"Damn."

Ethan filled Bailey in on everything from the church in Napa to how Jack ran the wedding picture through the Hounddog system and learned that Benjamin Carver is former Hounddog employee Rufus Wall.

Bailey didn't seem surprised. "The onion's starting to unravel," Bailey said. "How's Jack doing?"

"He moved into a place that looks like a brothel," Ethan said with a laugh. "I'm telling you, the place had red-velvet-draped windows, clashing dark-colored walls, faux-gold molding trim, and he thinks it's all awesome."

Bailey said, "One man's trash is another man's treasure."

Ethan thought about how proud Jack was to show him his new digs. "It was good for him to move on. He needed something that was just his."

"I'm sorry to see him go," Bailey added, "but you two were going to kill each other if he stayed."

"Was it that obvious?"

"It was a fast descent from the moment we started Stalker. You two never agree on anything anymore."

"I guess people change."

Bailey said, "People don't change, they reveal themselves."

"That's good, Bailey." Ethan paused to think about that. "Is that another Oscar Wilde quote?"

"To tell you the truth, I don't know where I stole that gem."

"Has any of your deep insight and wit come up with anything on Brooke?"

"Not a thing. But we do know that we're not the only ones who have been looking for her," Bailey told him. "Emily found a Stalker account from London that uploaded old pictures of Brooke the day we launched our Face Match Mode—"

"That feature could be used to find missing people," Ethan said, realizing, "even people that have changed their names."

"Exactly," Bailey agreed. "And now this person from London knows she's using the name Brooke Shaw."

"How?"

"When Brooke got a driver's license and filed for the wedding license," Bailey explained, "her photo went into public record databases, right? That's how we learned she was getting married. This Stalker account got the same match."

"Who is he?" Ethan asked. "What's the name on the account?"

"Don't know. Don't even know if it's a 'he' or a 'she' or a 'they.' The account is blocked. Whoever set it up used all our privacy options."

"But they had to use a name to get an account—"

"C. G."

"C. G.?"

"The letters 'C' and 'G.'"

Ethan tried to remember if Brooke had ever mentioned anyone with those initials.

Bailey said, "That's all we have, Gov. CG from London. No idea who it is or why they're looking for her."

"We could bypass the security block," Ethan said. "We have the ability to get this person's details and contact them—"

"You know that's against our client agreement."

"Not to mention against the law," Ethan added. "But it's looking more and more like she's in trouble and we don't have grounds to go to the cops. We have to do whatever it takes."

Ethan heard Emily laugh in the background. "Glad to hear you say that, Gov," Bailey said, "because we already took the 'whatever-it-takes' liberty." Emily grabbed the phone and told Ethan, "There wasn't a phone number or address. But I found the credit card number used to set up the account."

Ethan said, "We can't do anything with a credit card number—"

"Unless we hack it," she said.

Ethan took a deep breath. "So you hacked it?"

"You just said we have to do whatever it takes."

Ethan sighed. "Who is it, Emily? Tell me."

"I have no idea," she said. "The credit card is under a family trust, filed under a tax ID number. That's as far as I got."

"There has to be an address. The mail for the trust must be sent somewhere."

"The mail goes to a house, but the house is owned by the trust, and the trust is in probate. Dead end."

"Where's the house?"

"Four-four-zero-eight Kings Road. I looked it up on Nethousprices. com—England's version of Zillow. It's not on the market but it's worth three-point-three million pounds. Not too shabby, right?"

"I told you she was hiding something from her past," Bailey said as he grabbed the phone back. "Kings Road is in Kensington, by the way."

Ethan remembered Bailey telling him that Brooke had an unmistakable Kensington accent. "I really need you to keep on this," Ethan said. "We have to find out who CG is. At the very least, it'll tell us why she's running."

"There are a lot of people in Kensington with those initials."

"I'm not saying it's going to be easy."

Bailey said, "So you're okay with this 'whatever-it-takes' tact?"

They were all well aware of the criticism their site drew about privacy issues. Brooke had often made Ethan promise to be painstakingly careful about crossing the line. But now he felt that he had no choice. It was a means to an end. "I'll take full responsibility if there are consequences," he told Bailey. "This is about helping someone we care about, who we think is in danger."

"That's quite noble," Bailey teased. "I'm glad that you didn't say you were asking us to break the laws just to help you get your girl back."

Of course, that was what Ethan wanted more than anything, but he told Bailey, "I just want to make sure she's safe."

They hung up and Ethan accelerated, thinking about Emily's theory and Bailey's comments about not knowing the details of Brooke's past. After a few miles, his mind wandered back to a day when he and Brooke had gone to Rustic Canyon, a popular hiking trail on the Westside of LA. He recalled a conversation they'd had when they reached the top of the trail.

—

HE ASKED HER, "Do you ever miss London?"

"I miss some things," she said as she sat down on a rock and looked out at the view of the ocean.

"You don't talk about it much."

"I think people dwell too much on their pasts, things you can't change, and if you're trying to have a future with someone, really, what's the point?"

"Some people think it's important to know everything about the person you plan on having a future with."

"The devil's in the details," she joked. "I'll bet every girl you've ever dated wanted to know every nitty-gritty particular of every other girl you had been with. Am I right?"

Ethan laughed. "Pretty much."

"Did you like it? Did it do any good?"

"Nope."

"And really," she concluded, "what's the point? We're here now. This moment is all there really is, all that matters. And I don't want to ruin it."

"Neither do I," he agreed.

She kissed him long and hard.

"I never met anyone like you in my entire life," he told her as they pulled apart. "I only want you to share whatever you want me to know."

—

AFTER THAT, HE HAD stopped asking questions about her past. Now he had to find out the truth about her, the hard way.

CHAPTER 20

*W*HAT MADE BROOKE RUN?
Ethan couldn't imagine who or what could cause such fear that she had to change her name and marry someone else who was also using a false identity. Had she done something so horrible that she couldn't go to the police for help? Had her past been so wrought with secrets and demons that she couldn't even tell the man who loved her what had happened? He needed to know, and, he imagined, so did Mrs. Wall.

Ethan arrived at the Walls' home just after five. He drove up a long driveway leading to a bloated McMansion, an overscaled faux-Greek revival fortress with six bedrooms, seven baths, and a synthetic lawn they put in when the California drought got serious.

With prices in the area pushing $2,000 a square foot—thanks to the tech boom—Rufus Wall had to be an exceptional programmer, making bank.

So what made Rufus run?

Sarah Wall was waiting for Ethan at the front door. She greeted him with a welcoming smile. "You didn't mention on the phone that you were so tall, dark, and handsome."

"I guess I left out the most important details," Ethan joked.

She invited him inside and told him to take a seat on the couch in her living room while she prepared refreshments. She didn't seem too broken up so Ethan figured that the Big Sur police hadn't told her that they were looking for her husband at the bottom of the sea, or she just didn't care.

She reeked trophy wife—overly bejeweled, unduly Botoxed, and dressed incongruously; her fake Double D's defied gravity heading north of her halter top, her skinny Zobha stretch pants squeezing her enviable tight ass, where most of her day was spent (in yoga, not on her ass).

A few minutes later she emerged from the kitchen with two full martini glasses. "You said that you worked with my husband at Hounddog," she began, "but you didn't tell me your name."

"Jack...Jack Stone," Ethan lied.

If she were to follow up after he left, at least his brother was a real employee there, and if she were to meet him at a later time, she would just think that he had shaved his beard. The twins had done the bait and switch many, many times and both knew the deal: whenever approached by someone about something that made no sense, just play along.

"I've already had a few," she confessed, "so excuse me if I'm a little loopy. Under these circumstances, I've decided to start happy hour a little early."

Something told Ethan that she started happy hour early every day. "It's understandable," Ethan agreed, "considering your husband has been gone now, for what, a week?"

"Has it been a week already?" she said as if her husband had just been late for dinner.

"Did he tell you why he was going out of town?"

She shook her head. "Just that he had business in New York."

"He told you that he was going to New York?"

Sarah glared at him over her martini glass. "I explained all this to the police. And I'm sure you didn't drive all the way out here to ask me things they already know. I'm assuming you're here to tell me something you couldn't tell me on the phone. So let's get this over with."

Ethan looked back blankly.

She prodded, "Did they find him?"

Ethan realized that she thought he was there to tell her that her husband was officially dead, and she definitely didn't look too distraught.

"No," Ethan told her, "that's not why I'm here—"

"Hounddog sent you to confiscate his computer?"

"Just as a precaution." Ethan went along, figuring he could search for any communications between Brooke and Rufus. "Just until he returns."

"He always takes his laptop with him. We have a family computer upstairs but there's nothing on it from Hounddog."

"May I take a look upstairs, just to be sure?"

"Not unless you're a cop and you have a warrant."

She was grinning, as if this were fun. He told her, "I'm not a cop."

"I worked for Lehman Brothers when they went down," she explained. "I know my rights."

Ethan wondered if she was the reason the Walls could afford the Palo Alto McMansion. "Do you work for another investment firm now?"

"I don't work anymore," she said with a chuckle, as if work itself was beneath her.

This spread and this wife were funded by tech money, Ethan concluded. *So why isn't she upset that he's missing?*

"But I handle all our family finances," she added with a giggle.

Maybe that's why.

"Sorry you had to drive all the way out here," she said.

Ethan felt the gin go right to his head. "That's not the only reason I'm here, actually…"

Ethan opened the wedding photo on his iPhone, expanding it with his thumb and forefinger so that only Brooke was visible, and then showed it to Sarah.

"Have you ever seen this woman?"

Sarah took a hard look. "She's pretty," Sarah said with a clip, like a lady about to be scorned. "Who is she?"

"You don't recognize her?"

"Should I?"

Ethan prompted, "From Hounddog maybe?"

Sarah took another look and shook her head. "I don't know many Hounddog people. And I've never seen that woman before. Is that

Anna Gopnik? The police told me that my husband might have been with a woman named Anna Gopnik—"

"No, this woman's name is Brooke Shaw."

"I don't know her, no." Sarah sat back resolvedly, unblocking Ethan's view of a Dancing Rabbit statue on the mantel, the same kitschy eyesore he and Jack were given after their corporate retreat.

"Maybe you would know her from one of the company functions," Ethan said, "like Dancing Rabbit."

"What's a dancing rabbit?" Sarah asked.

"It's a place in Big Sur. It's popular with tech companies for corporate retreats. That statue is from there."

She turned around and her face soured. "I never liked that thing. My husband insisted on putting it there." Sarah got up and headed back to the kitchen. "Would you like a refill?"

"I'm good. Thanks."

"Will you be staying for dinner?"

He glanced his watch. "I should be getting back."

"Too late to go back to the office, especially with rush hour traffic." She returned with the martini shaker and topped off both glasses.

"Your husband must have mentioned going there," Ethan pressed, "to Dancing Rabbit."

"I vaguely remember something. I don't know."

Sarah sat next to Ethan on the couch this time. Ethan could feel her warmth and smell her perfume, which was as overpowering as she was. She touched the hand that Ethan was holding his iPhone with, the picture of Brooke still illuminated, and she asked, "Who is this woman? The truth."

"She's my girlfriend."

"Your girlfriend?"

"She's also gone missing," he told her. "I thought maybe you could help me, make a connection, something."

Sarah rubbed Ethan's knee. "Maybe we can help each other forget."

Her intent was unmistakable.

"I always have a hard time resisting tall, handsome young men," she moaned as she leaned in and kissed his neck.

Is that why Rufus ran?

Ethan pulled away. "What about your husband?"

She worked her tongue up to his ear and whispered, "He's not here to complain, is he?"

CHAPTER 21

I T WAS A SUBURBAN strip mall, broad daylight, and Jack felt safe. It didn't even occur to him that he wouldn't, or shouldn't. The sun was shining. People were milling about, going about their business, and Jack walked over to the bank to get some cash. After he pulled some some out of the ATM, he headed back to his car, which was in the parking lot around the corner—out of view from the bank guard and the security cameras. Just as he reached for his car keys, he heard a voice from behind.

"Nice day, huh?"

Jack immediately knew it was not a friendly greeting, but a taunt, like a scrappy UFS fighter getting ready to rumble.

Jack turned. He didn't see anyone at first, and then a man appeared from behind a dark blue Dodge Caravan. He had a shaved head and bulked-up body covered in tattoos.

Jack was not afraid to defend himself. Having a brother makes you a good fighter; having a twin brother makes you a better fighter; and studying Tae Kwon Do for seven years because you're always picked on at school makes you a lethal weapon.

Now that Jack was a full-grown, six-foot-five man, well versed in Tae Kwon Do, he rarely worried about getting mugged or harassed. But instincts told him he'd better prepare.

"I'm Ace," Shaved Head told Jack, as if the name made a difference. "Would you help us out with this thing over here?"

"What thing?"

He pointed at the van's back door. "It's in here."

Jack thought of his Sensei, Mr. Miyagi (not his real name, just what Jack called his Tae Kwon Do master), and his first rule: do whatever you can to avoid a fight.

"I don't think so," Jack told Ace. "If you'd excuse me, I'm in a bit of a rush."

The back door of the van swung open. Another tattooed man wearing a ragged T-shirt with an auto parts logo jumped out.

"Come on," Ace said, "it'll only take a minute."

"My mother taught me not to talk to strangers."

Rule two: run, if possible.

Jack turned to take off, but a third bulked-up goon was blocking his way. This one had to weigh in close to three hundred pounds, leaving Jack no room to squeeze by.

"We just have a few questions for you," the big guy said, gesturing toward their van. "Come inside."

He wasn't asking.

By the time Jack opened his mouth to object, he was already being lifted and dragged. It happened in seconds, and he knew he would have to resort to Mr. Miyagi's third rule: if there are no other options, fight.

Jack jabbed Ace in the nose. He went back, blood squirting over his shaved head. The other two heavyweights, Dale and Wade, laughed at their driver and overpowered Jack like he were a flailing rag doll, shoving him into the back of the van.

Ace hobbled back into the driver's seat, bitching and moaning.

Dale's thick hand wrapped around Jack's throat, and then he shouted at Wade, "Shut the door!"

The van drove off, wheels screeching. Jack felt his phone vibrate. He reached in his pocket and glanced the incoming call. It was his brother. Just as he tried to push the accept button, Dale twisted Jack's wrist, hard. Jack screamed as his phone fell out of his hand and into his lap.

"Don't even think about it," Dale grunted.

"What's he doing?" Ace shouted from the front.

"Trying to answer his phone."

Ace ordered, "No phones."

"Okay, okay," Jack pleaded. "Let go. That hurts!"

"No phones," Dale repeated, then he slammed Jack's phone on the floor. It shattered into pieces. Jack assumed they wanted the stack of twenties he had just pulled from the ATM. He prepared to take a few hits and capitulate a few hundred bucks. "My wallet's in my back pocket," he told them.

"Thanks," Wade said, reaching for it. "Bonus."

"Gimme that," Dale said, reaching.

Wade slapped his hand away.

Ace shouted from the driver's seat, "Put the wallet back."

Dale scowled at Ace and reluctantly stuffed it back in Jack's pocket.

They weren't after his money. Jack noticed they were circling the road around the mall for the second or third time. "What do you want?" Jack asked.

"You're going to take us to her," Ace shouted from the front. "Where is she?"

Wade twisted Jack's wrist for emphasis.

Jack grunted, then caught Ace's eyes in the rearview. "Who are you talking about?"

"Your girlfriend."

"I don't have a girlfriend!"

Wade bent Jack's entire arm back.

"Agghh!"

You can tell when someone gets pleasure out of inflicting pain. Jack needed to get out of there. These guys were just warming up.

Dale jabbed Jack in the ribs as if it would make Jack more cooperative. "Start talking."

Jack keeled over and noticed the prison and gang tattoos running up Dale and Wade's arms. He knew that these had to be the guys that tailed Ethan from the church. They were looking for Brooke. And they thought he was Ethan.

"I don't know where she is," Jack told them.

"Where have you looked so far?" Ace asked.

"I haven't—"

"Liar!" Wade slapped Jack.

Ace asked calmly, "Where do you think she might be?"

"No idea."

"Try harder," Wade said with a backhand across the face.

Jack glanced down at his shattered iPhone. "I can call her and ask her where she is if you hand me my phone back."

Wade punched him in the gut and Dale crushed what was left of his phone with his giant steel-toe work boot.

Jack shook off the sting. "I really have no idea."

Dale hit him in the sternum. Hard. He gasped and wheezed and glimpsed Ace watching in his rearview again, enjoying the show. "Easy," Ace said, "we need him to be able to talk."

Jack sat back up and hissed, "Okay, I'll tell you." He focused on Dale, held his ribs as if he were hurt, and whispered, "I know where she might be…"

Dale leaned closer so he could hear better.

Jack sat taller so he had leverage, "She might be…" And Jack head butted Dale.

Crack!

Dale went back. His tremendous bulk bounced and made the van shudder. Dale's eyes stayed open but he looked comatose, which Jack thought was an improvement.

Wade sprung at Jack, but Jack used his heft for momentum, and the leviathan slammed into the side of the van.

Jack had never had to defend himself as an adult, especially in a life or death situation, and never knew if the years of Tae Kwon Do had served any real purpose besides giving him the ability to hold his own in the sixth grade. But, even though the back of the van prevented him from standing up fully, and every turn Ace made challenged his balance, it proved to be more effective than he could have imagined. Mr. Miyagi used to make them do exercises on their knees to emphasize speed, agility, and reaction force, using the principle that as the striking limb is brought forward, the other parts of the body should be brought backward in order to do damage to the striking limb.

This shit works!

Wade came back at him, angrier and sloppier. Jack snapped his right leg up, his right arm back to provide the force, and nailed him square in the nose.

Ace yelled from up front. "What's going on back there...? Talk to me!"

Wade grabbed his bloody nose and howled, "I'm going to kill this fucker."

Jack heard Ace object, but when he turned, Wade's colossal form was heaving at him, this time with a knife. Jack ducked and dodged, twisted Wade's arm behind his back, and shoved it hard. Jack heard Wade's limbs crackle. The knife dropped out of his hand and Wade collapsed like a rag doll. He appeared benumbed, but Dale was moving again, and reaching for a Glock 19, his hand already gripping the handle. Jack leapt forward, shoving his elbow into Dale's neck.

Dale tried to aim the gun at Jack. Jack latched onto Dale's wrist. The gun wavered back and forth.

Dale thrashed; Jack pummeled.

Ace slammed on the brakes. The van skidded. Jack hit the floor, his head bouncing off the door handle on the way down. The gun exploded. Everything went dark. Jack blacked out, probably for only a minute or two. When he opened his eyes, Ace and Dale were shouting at each other.

Ace said, "He's no good to us now, is he?"

Dale said, "I didn't mean to fire. You were driving like a maniac!"

Jack realized they thought the bullet had hit him. That is until Dale noticed that Wade's clothes were soaking wet, a bloody bullet hole in his back. Dale turned Wade's body over. A prosaic gaze stared back.

Wade was dead.

Dale screamed, a guttural hateful cry.

Jack took the opportunity to release a sidekick into Dale's shoulder. The gun flew out of his hand and Jack leapt up, grabbing it midair.

"Nice move, if I do say so myself." Jack had never handled a gun before. It was heavier than he thought it would be. He pointed it at Dale and ordered, "Open the back door."

Ace shook his head at Dale. "You idiot."

"Open the door," Jack repeated.

Dale obliged.

Jack jumped out, stumbled, and fell onto the pavement. As he got back up, he saw Dale roll Wade's body out of the back. The corpse landed with a thud. The back door slammed shut and the van screeched away like a bat out of hell.

It all happened so fast. Jack stared down at the corpse in disbelief. He didn't know how long he was standing there before he heard a few people screaming and shouting from the curb. When he looked up, he saw the security guard from the nearby bank ordering everyone to stay inside and get down. One of the bystanders didn't obey, a young woman standing on the curb in front of the bank pointing her cell phone. Jack knew that she was videotaping him. He also realized that he was standing over a dead body, and he was holding a gun.

It looked bad.

Jack started toward the guard thinking of a way to explain the situation, but before he could say anything, the guard shouted, "The police are on the way!" and then ran back inside the bank.

Jack could only imagine what the bystanders would tell the police, and what the video would corroborate.

It looked really bad.

Jack did the only thing that made sense at the time.

He turned around and ran.

CHAPTER 22

ETHAN SPED AWAY FROM the Walls' McMansion and called his brother to see if they could affirm their findings about Rufus and Sarah. But when he called, Jack's cell phone went right to voicemail.

So he called Bailey, who picked up right away, "Talk to me, Gov. What did Wall's first wife have to say for herself?"

Ethan told him, "She hit on me."

"She hit on you?" Bailey repeated, now even more intrigued. "Did you close?"

Ethan heard Emily whack Bailey in the background, and call him a pig. Ethan had to smile. They made for a cute duo. "She's right," Ethan said, "you are a pig. And no, I didn't close."

"Then why did you mention it, just bragging?"

"Because it indicates that the Walls had marriage issues. She looked like the kind of lady that married for money, and by the way she handled her liquor and came on to me, I'm sure I wasn't the first guy she made moves on."

"So instead of asking for a divorce and letting her take him to the cleaners, you think he faked his death, stole an identity, and married Brooke?"

Ethan knew Bailey was mocking him, and the theory did sound far-fetched, especially when Bailey added, "So his cheating whore of a wife could cash in on his life insurance policy or something?"

"It might be a shrewd way to avoid an expensive divorce," Ethan said, "just become another person."

"Nice exit strategy for him, I suppose, but then why did he need to marry Brooke?"

"Don't know," Ethan said. "But I have a good idea how they know each other—"

Ethan heard Emily say to Bailey, "Tell him."

Bailey whispered, "I will."

"Tell me what?" Ethan asked.

"Just finish what you were saying," Bailey said. "How do they know each other?"

"Dancing Rabbit," Ethan told him. "They must have met there. There was one of those rabbit statues in the Walls' home. Remember those silly rabbits Brooke gave us when we left the retreat—?"

"'Silly rabbit, Trix are for kids,'" Bailey laughed and performed the entire TV commercial from the seventies. "Did you have those ads here?"

Bailey had started his career in advertising and had a slogan ready for every social reference. Ethan thought it was funny sometimes.

Just then, he did not.

"Stay with me," Ethan said, "planet earth. Sarah Wall didn't know what the rabbit statue was. She had never heard of Dancing Rabbit, which was strange, considering. Remember the Dancing Rabbit mantra—"

"A place to transform."

"Exactly. We assumed they were talking metaphorically, about internal growth and all that psychobabble, right? But maybe they were talking about actual transformation, or as you put it, 'exit strategies.'"

Bailey laughed again and said, "Come to Dancing Rabbit for the kale, leave with a new name?"

"I don't know why you left advertising, Bailey."

Bailey sighed. "You think the tech biz is a young man's game, advertising's worse."

"Tell him," Emily said again.

"Tell me what?" Ethan asked. "Did you find out who CG is?"

"Not yet, but Emily has a theory."

"I'm listening."

"Don't take it the wrong way—"

"I don't like the sound of it already."

Bailey took a deep breath and then said, "What if Brooke was with you just to get close to Stalker?"

"Why should I take that the wrong way?" Ethan snapped back, considering the possibility. "You think she was a corporate spy?"

"I don't know," Bailey said, "but I'm sure you've heard the expression, 'Keep your enemies close.'"

Ethan scoffed. "So I'm supposed to be the enemy in this theory?"

"Just think about it…You met her at Dancing Rabbit where she was living this alternative lifestyle and she immediately gives it all up, everything she was doing, and moves down to Santa Monica to be with you. Always seemed a tad dodgy—"

"We fell in love," Ethan interjected.

"I know…" Bailey rolled his eyes. "Just hear me out. Please."

"Go on."

"What if she had known that this CG chap was searching for her on Stalker. He was one of our early subscribers. And she knew that he might find her when our Face Match Mode became available—"

"So Brooke faked our entire relationship just to monitor her stalker—?"

"To stay a few steps ahead—"

"That's ridiculous."

Emily whispered to Bailey, "Ask him if he told her we were going to upload?"

Bailey asked, "Did you tell her that we were moving forward with Face Match Mode?"

"I did, but—"

Emily grabbed the phone and asked Ethan, "When? When did you tell her?"

Ethan remembered how upset Brooke was when he told her they were launching the face recognition feature early. "I called her after Jack left—"

"And then she ran."

Bailey took the phone back and said, "You told her that we were launching that afternoon, and then she was gone that evening!"

Ethan went quiet.

Bailey said, "Don't take it so personally, Gov. She might have a very good reason for having to do it. We don't know how dangerous this nutter is or what he wants from her."

"Nothing is more personal," Ethan sighed. "I don't believe that Brooke used me. If anything, she left to protect me. She didn't want me to come for her because she didn't want to drag me into it."

"Into what, pray tell?" Bailey asked. "Why is she running? Why is this CG looking for her—?"

Ethan noticed a Highway 101 sign up ahead. "I don't know, but I'm about to find out. I'm going back to Dancing Rabbit, ground zero, where this all began. I want some answers."

"That hippie pulled a Taser on you last time," Bailey reminded him.

"And now he's gonna regret it," Ethan said as if he were Clint Eastwood. "I'm tired of theories. I want answers."

Ethan accelerated onto the highway and headed toward Big Sur, unaware that an all-points bulletin with the security video from the bank outside of San Francisco had been released to nearby police departments and a still of Jack holding a gun and running away from the scene of the crime was shared with the media.

Sometimes being mistaken for your twin is a good thing.

This wasn't one of those times.

—

SEAN MCQUEEN OPENED HIS door and the blood drained from his face. Jack was standing before him, visibly shaking, the nightmare still in his eyes. His clothes were ripped and soiled. And there was blood splattered up and down his clothes.

"What happened to you?"

Jack told him: "I think I'm in trouble."

CHAPTER 23

B IG SUR IS A sparsely populated region of the Central Coast of California, from the Carmel River in Monterey County south to the San Carpoforo Creek in San Luis Obispo County. There are only about a thousand year-round inhabitants—descendants of the original ranching families, visiting artists and writers, wealthy second-home owners, and people who retreat at the high-end resorts and spas cantilevered off the mountains with panoptic ocean views. Most of the locals would say they were drawn there by the natural beauty, solitude, and tranquility. And because it felt safe. The crime rate had always been low, and the small police department, with their small-town friendliness, prided itself on keeping its soulful residents and visitors secure. It also had Sergeant Cruz.

Sergeant Cruz was a fourth-generation officer who had run the Big Sur Police Department for two decades. His surname was Mexican but he came from Native American stock, Ohlone specifically, the first known inhabitants in the area. Like his father, grandfather, and great-grandfather, he had taken a vow to keep their home safe.

But in the past year, there had been nearly a dozen missing persons reported—a record number for the region. Rumors were mounting from a kidnapping ring to a serial killer on the loose. A conspiracy website even speculated about an inexplicable gravity force akin to the Bermuda Triangle. The locals were growing concerned and it didn't bode well for tourism, their primary industry.

Cruz and his department were well aware many of the missing people had some connection to Dancing Rabbit, but they had to tread cautiously. The resort was a long-standing pillar in the community, one of the biggest employers in the area, and a popular destination for visitors from San Diego to Sacramento and beyond. They needed more to go on in order to invade its walls.

Until the San Francisco Police Department released a video showing Jack standing over a corpse, holding a gun, and fleeing the scene.

Because when Sergeant Cruz showed the clip to his department, Detective Ramsey jumped to his feet. "That's the young man that approached us when we were pulling the Mini Cooper out of the ocean!"

"The tall young man—" Detective Johnson agreed. "He was looking for his girlfriend and brother, said they were coming from Dancing Rabbit."

"Did you follow up at Dancing Rabbit?" Cruz asked.

"We made a routine visit to inform them about Anna Gopnik," Ramsey said, "but you know how tight-lipped they are."

Ramsey flipped through his notes and told the sergeant, "His name is Ethan Stone."

"I'll let San Francisco know," Cruz told them.

"Wait a minute," Ramsey said. "Play the tape again. The guy that stopped had a beard, didn't he?"

The sergeant replayed the video.

"You're right," Johnson agreed. "Good eye. He must have shaved. But that's him. Definitely him."

The last thing Big Sur needed was a retreat harboring murder suspects. So Cruz decided to pay one of its most beloved residents a personal visit.

———

ELVIS GREETED SERGEANT CRUZ with a Native American hello: "Yatahey."

As a longtime student of the Big Sur counterculture movements, Elvis often reached out to the local Native American community to help implement some of their rituals, often trying to lure them to the Dancing Rabbit property to share their traditions with their guests.

The last time Cruz had been on the property had been for a craft and jewelry exhibit. Now he was there on official police business.

Elvis suggested they go to the gazebo on the bluffs so they could talk in private. "I have to tell you that I've done some digging into your past since the last time you were here," Elvis said, as if he were the cop.

"My past?"

"Did you know that your grandfather had shortened your last name in the early 1900s? Your name was Costeños. It means 'coastal people.'"

"My grandfather changed our name to avoid problems back then, to fit in and assimilate," Cruz explained.

"Such a shame," Elvis said. "Such a beautiful name. Did you know there's a native ceremony you could do to change it back?"

"No. I didn't know that."

"Doesn't Sergeant Costeños have a nice ring to it?"

Cruz liked when locals acknowledged his heritage. But he also could tell that Elvis was pouring it on a little heavy to butter him up.

They went inside the gazebo and Elvis served iced tea. "Your detectives were here the other day, asking about Anna. I couldn't tell them much. You know, people at Dancing Rabbit don't talk about their past."

"Right." Cruz tried the tea and then asked, "Tell me why that is again?"

"It's about living in the present."

"Makes sense," Cruz said. "But I'll tell you what doesn't make sense. That Big Sur has more unsolved disappearances than ever and almost all of the missing persons have stayed at Dancing Rabbit at some point."

Elvis shrugged. "People come, people go. We don't ask, they don't tell. We're all about free will."

"I'm glad to hear that but—"

"And privacy," Elvis added. "We protect their right to privacy so they can recapture balance in their lives... What the Native Americans call *Koyaanisqatsi*—life out of balance—is by definition, the nature of balance. Matter of fact, Dancing Rabbit's philosophy is based on the inspirations of *Koyaanisqatsi, Powaqqatsi,* and *Naqoyqatsi.*"

"Within every crisis you can find a blessing or more," Cruz said. "Well done. I respect all that, as well as your need for privacy, whatever your reasons." Cruz reached for a folder inside his shoulder bag, "Even before Dancing Rabbit, back in the sixties and seventies, this property was known for its privacy—not to mention easy sex, drugs, and rock 'n' roll—and we never intruded. But our first priority has always been safety." Cruz took out a blown-up printout of Jack holding a gun and placed it in front of Elvis. "Do you know this young man?"

Elvis had a poker face.

"Harboring a fugitive puts other people at risk, not to mention that it is against the law," Cruz said with a more threatening tone.

"Might be the cat that broke into our property the other night," Elvis said.

"He broke in... Why didn't you call us?"

"Didn't need to. I chased him away."

"He's wanted for murder. He may be dangerous."

"I see that."

"If he's making a run for the Mexican boarder, he'll have to pass through here again."

"If he comes back, we'll be ready."

"If he comes back, promise me that you'll call us immediately." Cruz met Elvis's gaze and put his fist over his heart. "The real meaning behind *Koyaanisqatsi, Powaqqatsi,* and *Naqoyqatsi* is about not adding to the chaos."

"I definitely don't want to add to it, man."

"So we understand each other?"

"We do." Elvis put his fist over his heart to confirm. "We're cool."

———

CARPE DIEM IS A trendy wine-tasting bar tucked away in a remote hillside, popular only with the Napa locals. Brooke had been sitting there for nearly two hours, sipping wine and killing time like a bored, lonely lush, planted on a stool in the middle of the afternoon.

"Je parle très peu l'anglais," she said to the handsome bartender, Fritz (probably a nickname). Then in broken English and a fake French accent, she told him that she was visiting from Paris so that she would be left undisturbed.

Just her luck, Fritz had been brushing up on his college French and thought it would behoove them both for him to practice. *"Essaye ça* Failla 2010," he announced, bringing her a fresh glass, her third or fourth. *"Ça a* full-throttle notes of pears and green apples—*des poires and pommes*— complex layers of buttered toast, honey, and creamy lees. *De Sonoma."*

"Sounds *delish."*

"Prendre plaisir!" Fritz said as he moved down the bar to push a $200 Cabernet Sauvignon on a tipsy gay food critic vying for more pours and Fritz's phone number.

That's when Brooke noticed the breaking news on the TV above the bar, reporting the murder. They showed the security footage and zoomed in on Jack as he ran away waving a gun. Brooke spilled her Failla.

"Fritz—" she called out louder than she meant to, "would you please turn up the volume?"

Fritz didn't seem to notice that she had dropped the French accent and suddenly sounded British. But he did notice the panic in her face and turned up the sound on the TV.

"If you see this man or have any information of his whereabouts, please contact the number below…"

The last thing she had expected was for Jack to shoot someone and flee on national TV.

And then she heard the TV announcer say, "The suspect has been identified as Ethan Stone. He is still at large and likely to be armed and dangerous…"

"What have they done?" Brooke groaned.

Rabbits can never get caught; they have to be fast on their feet, always a few steps ahead. That's why Brooke had two invisible applications built that guaranteed that she—or any Rabbit on the run— never got caught. (The apps were invisible because they were hidden; you could only access them through settings; only if you knew where to look.) These apps were custom-made by Hounddog, exclusively for Brooke, never meant for public use. They were in permanent beta, knowing they would never get approved for market, but McQueen had agreed to make them when Brooke convinced him that a biometrics company could be used to protect people who needed protection.

Long before Brooke left Ethan, she had installed the invisible apps on the twins' smartphones. One was called Black Box and the other was Pocket Dialer.

Pocket Dialer gave Brooke the ability to connect the twins' phone lines, as if one of them called the other. She had a silent ring setting on her phone so they wouldn't know when she called, and when their phone answered, she had the ability to overhear whatever they were doing. It could function like a wiretap, without a wire or a tap.

Black Box was a tracking device with real-time access. The GPS on their phones would signal their whereabouts. Other applications tracked GPS signals, but Black Box was unique because it recorded everything in close range of the phone at all times, even if their phones were shut off—just like a black box in aviation, maritime, or rail transport—so it could be used in case disaster struck, to prove what happened, assist in the investigation, or just to get answers. The apps drained their batteries a *scootch,* but not enough for them to notice.

She did this for their protection and safety.

Knowing that there was a good chance Ethan would come for her, despite her plea for him to stay away, she had planned accordingly.

But she couldn't have been prepared for this.

She grabbed her phone, opened up her Pocket Dialer app, and got busy.

Fritz noticed the look on her face. "Are you okay?" he asked. "*Est-ce que ça va?*"

"I'm fine," she lied.

"The Failla is not for everyone," he said. "Would you like to try something lighter?"

"Just the check, please. I really have to get going."

That was an understatement.

CHAPTER 24

E THAN SEARCHED THE ABANDONED reception area and rang the bell. He was now convinced that Dancing Rabbit was more than the resort it claimed to be—more than a place of seclusion, more than a berth of escapism, more than a hideaway for lost souls, more than a place to transform. He was prepared to learn why Brooke had to keep her real identity from him, why she really came to America, and why she was running. He was sure the answers were buried there and he desperately wanted to hear the truth, even at the risk of getting another electroshock.

"Hello! Anybody here?" he shouted.

The door leading out to the property unlocked and opened. "Hello, Ethan," Elvis greeted him with a smile, as if he were expecting him. "Nice to see you again."

He remembered me this time. That's a good start.

"I apologize for the way I barged in last time," Ethan began, searching to see if Elvis was holding his stun gun, "but I'm still worried about her—"

"I feel you, man."

"I realize there are things she didn't tell me, and maybe she had a very good reason, but if she's in some kind of trouble, I want to help her."

"I totally get that," Elvis said, chill as a hippie on dankity dank. "It's suppertime. Come join us. We'll talk."

There was no resistance this time. Elvis was treating him like he was one of them. Something had changed. Ethan wondered if he was walking into a trap, an ambush, or worse, but he nevertheless followed Elvis onto the grounds. They walked in silence, facing the sun setting over the sea, luminescent warmth that could calm anything, except Ethan just then.

"Any news on Anna Gopnik yet?" Ethan asked, breaking the lull. "When I was here last, the police had found her car but not her body."

Elvis paused, looked out at the ocean, and shook his head. "No one could survive a drop like that."

Ethan pressed, "The police told me there have been other missing people from Dancing Rabbit."

Elvis repeated his stock response, "People come, people go," but he didn't elaborate.

Ethan followed him to the mess hall and wondered why there weren't more people out and about this time of day. "Seems quiet," Ethan said. "Is the resort slow?"

"It's a weekday. Only Rabbits allowed."

Ethan had heard Brooke refer to the people that worked there as Rabbits. For some reason, when Elvis called them Rabbits, it sounded more exclusive.

Was Brooke a Rabbit even though she was no longer an employee? Once a Rabbit, always a Rabbit? What do Rabbits do?

Rabbits run!

Ethan noticed a few sets of eyes watching him from a doorway. Doors shut and curtains closed as they passed by some of the cabins. A man cutting grass stopped to look at them, wiped his brow, and turned away when Ethan made eye contact. A couple behind a tree seemed to be arguing in whispers.

Ethan decided that he was being paranoid and just then, like he was receiving a message from the God of technology, his iPhone pinged.

He lifted the device from his pocket and glimpsed an incoming text: *They're coming for you.*

He scrolled down to see who had sent the warning but his alarmist seemed to want to remain anonymous: *Sender unknown.*

"Do you have to take a call?" Elvis asked. "I can give you some privacy."

"It was just a text from a friend," Ethan told him. "It can wait."

They arrived at the mess hall. "You must be hungry," Elvis said, revealing an inscrutable grin. "Let's grab some grub and have a little chat."

Ethan was pretty sure he was about to enter a lion's den, or rabbit trap, but he had come for answers, and he wasn't going to bow out now. He needed to know what this place had done to Brooke.

Elvis saw Ethan's encumbrance and nudged him inside.

The mess hall was a wide-open lodge with high ceilings and a help-yourself cafeteria where servers in hairnets spooned out vegetarian fare that left you hungrier than when you came—what you'd expect from an adult camp for earth-crunchers. Rows of long community tables extended from each side, and when Ethan and Elvis entered, most of the seats were taken. All of the Rabbits glanced up as they moved through, then went back to their crimson-colored soups, stews, and chilies, minding their own business, which he already knew was what Rabbits did best.

Elvis pointed toward the back. "How about that table in the corner?"

"May I use the bathroom first?" Ethan asked, hoping to rattle his agenda.

Elvis pointed to the other side. "It's over there."

"I remember. Thanks."

Ethan crossed the room and glanced at the entrance, noticing a bulky man close the doors. Two other men sporting man buns and unkempt beards were loitering oddly, as if they were sidelined players waiting for their coach to let them in the game. Ethan assumed that it was the only entrance, unless there was a back door in the kitchen, which would be difficult to get to. He was sinking further into the rabbit hole.

He scanned the Rabbits, wondering if one of them had texted him the warning. The unisex lavatory had three stalls, three urinals, and three sinks. There was no lock on the door so Ethan had to move fast.

He tucked into the last stall, shut the hinge, and responded to the text message: *Who is this?*

The response: *Sender account no longer valid.*

Ethan relieved himself as he considered his options.

When in Rome.

Then he heard sirens in the distance.

He glanced another text: *Get out of there.*

Shit! Nowhere to run. Nowhere to hide.

He noticed an open window, possibly large enough to climb through. He stood on the toilet, extended his long arms, and reached the ledge, never more grateful that he was six foot five.

Just then, the bathroom door opened. Ethan ducked back down, squatted on the toilet, never more annoyed that he was six foot five. He peeked through the crack.

One of the Man Buns that had been guarding the door washed his hands at the first sink, checked himself out in the mirror, and then toyed with his hair.

He's stalling.

Ethan grunted noisily, to express his need for privacy, and it seemed to work. Man Bun walked out. Ethan moved quickly and swiftly, pulling up, over, and through the window. He heard the bathroom door open again, and he jumped.

The drop down was greater than he had anticipated, more than a dozen feet, but luckily he landed in a dirt pile that helped break the fall. The sun had fallen behind the horizon and it was getting dark fast. No one saw him behind the building—yet—but he took cover behind a cluster of bushes and searched for another exit besides the reception area he had entered through. The sirens were getting louder. Red-and-blue flashing lights from the road, approaching.

He heard a voice coming from the bathroom. "Mr. Stone? Are you okay?" It was Elvis. Ethan could hear him checking the stalls, slamming the doors open. Then he shouted, "He's gone!"

Elvis noticed the open window but it was too high for him to reach. He rushed back into the dining room and ordered, "Shut the gate! Lock the exit!"

Ethan made his move. He ran low and swift, staying in the shadows, disappearing behind the cottages, and then evanescing into the woods. He hoped that his long legs and the endurance he'd built up jogging on the Santa Monica bike path would be enough to outrun a mob of vegan yogis.

He climbed the fence at the edge of the property. When he glanced back, he could see that Dancing Rabbit was up in arms. Rabbits were rushing from the mess hall, pointing and yelling bloody murder in all directions. The police were talking to Elvis, probably to get a detailed description of what Ethan was wearing, all the gory details of the two-time trespasser. Never in Ethan's wildest imagination would he have thought the police were actually there to apprehend him for the murder of Wade Franks, an ex-convict found dead in a strip mall parking lot earlier that day, or that his brother was seen on the TV news running away from the dead body, murder weapon in his hand, and Ethan was now being mistaken for Jack.

Ethan considered going back and telling them he had only trespassed again because he was worried about Brooke, who was still the latest missing Rabbit. He already knew that the Big Sur detectives—Ramsey and Johnson—were suspicious of Dancing Rabbit and their possible connection to the missing people in the area. But he was aware that this was a small town and Dancing Rabbit was one of the few businesses that the police needed to protect. And Ethan had trespassed on the property last time he was there, uninvited, and stormed into one of the cabins.

It looked bad.

Then, one of the Rabbits pointed toward the bushes where Ethan was hiding and nudged one of the police officers. Running from Rabbits was one thing. Running from cops was another.

It looked very bad.

Ethan's phone pinged and he looked down at another text: *Go! Now!*

So just like Jack, he did the only thing that made sense at the time. He turned around and ran like hell.

CHAPTER 25

Ethan's instincts took over. He charged through the dense woods, vaulting shrubbery like in a hurdle race, and hightailed it onto the main road. Staying in the shadows of tree barriers, he moved then hid, again and again, hoping to gain some distance. The police would likely apprehend his Tesla in the Dancing Rabbit driveway, and he considered calling Jack or Bailey to come pick him up. But where would he hide for the few hours it would take either one to get there? The police would be able to search every square inch of Big Sur by then. And he was on the only road in or out of Big Sur. No doubt they would troll Highway 1, slowly and thoroughly, until they found him.

He needed a Trojan horse escape. He'd have to sneak away unseen somehow. So he decided that he needed to hitch a ride out of there.

When he saw a car approaching, he jumped out on the road and waved his arms like a madman. The driver sounded his horn as he swerved around the thrashing giant, just missing him.

No one in their right mind would stop for me.

He looked back and saw two police cars backing out of the Dancing Rabbit driveway. There was a third car parked on the shoulder of the road. An officer pulled search dogs out of the back seat and prepared them for a hunt.

There was no place for Ethan to hunker down. He was out of options.

Just then, his cell phone pinged and he glimpsed another text: *Across the street, behind the pines.*

He looked across the street and behind two large pine trees was a rustic cabin with the lights on, just up the road.

He scrolled down: *Sender unknown.*

Whoever was helping him wanted to be anonymous. He didn't know how they were tracking him or why, but he was grateful.

He stayed low and lumbered closer. The front door of the cabin had an *open* sign. A small parking area was empty, save for an old Ford pickup that looked like it'd been sitting there since the sixties.

Chimes sounded when he went inside, but he didn't see anyone. It looked like an arts and crafts museum with a lot of books and memorabilia; a hoarder's posthumous tribute; a tomb.

"What is this place?" he exhaled.

He heard some ruffling from a back room and a chirpy female voice, *"El sur grande,* the splendor of the Central Coast, for those seeking isolation and natural beauty just like Hunter S. Thompson, Jack Kerouac, and Henry Miller. This is an aggregation of the most literary flower children, an informal respite. Are you looking for memoir or fiction?"

"Who is that?" He moved toward the voice. "Where are you?"

Ethan walked through the stacks, expecting to find an aging bookish hippie librarian, maybe one of Elvis's old squeezes prepared to give him a dissertation on the beat generation, but when he turned the corner, he saw Brooke's former roommate, Anna Gopnik—aka, the girl who drove over the cliff. She was alive and well, and tucked away in the safety of the Henry Miller Memorial Library.

Ethan gasped. "I thought you were dead."

"I thought you were a womanizer," Anna replied.

"But I saw them pull your car out of the ocean—"

"I saw you seduce my roommate and lure her down to the netherworld of Los Angeles, but here we are, both survivors of unfortunate fates and predicaments."

"They're still trudging the ocean looking for you, but you're here, you're alive—"

"Sorry to disappoint you, but cruise control did the deed for me. It's more dependable than I am, and it's not afraid of heights."

"You sent your car over the cliff…to fake your death?"

"You're smarter than you look." She headed toward the front counter, near the entrance.

He followed her. "They can't declare you dead without a body."

"I left plenty of blood all over the inside of my car to give them DNA proof," she explained. "It was painful, too." She showed Ethan the bandages on her arms where she had cut herself.

Was this another trap? Ethan wondered.

"Did you send me those texts?"

"What texts?"

He showed her his iPhone. "These."

"No."

He scoped out the library to see if there were any cameras, or anyone else watching. As he looked out the rear window to see if there were any cars parked out back, he asked her, "Just tell me why?"

"Why what?"

"You know what I'm asking, why would you want people to think you were dead?"

"We all have our reasons. Mine are personal."

"Does Dancing Rabbit help people fake their deaths and disappear?" he asked. "Do they give you someone's identity, someone who won't be missed? Is that what they meant by 'a place to transform'? Is that what Brooke did?"

"I really don't know," Anna explained. "No one tells anyone why they do it, who they were, who they're going to become, where they're going That's how this works. Never tell anyone, and no one will ever know."

"But you know that Brooke is hiding," he pressed, "running from something—"

"I don't know anything. I just told you."

Ethan studied her face. She meant what she said.

"I got these texts just as the police arrived, helping me get away. I think they were from Brooke. I think she was trying to help me get away."

"I think you're right."

"She has to be close by then."

"Not necessarily," Anna told him. "There's a GPS tracker in your phone."

Ethan checked to make sure his Stalker app was off, and it was. "No one can track me if I shut off the tracking capabilities in the settings. It's something I developed to make sure that I'm never tracked."

"You must be hiding something then," she insinuated, for effect.

"I'm not hiding anything."

Anna smiled. "Brooke uses an app that doesn't shut the GPS down. It always knows where you are, like it or not."

"There's no app on the market that does that."

"I didn't say it was on the market," Anna explained. "I said it was in your phone."

"Like a bug? She had a bug planted in my phone? Brooke doesn't believe in invading people's privacy. She hates technology."

"She doesn't trust the way people *abuse* technology but she believes that technology can be used to help people."

Ethan glared back, confused.

"She's tracking you for your own protection," Anna explained. "She had hoped you would stay away like she asked you to, but knowing how persistent you are, she knew it was unlikely."

"Is she doing it to keep me away or keep me on a leash?"

"Maybe both, I really don't know. Nobody shares how or where or why." Anna pulled a copy of *Tropic of Cancer* from the shelf. "I always thought Henry Miller was a foul-mouthed, crude, hyperbolic druggy hack. But Brooke seemed to like him and she wanted me to give this to you."

Ethan noticed a familiar coffee stain on the cover, and the receipt used as a bookmark was from Bulletproof, a coffee shop in Santa Monica that Brooke used to frequent. "This is her copy. She was here!"

"Yes."

Ethan looked around.

"She's not here now," Anna assured him.

"Was she here to arrange your disappearance? And Rufus Wall's? To stage the car accident? Is the timing of her disappearance linked to yours—?"

Anna opened the book to a bookmarked page with an underlined passage, and told him, "She thought this would help you understand."

Ethan read the passage aloud, "'As soon as a woman loses a front tooth or an eye or a leg she goes on the loose. In America she'd starve to death if she had nothing to recommend her but mutilation.'" Ethan looked up. "I don't get it. I'm not missing a tooth or an eye or a leg. And I've never hunted in my life. Is this some kind of message, a metaphor, a clue, or what?"

"She thought it would make sense to you. Honestly, that's all I know."

"I told her that she was my missing piece," Ethan blurted, as if a light bulb went off. "When we met—"

"Gag me with a spoon." Anna sighed impudently, as if he struck a nerve. "When Brooke told me she was moving to Santa Monica to live with you, I asked her what she liked about you, why she was so sure. I actually thought your brother was more sensitive—"

"So I've heard."

"But she said you were a hunter, the kind of guy who wouldn't give up until you found your missing piece. I thought it sounded overly sentimental. I also thought it was rather callow, both of you so sure that you would end up together—"

"It wasn't," Ethan snapped. "When you know, you know."

Anna rolled her eyes. "That's what she said."

Dogs barked outside. Then a car door shut.

Anna looked out the window. Police were approaching. "If they catch you, you never saw me."

She put her finger to her lips and disappeared into the back room. Then he heard her voice once more: "There's a trail just out the back exit that goes up into the hills."

And he took off.

CHAPTER 26

THE CLOUD-COVERED MOON CAST an ambient glow over endless verdure, overgrown and dense, and a narrow trail up the steep hillside. Ethan plowed upward, maneuvering through the thick vegetation. He hoped it led somewhere, hopefully not to another lion's den. He could hear the dogs barking; they were ascending the trail, not far behind.

Twenty minutes in, Ethan reached the zenith, a narrow ledge with a gnarly drop down to a dried lakebed. He looked for another option but the posse was getting closer. He sidestepped the ridge, slowly at first, and then he picked up speed. After traversing fifty yards or so, his foot hit a loose patch of dirt. He slid and went over, bouncing hard off the jutting, rocky slope as he tumbled. Luckily, he grabbed a thick tree root embedded into the protuberance and broke the fall, just in time.

He watched Brooke's copy of *Tropic of Cancer* soar into the frondescence abyss, as if he were watching her—or her last words to him—fly away.

Then he had an epiphany.

The reference about her being his missing piece could only mean one thing: she wanted him to know that it was real, their love, their bond.

When you know, you know.

Anna Gopnik had doubted their love, even when she'd handed him the book. Bailey and Emily had warned Ethan that he didn't really know her. And after she left, even Ethan had doubts. She knew he would, considering the way she left. She also knew that he would be so determined to find her that he would ignore her wishes that he leave her alone, especially if he thought she was in trouble. She wanted him to know that she wasn't running from him. She knew he'd need to know if what they'd shared was real. So she left him a passage that referred back to their first meet-cute, when he told her that he would never give up until he found his missing piece.

That was all he needed to know and it gave him the strength of a thousand men. He pulled himself up the side of the mountain, hand over hand. If the tree root hadn't spent the last hundred years growing exactly where it had, he would be dead. He looked down at the heart-stopping drop. He lost her book instead of his life and he remembered Brooke often talking about life being full of paradoxes, and her definition of mindfulness resonated: "Life is just a series of perspectives that shift from moment to moment."

But when he pulled himself up to safe ground, his perspective changed once again, as did his circumstance.

Half a dozen police officers were pointing guns at him. One of them said, "Hands over your head where we can see them."

Ethan squinted as a flashlight shined in his eyes. "I can explain everything. I'm unarmed—"

"Hands!" The officer shouted.

Ethan obeyed.

Another officer pulled back on snarling canines. "Relent!"

Two more officers approached. One of them pulled Ethan's arms back and clamped handcuffs on his wrists, the other patted him down and said matter-of-factly, "You are under arrest for the murder of Wade Franks."

"Wade Franks? I don't even know who that is. I didn't kill anyone—"

"Save it," the cop patting him down said, now satisfied that Ethan wasn't packing a gun. "You are a criminal suspect in police custody, and I'm going to explain your rights, do you understand?"

"Yes, but—"

"You have the right to remain silent. Anything you say can and will be used against you in a court of law..."

"This is a mistake," he protested.

"Walk!" The officer shoved Ethan forward and finished the Miranda rights as they all headed back down the mountainside.

Next thing Ethan knew, he was in the back seat of a police car, alone and cold; the damp chill in the air made him shiver, as did his worsening situation.

As they drove by Dancing Rabbit, he saw Elvis and other Rabbits standing out front, watching Ethan pass in a caravan of police cars, as if they had captured him themselves.

Was it pride or pity on their faces? Ethan wondered, feeling angry, betrayed and more confused. He had gone back to Dancing Rabbit for answers, and he was being carted off to jail with more questions.

The policeman riding shotgun told his partner that they had orders to take him to the Monterey County Sheriff's Department. He didn't say why, but he mentioned that it was a bit of a drive and he wanted to get home as soon as possible to celebrate his birthday.

Ethan and Jack had recently celebrated their thirtieth birthday, the big three-oh. He thought about how his worst problem back then was not making Fast Company's top thirty under thirty.

Perspective.

He remembered how Brooke had pulled off his birthday celebration without a hitch, when he walked onto the Pacific Terrace at One Pico, the elegant restaurant at Shutters on the Beach, and a cacophony of a hundred or more shouted, "Surprise!" Stunning LED light balls dropped from the sky and the entire courtyard overlooking the beach was illuminated by hundreds of tree bulbs. A sea of people cheered. Music blared. Champagne flowed.

"Told you I could pull one over on you," Brooke bragged when she saw the look of surprise on his face. "You have to be on your toes with a girl like me."

Now Ethan was staring out the window of a police car and thinking he should have paid closer attention to the details.

—

MONTEREY SHERIFF'S DEPARTMENT WAS swarming with news reporters and cameras as the Big Sur police car drove up. Ethan covered his face until they disappeared into the underground parking. The arresting police officers led him inside and delivered him to the Monterey team. They booked him, took his mug shot and prints, and locked him in an empty jail cell.

He lay down on the cot and stared at the ceiling, thinking that it would be a long night, but it wasn't five minutes before an officer summoned him.

"Let's go, Stone," the officer said as he unlocked his cage.

"Am I being released?"

The officer laughed. "Not a chance."

Ethan was told to wait in the interrogation room. A few minutes later, Big Sur Detectives Ramsey and Johnson came in and took seats across from him.

"Remember us?" Ramsey started, flashing his Big Sur badge.

Ethan felt relieved to see familiar faces. They were honest-looking faces. "Yeah, from the car accident."

"Do you understand why you're here?" Ramsey asked.

"It's obviously a mistake," Ethan tried to explain. "They said I was being arrested for murder, which is ridiculous. I didn't kill anyone, I've never even heard of the guy they say I killed...It's all just absurd!"

"Is it?" Johnson held up his smartphone so Ethan could see and played a shaky video.

Ethan watched the video clip of Jack standing over Wade's dead body and then running away.

"Jesus, Jack!" Ethan muttered.

"Who's Jack?" Ramsey asked.

"My brother. We're twins."

Johnson laughed. "Haven't heard the evil twin excuse in a long time."

"He's not evil," Ethan snapped. "And how can that possibly be me since the guy in the video is clean-shaven?" Ethan tugged on his facial hair. "Do you think I grew this in a few hours?"

Johnson adjusted his thick geriatric glasses and turned to Ramsey. "You caught that."

Ramsey nodded.

"Let's say that this is your brother," Ramsey pressed on. "Any idea why he did this?"

"He couldn't have." Ethan folded his arms and shook his head. "He was obviously scared. Something made him run."

"Innocent people don't run," Johnson said, "they call the police. He's standing there in broad daylight holding a Ruger nine-millimeter semiautomatic." Johnson held up his phone again so Ethan could see the frozen image of Jack.

"The murder weapon," Ramsey added.

Ethan shook his head. "I don't know."

After a long pause, Ramsey continued, "Tell us about Dancing Rabbit. You had said that your girlfriend worked there."

"Yeah. She did. About a year ago."

"Her name?" Johnson said as he pulled a pen and small notepad from his shirt pocket.

"Brooke Shaw." Ethan watched Johnson scribble her name down and wondered if he should say something about her false identity.

"What did she tell you about Dancing Rabbit?" Ramsey asked.

"She liked it."

Ramsey stared back, waiting for him to elaborate.

"It's one of those self-sustaining ecovillages. They promote community, teamwork, social responsibility. We did our corporate retreat there."

"Is that how you met Anna Gopnik?"

Ethan nodded. "That's right."

"The Dancing Rabbit folks didn't have any information about Anna, no forwarding address, no idea where she came from. We found that strange."

Ethan was just about to tell them what Anna told him—without telling them he had seen her—when it dawned on him: he was picked up in Big Sur.

"Why did you drag me all the way up here to the Monterey station?" Ethan asked.

"This was closer for the FBI," Johnson told him.

"The FBI?"

As if right on cue, the door swung open and a hard-boiled, steely-eyed woman in street clothes and an FBI badge around her neck barged in.

CHAPTER 27

M<small>R. STONE, I'M SPECIAL</small> Agent Matz." She shook Ethan's hand—her grip as unassailable as her entrance. An Asian male twenty years her junior traipsed in behind her and announced, "We'll take it from here, fellas," as if he were parroting an episode of *Law & Order*. Only he wasn't trying to.

"Shut up, Shu!" Matz barked at her lackey.

"What did I say?"

"It's the way you said it. Introduce yourself and state your purpose."

"Okay fine. I'm Agent Shu. FBI. And we need to talk to this man. In private."

Ramsey said, "We just have a few more questions, if you don't mind—"

"We do mind," Matz interjected. "We gave very strict orders to hold him until we got here. You might have just mussed up a federal investigation."

"No disrespect," Johnson said, "but you might have just mussed up a local one."

"Good to know," Matz said, incensed. "That's why we have the pecking order that we do."

Off her glare, Detectives Ramsey and Johnson begrudgingly walked out.

Once the door shut behind them, Matz asked Ethan, "Do you know why we're here?"

"They think I killed a guy, but like I tried to explain—"

"We know it's not you in the video," Matz said. "It's your twin brother, Jack."

"Yes, but Jack wouldn't hurt anyone unless he was being attacked." Ethan's impulse was to defend his brother even before he knew what he was defending. "He had years of Tae Kwon Do, which is all about being nonaggressive, using it only for self-defense—"

"We know what Tae Kwon Do is," Matz said. "And we agree that your brother was most likely attacked. The victim was no angel, God knows. No one is going to miss him besides an inmate or two. But there's another matter we need to discuss." She turned toward the two-way glass and yanked the privacy shade over the lurking detectives. "They have a missing persons dilemma in their district," she told Ethan, as she took the seat across from him. "They think Dancing Rabbit might be involved. And since you were there, they think you might know something about it."

Ethan nodded.

"We have reason to believe Dancing Rabbit is actually *helping* people disappear, like a witness protection program for people who aren't witnesses and probably don't deserve protection."

They're going to ask me about Anna.

"We're here to discuss one such person."

Here it comes.

"You know her as Brooke Shaw," Shu said.

What? Hearing her name hit Ethan like a smack on the head.

"You have no idea why your girlfriend left you," Shu chimed in, "and you don't even know her real name."

"You're right," Ethan admitted. "I don't."

"And there's something else you're not aware of," Matz told him: "She's on the FBI's most wanted list."

Ethan went numb.

"We just learned she was using the alias 'Brooke Shaw' yesterday," Matz said, "when our Stalker account alerted us."

"Your new face recognition feature made the match," Shu added.

"You hacked us?"

"He didn't say that," Matz said.

"You created an app that helps people do suspicious things," Shu said. "It attracts dangerous people. So yeah, we monitor the site."

"That's bullshit."

"Look who doesn't like their privacy invaded?" Shu taunted.

Ethan wanted to take a swing at the guy. "We only use public information."

"I don't give a flying fuck what you use," Shu spewed, "it's still creepy, just like you stalking your ex-girlfriend—"

"Shut up, Shu," Matz snapped. "No one wants to hear your opinion, or your politics." She leaned in closer to Ethan and said, "This is a lot for you to digest right now, but you need to know the truth about her."

"You're right," Ethan said, preparing himself. "Why is the FBI looking for her?"

Matz told him: "She's wanted in London for the murder of her father."

"Murder—?" Ethan choked.

It keeps getting worse.

"She loved her father," Ethan said defensively. "She wouldn't hurt him. She couldn't kill a fly. She can't even eat meat."

"She must be completely innocent, then," Shu said, condescendingly.

"Jealousy can make people do terrible things," Matz said, as if she were making a profound point.

Ethan recalled the first conversation he had with Brooke about why he started Stalker. Ethan had said, *"Our site finds people that don't want to be found, for a fee... Sometimes people can't move on. We help them get closure."*

Brooke responded, *"Because jealousy makes people do terrible things?"*

How would Matz have known that?

"Have you been listening to my conversations? Is my phone bugged—?"

"Don't be paranoid," Matz said. "I'm trying to tell you what your girlfriend's motive was. The Godeaux family had an awful lot of drama—"

"And an awful lot of money," Shu injected.

"—Betrayals, infidelities, inheritance discrepancies, and bitter jealousies that eventually led to murder."

"Godeaux?" Ethan whispered. "Is that her real name? Godeaux?"

"Yes," Matz confirmed, "her real name is Stella Godeaux,"

"Stella Godeaux," Ethan repeated as he thought again of the passage she had underlined in *Tropic of Cancer*: *As soon as a woman loses a front tooth or an eye or a leg she goes on the loose. What did she lose that was so irreplaceable? Why was she on the loose? Maybe she never told me anything so I wouldn't be able to talk if the FBI ever picked me up.*

"British Semi-Salic law says that children inherit an estate after the extinction of the last parent," Matz said. "This was about money."

"It's always about money," Shu added.

"After her father passed," Matz continued, "the family estate would presumably be divided between Stella and her brother. There must have been some unexpected surprises because the brother wasn't happy. He made accusations that the will had been tampered with, and worse, he was suspicious about the circumstances surrounding their father's death. He demanded an autopsy and, sure enough, the results proved that the old man's heart failure was provoked by a dose of cyanide."

"Maybe the brother poisoned the father," Ethan suggested. "He also had motive."

Matz shook her head. "After the autopsy, the court ordered the hospital to release the security footage in their father's hospital room. The hospital rooms all have cameras to monitor the patients. This was Stella Godeaux's last visit." Matz nodded to Shu. "Show him the footage."

"This is what we call indisputable evidence," Shu said as he pulled an iPad Mini from his pocket and played the security video. The footage was taken from a high, wide angle, and it was grainy, so details were not perfectly clear, but Ethan could make out a woman enter a hospital room. She had long black hair and was wearing a full-length raincoat over a red dress. She approached the patient, an older man with his eyes shut. The woman looked down on the man for a long while and then pulled a syringe from her purse and inserted a liquid into the IV. When the woman turned to leave, she glanced in the direction of the camera. It was brief and it was blurry. And it certainly looked like Brooke.

Ethan heard himself gasp.

"Her father had been admitted to a hospital and treated for a mild heart attack," Matz said. "According to the doctors, he would have made a full recovery. An hour after Stella Godeaux signed out at the visitors' desk, a nurse found her father dead."

"Then why didn't they arrest her?" Ethan asked.

"She had already fled the country. As soon as the autopsy was ordered, she split. They knew the flight she was on when she had entered the US as Stella Godeaux. But she'd had a few days' head start and didn't leave a trail. Our friends at the SIS asked us to help, but we couldn't find her. Like I said, we didn't know that she was using the identity of Brooke Shaw until your site made the connection."

Ethan looked shell shocked. "The SIS?"

"British Secret Service," Shu grinned, "MI6…Bond. James Bond."

Matz and Ethan both snapped, "Shut up, Shu!"

Ethan turned to Matz. "What do you want me to do?"

Her voice softened. "Just keep looking for her. She's not done with you."

Ethan smiled, without giving his face permission, hoping that Matz was right, that she wasn't done with him. He wasn't done with Brooke—or Stella—either.

It must have shown on his face because Matz explained, "If she were done with you, she wouldn't be tracking you still."

"The GPS signal on your iPhone doesn't shut off," Shu said.

"You searched my phone?" Ethan asked.

"He didn't say that," Matz said.

Shu smirked.

Anna Gopnik was right about Brooke tracking him, but all the new information about her still didn't mesh with what Ethan knew, or thought he knew. She was the least materialistic, most spiritual person he had ever met, and now these agents were claiming that she killed her father for her inheritance. He was sure they were all missing something.

"Think of the press you'll get," Shu said, "'Stalker founder uses his controversial site to track down his killer runaway bride.' That's advertising you couldn't pay for."

Getting press for Stalker was the last thing Ethan cared about just then, but he knew what they were getting at. "You want me to set her up?"

Matz nodded; Shu grinned.

"No one has heard her side yet," Ethan protested. "I'm telling you, none of this sounds anything like her."

"You saw the footage in the hospital," Matz said.

"And innocent people don't run," Shu said, repeating what Detective Johnson had said about Jack.

"Unless there's another explanation."

Matz was growing impatient. "Like what?"

Ethan searched for possibilities. "Maybe someone made her kill her father. Maybe her father asked her to do it. Maybe she's protecting someone. Maybe she has a twin sister."

The agents both laughed.

Ethan was at a loss. He didn't have a clue whom she'd be protecting, and he was running out of ideas.

"Anything is possible," Matz said empathetically. "We all want to find out what really happened, the truth. Once we find her, she'll be sent back home, and she'll get a fair trial. So help us."

"Let the courts decide if she's innocent," Shu added. "Have some faith in the system."

Faith was something Ethan usually had plenty of. Sitting there hearing about his brother and girlfriend both killing people was surely testing every last bit.

"We'll get you released from here tonight," Matz said. She snapped her fingers and Shu pulled a plastic bag from his pocket with Ethan's iPhone inside. "Keep your phone with you at all times so she can keep tracking you."

Shu handed Ethan his phone. "And so we can stay in constant communication."

"What about Jack?" Ethan asked.

"I was just getting to that," Matz said. "We'll make sure he walks."

"Do you really have the authority to release someone in this situation?" he had to ask.

"If we really wanted your brother, he'd be here right now instead of you," Shu crowed.

"Then you know where he is?"

"The phone company gave us his last few calls, and what do you know?"

"Shut up, Shu." Matz turned to Ethan. "We'll exonerate your brother. We can make that happen, if you promise your full cooperation." Matz extended her hand. "Do we have a deal?"

CHAPTER 28

THE RISING SUN GLIMMERED off the Monterey police complex. Ethan shielded his eyes so he could see the tow truck release his car from its hooks. The driver who was ordered to bring it up from Big Sur at four in the morning to convenience a yuppie murder suspect was not looking happy, but he smiled as Ethan's brand-spanking-new Tesla Model X dropped hard.

Karmic justice.

Ethan approached. "Any chance it's been plugged in?"

"Car's exactly as you left it."

The driver sorted out the paperwork and handed Ethan the keys. Ethan got inside and checked the dashboard. His battery had enough of a charge to get back up to San Francisco.

Ethan drove away and called Bailey. While the phone rang, Ethan thought of something Jack had often said: *Every advantage has an equal or worse disadvantage.* It was true with every app entrepreneurs created to make lives more efficient and convenient. It was true for his car that was invented to save the planet. Ethan realized that it was also true about people, and especially true for twins.

Bailey sounded anxious when he picked up. "I've been calling all night. For the love of God, where have you been?"

"Jail," Ethan told him. "They thought I was Jack. They have a video of him running away from a dead guy holding a gun."

"We've all seen it," Bailey said. "It was on the news, for Christ's sake! The office was abuzz last night. Everyone stayed until midnight. Good thing we don't pay overtime."

Ethan smiled. "Glad you always put the business first."

"Somebody has to, especially since your brother quit on us and you went AWOL."

"I'll be back as soon as I find her."

"So you're out? They released you?"

"Yeah, and the FBI will make Jack's charges go away if I help them find Brooke," Ethan explained. "But you'll never believe why they're looking for her."

"At this point, I'd believe anything."

Being the first time Ethan said it out loud, he nearly swerved off the road when it came out of his mouth. "She's wanted for the murder of her father. They think she was after her family fortune."

Bailey fell silent, for once.

"You still there?"

"High-class problems never cease to astonish," Bailey said. "I should have known. Her being from the Royal Borough of Kensington and all. Is she a princess, duchess, lady, majesty—?"

"I don't know."

"I'll bet her surname is Mountbatten or Windsor—"

"Godeaux," Ethan told him.

Bailey's voice dropped an octave. "What did you just say?"

"Her real name is Stella Godeaux."

"Bugger!" Bailey blurted. "Please, don't tell me this!"

"Why? Is she really a duchess?"

"We should only be so lucky," Bailey said. "You know our angel investor—?"

"No," Ethan reminded him, "because I've never spoken to him."

"Well, his name is Clinton Godeaux, an Englishman with a French surname, for fuck's sake! He's also the guy from Kensington who's been looking for her with the initials C. G. Now we know why he wanted to remain nameless. I'm such an arse, I should have known!"

"He obviously didn't want you to know."

"Maybe Emily was right about her," Bailey said. "Maybe she was already married when she came to America. I can find out in a jiffy."

Bailey moved over to his desktop computer. "A quick search will suss out if Godeaux was her maiden or married name."

"'I'he FBI told me that she had a brother who contested the father's will. Clinton Godeaux is probably the brother—"

"Eesh!" Bailey shrieked as articles emerged from *The Sun, The Mirror, Daily Mail*, and local tabloids. "This was a big scandal. It's all over the red tops." Bailey skimmed a few articles and then read out loud, "'Stella Godeaux fled the country after the autopsy proved that her father, Arthur Godeaux, was poisoned to death.'" Bailey paused to consider the weight of this, and then asked, "What if the reason CG backed Stalker was just to find her? That must be why he pressured us to put our Face Match Mode up before it was ready, and the reason I can't get ahold of him now I have three calls into him."

Ethan reasoned, "Funding a company just to find someone is pretty extreme."

"Not if you're looking for your sister who murdered your father and messed with your inheritance. Says right here that her father, Arthur Godeaux, was a successful businessman and her mother, Beatrice Goodchild-Godeaux, was the daughter of an English aristocrat. This doesn't look good, Gov—"

"I still don't believe it. She couldn't murder anyone. She couldn't."

"All evidence is pointing to the contrary."

"She told me that she loved her father, that they were close. And she never lied. You know her. She was blunt and forthright about everything."

"About everything that she wanted you to know." Bailey's voice dropped to a whisper. "She avoided talking about anything personal. That's not normal. Women love to share everything. They love to talk. At least, all the women I know do."

Ethan stared out at the road. Was it possible that her brother financed Stalker just to find her? Could this be an elaborate cat-and-mouse game that he had gotten mixed up in?

"Remember how you originally pitched Stalker?" Bailey reminded Ethan, "For people who are too preoccupied and hung up on the past—?"

"To help people find resolve in their past so they can have a future," Ethan corrected.

"Same difference. It's for desperate people, if we're being honest."

"Desperate measures!" Ethan countered. "It's for people who can't move on until they have answers..." His voice went raspy and dire. "Like me now."

"This has been a rough patch for you, Gov. But you'll get through it. You've taken Stalker this far because you're a believer. You think everything is possible and it's a great quality. It's contagious. It's the reason we're all here."

"My brother calls it blind faith."

"You can be starry-eyed at times. It's true. And that's why you can't see Brooke—or Stella—for what she really is, maybe."

They both went silent for a bit. Ethan felt ridiculous for being so mulish, despite the facts.

"Your blind faith or optimism or belief in the underdog or whatever you want to call it, is rare," Bailey said, "and it's the reason you'll get through this. You'll find love again. There are plenty of fish in the sea, some of whom are not wanted for murder."

Ethan appreciated the encouragement but the thought of moving on from Brooke was too much to bear. "The FBI gave me the address of where my brother's hiding. I'm on my way there now. Do me a favor?"

"Sure. Anything."

"Keep trying Clinton Godeaux and see what his intentions are?"

"Sure," Bailey promised. "I'll call if I get through to him."

It was the last time they ever spoke.

CHAPTER 29

SEAN MCQUEEN'S AWARD-WINNING *ARCHITECTURAL Digest* glass home was perched atop the most desired vantage point overlooking the San Francisco Bay. Ethan drove up the long waning driveway, wondering if McQueen traded up homes the way he traded companies.

Sean McQueen was at the peak of the Silicon stratosphere—literally and figuratively—a twinkling star in a culture so often compared to Tinseltown because of the hypersonic successes, disastrous failures, and all the hyped-up nonsense along the way. High school with fuck-you money. And because McQueen stayed out of the limelight, it added to his mystery, intrigue, and valuation.

The blog TechCrunch coined the terms "unicorn" to define start-ups that are worth $1 billion, "deacorns" that are worth $10 billion, and "super unicorn" that are worth $100 billion or more. These hacks billed Sean McQueen, the Wizard of Silicon, as most likely to reach super unicorn status this decade. They had also projected that his latest start-up Hounddog—was likely to surpass Stalker and lead all transparency apps within a year. And it irritated Ethan to no end. Not only the overused, exaggerated tech speak and nescient speculation, but also how venture capitalists would blindly throw money at image entrepreneurs like Sean McQueen, who bought and sold companies on a whim and were surely creating another bubble that would burst all over the rest of the up-and-comers.

But as Ethan walked up to McQueen's massive oak door, he thought of Brooke (the mindful Brooke he knew, not the killer-on-the-run Brooke) and how she would have called him on the real reason he thought ill of a man he had never even met: McQueen had poached his brother.

Ethan laughed at himself and the oak door opened before he could knock—right on cue.

Sean McQueen extended his hand and revealed a warm smile. "You must be Jack's brother."

"What was your first clue?" Ethan said, rubbing his scruffy beard.

"I'm Sean," he said like his status didn't require a last name. "Come inside. Please."

Glad he didn't introduce himself as "The Wizard."

"Nice digs," he said matter-of-factly as he looked around what might have been the most awesome home he had ever set foot in. "Where's Jack?"

"In the shower," McQueen said. "I can give you the three-dollar tour until he comes out." McQueen pressed a remote that raised a motorized curtain. The floor to ceiling glass windows revealed a drop-dead 180-degree panorama of the sun setting over the bay. The view looked like an Albert Bierstadt painting, one of Ethan's favorite artists who painted wonderful, almost surreal landscapes, and one of the reasons Ethan had originally wanted to move out west.

"I get so sick of looking at this view," Sean joked. "Can I get you something to drink or eat?"

Ethan wanted to hate the guy but Sean had the kind of charm that made it impossible.

"I'm fine," Ethan said. "Just tell my brother that I'm here. Please."

Just then, Jack came out from the bathroom, skimpy towel around his waist, and he didn't look happy. "What are you doing here?"

"I'm here to see you," Ethan said.

"How'd you know where to find me?"

"The FBI told me what happened and where you were. They know everything."

"How? How do they know?"

"They used the Stalker app," Ethan half joked. "They have no boundaries. Why'd you run?"

Jack stared back.

"They showed me the video—"

"I was standing over a dead body, holding a gun. Why do you think I ran?"

Ethan exhaled, relieved. "They believe that it was just self-defense and they're going to clear you. You're off the hook, they assured me. You're good—"

"Good? Goons the size of this house attacked me because they thought I was you! They were looking for Brooke. I'm lucky to be alive—"

"I know. We've both been through a lot. Let's sit down and have a little talk. I have a lot to tell you. And you have a lot to tell me."

Jack glanced at Sean through the kitchen passway, as if looking for approval.

"Better to get it all in the open," Sean said.

"Yeah, okay." Jack went pale and headed down the hallway. "I'll put on some clothes and we'll talk."

Ethan knew Jack would be shocked to hear about Brooke's supposed crimes. But Jack was about to disclose a shocker or two of his own.

—

THE MARINE LAYER WAS so thick that the bright multihued Ferris wheel on the Santa Monica Pier was virtually undetectable from the shoreline.

Bailey trudged through the sand alternating his humming with periodic curse words, his breath heavy, his smoker's lungs wheezing the entire time.

When he approached the third concrete caisson under the dock, Clinton Godeaux stepped into view and announced, "Good morning, Mr. Duff."

Bailey gasped, taken by surprise.

"Don't get your knickers in a twist," Clinton said, "I told you I'd meet you here."

Clinton had always controlled where they met, how long they met for, and what they discussed. It made Bailey uneasy, as did the oversized Tom Ford tinted glasses that hid Clinton's eyes.

"It's monkeys outside," Bailey complained. "Our offices are not bugged. Hardly anyone shows up this early, not to mention that none of our employees would have any idea who you are."

"I can't take any chances, in the case you told some of them about our arrangement—"

"You made it perfectly clear that you wanted to be a silent angel," Bailey assured him. "It drove my partners mad that they could never meet you."

"I'm sure they didn't mind so much when my checks cleared."

"They whinged me about that, too," Bailey told him, "why the checks were distributed from Highpoint Corporation, a dodgy, unregistered corporation."

"I told you to tell them that it was a shell company."

"I did." Bailey took a few deep breaths and looked out at the crashing waves. "You need to answer some questions now."

"You want to know why Highpoint wasn't registered as a corporation?"

"For starters."

"Because it's the name of a place."

"Is that right?" Bailey waited for him to elaborate, but he didn't. Bailey asked, "Did you finance our company to look for your sister?"

Clinton's eyes turned cold.

"I know that you've had a Stalker account with your initials, C. G.," Bailey admitted.

"So much for the privacy settings, I suppose," Clinton said mockingly. "Stalker. The stalking company that stalks you right back. Brilliant."

"Is that why you forced us to get the Face Match Mode online before it was ready?" Bailey pressed.

"I needed to find my sister," Clinton professed. "I'm a satisfied customer."

"You learned that your sister was using the name Brooke Shaw when she filed for a marriage license."

Clinton laughed, but it was a contemptuous laugh. "Nothing is sacred." He took off his large Tom Ford aviators and pulled the handkerchief from his pocket to clean them.

That was the first time Bailey saw Clinton's face in broad daylight, and his eyes. "I can't believe I never noticed…you look just like her!"

Clinton's brow furrowed and his smile lines faded. "You've given me no choice. I'm going to have to shut you down."

"What? Why—?"

"I didn't want anyone to know that I had anything to do with Stalker."

"No one knows—"

"Don't be a daft cow. I have to eliminate any loose ends. You're a loose end. It's over. You're finished."

"No, you can't do that. We are so close to profit!"

"Don't take it personally. Ninety percent of all start-ups fail."

Before Bailey could object again, Clinton pulled out a 9mm handgun that his contracted bounty hunter, Ace, had given to him when he picked him up at the airport.

Bailey backed away and tripped, falling on the sand, then scrambled like a crab. "You have my word, I won't tell anyone anything, I promise—"

"I know you won't." Clinton squeezed the trigger and the bullet hit Bailey right between the eyes. "Dead men can't talk."

Pigeons flapped noisily as Clinton walked away through the dense fog.

THE BLACK BOX APP that Brooke had installed in Bailey's phone recorded everything: the entire conversation with Clinton, the gunshot, and the 911 call that a jogger made when he noticed Bailey's body sprawled facedown in the sand.

The Santa Monica police was there in ten minutes. They taped off the area and questioned a few people. One of them told the police that he'd heard a gunshot. Another said he saw a man get inside a black Escalade in the nearby beach parking lot and the big car screeched away like he was in a big rush. None were able to describe the man.

The police found Bailey's office information on a business card in his wallet. Stalker employees were summoned to identify his body.

Since Stalker had been flagged in the hunt for Stella Godeaux, an FBI agent showed up an hour later and informed the police that the victim was related to a high-profile investigation. Per protocol, the FBI agent confiscated Bailey's cell phone. If he had taken it back for full analysis, the FBI likely would have found the Black Box app and learned what Clinton Godeaux had done.

But he didn't.

Instead, Bailey's phone was sent up to San Francisco, per the request of Special Agent Shu, who thought of himself as digitally savvy.

But who wasn't savvy enough.

CHAPTER 31

ETHAN SAT WITH JACK in Sean's living room reliving the past twenty-four hours.

Ethan asked Jack about his abduction, knowing Jack was still reeling from seeing a man die, and feeling responsible.

"It was the first time since I declared my atheism that I wished I had a God to absolve him," Jack told him.

"And I thought you were hopeless," Ethan teased.

"Right now, I'm just glad to be alive."

Ethan explained what had happened when he went back to Dancing Rabbit, how he had been mistakenly identified, arrested, and told that Brooke was wanted for the murder of her father.

"Everything I thought I knew about her is a lie," Ethan said. "She played me like *Grand Theft Auto*."

"I don't believe that," Sean said as he joined them, sitting next to Jack, as if Jack were his. "She's in love with you. She wanted to marry you."

Sean made Ethan uneasy. He was his direct competitor with an unfair advantage, who had lured his brother away, likely for some insane amount of money.

Ethan asked Sean glibly, "How would you know?"

"She told me so."

"When did you meet her?"

Sean and Jack exchanged a look.

"Sean's right," Jack said as he stood up, preparing. "It's time to get everything in the open."

"That's what I thought we were doing," Ethan said.

"Remember I told you that Brooke was the reason I moved up here?"

Ethan nodded. "You said that she introduced you to the guy that hired you."

"Exactly." Jack looked over at Sean. "Sean is that guy. Brooke introduced me to Sean—"

"She introduced us," Sean repeated. "I also had met her at Dancing Rabbit." Sean pointed at the rabbit statue on his fireplace, its large, black, glassy eyes staring back as if it were watching them, gauging. "She gave me one of those trophies after our retreat."

"Just like the one she gave us," Jack said.

Just like the one she gave the Walls, too, Ethan thought.

"I was so impressed with her," Sean continued, "I hired her as a consultant. She helped us refine our mission, how we can use our technology to help people. We even developed a few apps for her."

"She was a consultant for Hounddog?" Jack looked genuinely surprised and said to Sean, "You never told me that."

"I couldn't tell you. We signed a confidentiality agreement. Silicon Valley is competitive. We need to be discreet about everything as we grow."

"So do we," Ethan said sharply. "And there are laws against hiring a consultant who was living with the CEO of your biggest competitor."

Sean didn't waver. "She never discussed your business with me and, obviously, she never discussed my business with you. She wasn't duplicitous. I wouldn't have hired her if I had any doubts about her loyalty."

"You don't get any more duplicitous than using a false name. She isn't really Brooke Shaw. Did you know that her real name is Stella Godeaux and she's wanted for murder?"

"No. I did not."

"Sean's right," Jack said. "Until we know her side of the story, we can't make assumptions."

Ethan took a deep breath and lowered his voice. "I've been telling myself the same thing, over and over again, trying to believe that she must have a reason. I fell in love with a woman that couldn't do any of these things. I would never describe her as duplicitous or deceptive or dangerous. But the facts keep hammering away at my loyalty. The FBI showed me a security video of her injecting some kind of syringe into her father's IV."

"What?" Sean and Jack said simultaneously.

"Her old man died of cyanide poisoning," Ethan said, looking out the window shaking his head. "I don't know how to spin that one."

"We have to consider all the angles and possibilities," Sean countered. "They played a video on the news of Jack running away from his attack and made it sound like he was a murderer, too. The truth isn't always obvious."

"Brooke is not a killer any more than I am," Jack agreed. "Now is not the time to lose faith in her."

This hit Ethan hard. He was giving up on the woman he loved enough to commit the rest of his life to. Everything he learned in the last few days was painting a completely different picture of the woman he thought he knew so well. The FBI had convinced him that she had killed her father. The security video was proof. Her family inheritance was motive. Bailey told him that her brother Clinton had financed Stalker just to find her. She had secretly worked as a consultant for Hounddog, his competition. And worse of all, she disappeared without any explanation. All logic told him that she was deceitful, at the very least. But his heart still beat for her. Jack and Sean were right, he decided. Now was not the time to give up on her.

"Sometimes you live your life with blinders and choose not to see what's really going on," Jack added. "You won't see the real truth if you don't see the entire picture. Like when Barry died—"

"Let's not beat a dead horse," Ethan moaned. "Why would you bring up Barry now?"

"Because it's a perfect example. You're still angry at Barry, and for all the wrong reasons—"

"Like everyone else, I'm angry because he killed himself."

Jack added, "And because he didn't come to you before he did the deed. Am I right?"

"Yeah, you're right," Ethan relented, "I think I could have helped him if I knew."

"Did you ever think that maybe he didn't want you to judge him and that's why he didn't say anything?'"

"Judge him?"

Jack glanced at Sean for reassurance. Sean nodded back. This made Ethan even angrier and he asked them, "Am I missing something here?"

"I loved Barry," Jack told Ethan.

"So did I," Ethan snapped back.

Jack's voice shook, "Not in the same way as I did."

A long silence followed.

A deadly silence.

Sean nervously grabbed the snacks no one had touched, and headed back to the kitchen saying, "See, we all feel much better now that everything is in the open, don't we?"

Ethan stared at his brother, trying to cipher the bomb he just dropped, if he understood him right.

"Barry was my first love," Jack explained, "and neither one of us were ready to accept what we were."

"That's why…" Ethan cleared his raspy throat. "That's why he killed himself?"

Jack nodded. "His family would have disowned him. Remember his dad? Remember his brothers? They would have flipped out. Barry was a star athlete. He was popular. No one would have accepted him. Or at least that's what he thought. He couldn't live with himself, disappointing the people he loved."

"He could have kept it to himself and lived a lie, like you apparently have."

"He doesn't mean that," Sean shouted from the kitchen.

Ethan glared at Sean, as if he were to blame, and spotted Sean's monogrammed kitchen towels. "S. M. Sean McQueen. It's your initials."

"Genius," Sean said. "He can read."

Ethan turned to his brother. "Those skimpy red underpants I found in your bathroom had the same embroidered initials. I thought it was a stupid logo, like an S&M thing. But it's him... It's you... You two... You two are...?"

This time Sean and Jack overlapped: "Gay!"

"He's quick, too," Sean joked to lighten the mood. "Jack chased me out of his new house this morning because you were on your way over," Sean told Ethan. "That's the reason I left my underwear behind. And monogrammed underwear is not something you want to leave behind."

Ethan couldn't help chuckling at that one. "Monogrammed underwear is not something you want to admit you have, either," he chimed in.

They all laughed.

Jack said, "Brooke introduced me to Sean because she knew we'd like each other. Not to divulge company secrets. She and I got pretty close while she lived with us. She was easy to talk to. I trusted her. I liked her."

Ethan nodded. "I know."

"That's why I had opened up to her about Barry and me. She understood why I hadn't come out to you. She knew that I didn't want to disappoint you. She got that. I knew you'd feel ashamed, maybe hate me, and I couldn't handle that."

Ethan's spine straightened. "You thought I would hate you? We've never had secrets, you and me."

"Except this one," Jack told his brother. "It's going to take some time to process this. I get it."

Ethan stood up, walked over to the windows, and stared out at the wondrous view of the bay. "You're not one to care what other people think. You're not afraid of being different. You've never backed away from controversy, and being gay isn't even as controversial anymore. This explains a lot of your odd, secretive behavior, but I don't get why you would hide it from me all these years."

Jack got up and stood by his brother. "You're right. I don't care what most people think. But I do care what you think. We could always laugh about our differences that no one else could see because we look alike, but if we're being honest, you have expectations of me, like I should live up to the standards you have for yourself. We can be different but we're still a reflection of each other, in the same way that macho dads can't handle gay sons—"

"You didn't think I'd approve?"

"I worried you'd be ashamed as a republican with a Mexican cousin wanting to cross the border."

Ethan smiled. "Good thing gay is the new black, right? Tim Cook is the new Steve Jobs. Anderson Cooper and Don Lemon are the new news."

"Are you saying that I'm destined for greatness?"

"Not at all. Especially since you left Stalker. But you don't need my approval, or anybody else's."

The twins both stared out at the bay for a bit. "You never understood why I get so depressed," Jack continued. "You can't imagine how low I go. I take meds on and off, depending on how bad things get, and the mood of my psychiatrist."

Ethan finally had a reason to justify feeling overprotective of his brother. "You once told me that you never wanted to have kids because it took the option of suicide off the table. That was long before Barry. Scared the hell out of me. I always worried about you after that. Who says things like that? Barry never said things like that and he actually did it."

"Barry didn't get the idea from me."

"I didn't say that—"

"I didn't know he was going to do it. I had no idea."

"Of course you didn't know," Ethan said. "I'm sorry you didn't think I would support who you are. I'm sorry I was so blind. I'm sorry I gave you reasons to think that I couldn't handle it—"

"And I'm sorry I didn't have enough faith in you," Jack cut in. "You're the one person in this world I should never doubt."

Ethan put his hand on Jack's shoulder. "You're my brother, my blood, we've shared everything."

"Even our birth," Jack agreed.

"I could never hate you," Ethan assured him. "Turning my back on you would be turning my back on myself."

CHAPTER 31

MINDFULNESS IS ABOUT LIVING in the moment, but it's hard to stay present when the past is coming for you. Brooke was convinced that if the past caught up with her, she would have no future, which presented a tremendous internal predicament. Even though she was adamantly opposed to using invasive technology to spy and manipulate, it was her only chance to survive.

It seemed to Brooke like an either/or quandary; either we are pawns living in an Orwellian world, or we go completely off the grid. And if we choose the latter, we need to use technology to stay safe, which often requires monitoring, spying, and, yes, privacy invasion. She had given much thought to this maddening paradox, especially since she had been on the run in America.

When she heard about the government monitoring phone calls, medical records, bank transactions, and private communication—all in the name of fighting enemies of the free world—it made her paranoid. Knowing that people were being recorded almost everywhere, she grew concerned for modern society, fearing that basic trust was in crisis. Even the thought of drones taking out terrorists in foreign lands with a push of a button kept her up at nights vexing that it was only a matter of time until our enemies acquired the same technology to wipe us out.

For every step of progress, there's an equal or greater danger.

But when Brooke weighed the pros and cons, and considered the cause and effect of using technology to its full advantage, she decided that it was worth the risk of dreadful consequences in the name of freedom—hers and her fellow Rabbits.

Rabbits weren't only people that worked at the Dancing Rabbit ecovillage—those wonderful people she met who committed themselves to sustainability, community, and leaving the world a better place. While she was living there, on the lam, she came to realize that there were a lot of people like her that desperately wanted to drop off the grid. Their reasons varied. Some needed to run. Some just wanted a change. And all of them didn't know it was possible. She had tapped into an underserved market, and, like all great entrepreneurs, she built a business that filled a unique void. She took on clients slowly, vetted them thoroughly, and turned aspiring escape artists into her own version of Rabbits, with mindful transformations that changed them forever. She was able to manage the business remotely—as a digital nomad—from iPhones that could only be traced back to employees at Dancing Rabbit, good citizens that never left the property, and who didn't even know the phones were registered under their name.

Since Brooke's select clients paid handsomely for this service, she was able to continually invest in custom tech artillery that kept her fellow Rabbits safe. In addition to the apps she had Hounddog build—Pocket Dialer and Black Box—she had a surveillance company called Eyecam build her miniature security cameras inside things she would give to potential clients.

When she was working at Dancing Rabbit, she gave porcelain rabbit statues to everyone that participated in her corporate retreat seminars, to remind them of the bliss they experienced in Big Sur, that nature was always with them, and transformation and growth were forever possible. She had Eyecam customize statues for people she believed had potential to become her future Rabbits, and would suggest that they place it in the center of their homes—in the most common room of their house—for a constant connection to mindfulness. Of course she never told them that it gave her ability to record activity in their homes to monitor them and determine if she were going to take them on as clients.

That's right, the Dancing Rabbit statues had security cameras installed in their heads, and she could access the real-time video it recorded with the Eyecam app called Security Video.

In the case of Rufus Wall, when he met Brooke on the Hounddog corporate retreat, he confessed a desperate desire to change his life but he didn't know how. Work had become a grind for him. His doctor had told him that his health was fragile and he couldn't keep up the pace he was going at. He wanted to work less and take life a little slower, possibly in some lovely place. His wife Sarah, who controlled the family finances, wouldn't hear of it, as she was also spending his money faster than he could make it. Further, her odd behavior whenever he returned from business trips—which was often—made him suspect that she was cheating on him. But divorce was not an option. Sarah was greedy. She had nothing to lose, everything to gain, and a best friend who was a ruthless divorce attorney.

For Brooke, finding out that Sarah Wall was having affairs only required one look at the Security Camera app the first time Rufus went out of town. When the Hounddog was away, the Hounddog's wife sure did play, and the porcelain rabbit saw it all. Sarah's deviant sexual exploits in the living room with her Pilates instructor were reason enough for Rufus to justify leaving the marriage. Rufus was an ideal Rabbit candidate and Brooke promised to help him transform. She advised him to be patient and wait for the right time. He was an extremely talented programmer and she laid out a future for him that made his long wait well worth it.

More than a year later, they executed their plan.

———

SARAH WALL WAS BESIDE herself when she had first received the call from the Big Sur Police Department explaining that they had found her husband's suitcase in a car that went over a cliff. She racked her brain for a reason why Rufus had been in Big Sur when he had told her that he was going to New York on business. There was only one explanation: he was having an affair. Despite her own infidelities, the thought enraged her. She wanted to get even, and the best revenge was living well. If he were up in Big Sur shtupping some young hippie chick, like the one he supposedly went over the cliff with, then she would get everything. She could cash in the $2 million life insurance policy she had made him buy, add it to their substantial investment account she had been managing, move back east (preferably somewhere warm), look for a new Pilates instructor, and make a fresh start.

But to do all that, she needed a body.

The morning after Ethan had paid her a visit, she woke up feeling anxious. She made herself coffee and checked the *Big Sur News* online to see if her husband's body had been fished out of the ocean during the night. But no such luck.

Then she went to the Fidelity website to see how her stocks were doing. Fortunately, the market was up. Unfortunately, her investment account was down. Way down. In fact, it had been emptied. Zero balance.

Since she and Rufus were the only two people who had access, she immediately called the Big Sur detectives who had notified her about her husband's supposed accident, to let them know that her husband was alive, a thief, and on the run. She demanded that they expand their search to find him. She wanted to press charges. She wanted to sue him. She even called her divorce attorney friend to prepare for battle, no matter the cost.

The Big Sur Police Department notified the FBI, and when the FBI got a face recognition match and learned that Rufus Wall had used the identity of Benjamin Carver and married murder suspect Stella Godeaux, they turned up the heat.

———

BROOKE HAD PROMISED RUFUS that she would monitor the situation until he was safely relocated. She turned on her Security Camera app and selected the Dancing Rabbit statue inside the Walls' home and saw quite a scene:

———

FBI AGENTS MATZ AND Shu ran inside the house waving their credentials, their voices overlapping, "Federal agents…" "The cavalry has arrived…" "Shut up, Shu! Collect intel… Do your job."

Sarah entered the living room sobbing.

Matz approached her. "Sarah Wall?"

Sarah sniffled.

"I'm Agent Matz, FBI. Okay if we sit over here?"

Sarah followed Matz to the couch.

"Tell me exactly what happened, when you noticed—"

"I always check the markets just after they open, six thirty our time." Sarah booted up her laptop on the coffee table. "I trade our stocks and bonds from this Fidelity account." She turned the screen toward Matz. "See?"

"What am I looking at?" Matz asked.

"The balance was over three million yesterday. Today, nothing. Zilch. The douchebag ordered a wire transfer."

Matz got the picture. "At least we know he didn't die off that cliff."

"Little comfort that brings me now," Sarah shouted, blowing her nose for effect. "These are our marital assets! I know my rights! I want to lock him up and throw away the key—!"

"First we have to find him," Matz said calmly. "Any thoughts where he might be—?"

Shu entered, interrupting. "Are these your husband's drawings?" He shoved an Android tablet in front of Sarah's face.

Sarah nodded. "It's his 'doodle pad.' He was working on a new emoji app."

"Is this cartoon character supposed to be him?"

"Ridiculous, I know," Sarah spewed. "It's his avatar, doing things he only wishes he could do. That's supposed to be him scuba diving, as if."

"Why is this relevant, Shu?" Matz demanded.

Shu held up the tablet and expanded the screen. "The last picture he drew has him looking out of a window on a plane that's heading for an island, grinning ear to ear. See what he drew on the island?"

Matz got up to take a closer look. "A flag?"

"A British flag…with the coat of arms."

Matz nodded, impressed. "Good work, Shu." She turned to Sarah and asked, "Does your husband have business in the Cayman Islands?"

"No. Not that I know of."

"If that's where he's gone," Shu explained, "there's nothing we can do. The Caymans don't extradite."

Matz looked at the emptied Fidelity account on Sarah's laptop. "It's likely that he transferred all the money into an offshore bank—"

Shu snickered, "Sucks for you."

Matz turned angry. "Remember when we talked about manners, sensitivity, and respect? This is one of those times."

"I feel faint," Sarah whispered.

Shu turned to an officer. "Can we get her some water over here?"

The officer headed to the kitchen.

Shu sat down beside Sarah and rubbed her neck. "That feel good?"

Sarah groaned, "I guess."

"You're a beautiful woman, Mrs. Wall. You'll have no problem starting over."

"Yesterday I was a multimillionaire. Today I'm flat broke."

"You have this ginormous house."

"Mortgaged to the hilt. How is that supposed to make me feel better?"

"What's the matter with you?" Matz interjected.

"You told me to be more sensitive—"

"I told you to do your job. There's still a chance he hasn't left yet. Check every flight to the Caymans. Now!"

———

Brooke forwarded this video clip to Rufus's new Benjamin Carver email account directly from her Security Video app. His flight wasn't scheduled to leave until later that afternoon and the FBI still had time to stop him. She hoped he'd received the message in time.

This Rabbit needed to run!

CHAPTER 32

"SORRY TO LAY ALL this on you when your focus needs to be on Brooke," Jack said. "For what it's worth, I know she loves you. She couldn't fake that. No one could. And it's hard to believe that she killed anyone, let alone her own father. She must have gotten caught up in something pretty awful."

"I have to find out," Ethan said as he headed toward the door. "I'm going to find her."

Jack exclaimed, "You don't have any idea where she is!"

Ethan turned back, a look of frustration on his face, and shook his head.

"What do you know about Clinton Godeaux?" Sean asked as he entered the foyer. "Other than he's her brother?"

"Just what the FBI told me," Ethan explained. "There were inheritance issues. Her brother suspected foul play, asked for the autopsy. The autopsy proved that the father was murdered. Seems straightforward."

"What else?" Sean pressed.

"He secretly funded our company and used an account with just his initials—C. G.—as well as all the privacy settings. And when Brooke married Benjamin Carver—your employee, Rufus Wall—he got a face recognition match on our site and discovered that she was using the name Brooke Shaw. That's all I know."

"So he can find her now?"

"That's why she's running, I assume..." And then Ethan's eyes brightened and he stuttered with excitement, "Unless...unless she just wants it to look like she's running. Maybe she wants her brother to come for her. Maybe she's leading him to her, setting a trap. She can't go to the cops. And knowing Brooke, she'd take care of the problem on her own, without putting anyone else in danger. Including me."

"Sounds feasible," Sean agreed. "She kept her brother away all this time, after all."

"As soon as our Face Match Mode goes up," Ethan added, "she gets a driver's license, which requires a picture that goes into the main databank we have access to."

Jack jumped in. "So the Face Match Mode lights up and her brother knows that she's using the name Brooke Shaw."

"She probably got the driver's license because she needed a legit photo ID to get a marriage license," Ethan said, "and that goes into the public record."

"So then the Face Match Mode lights up again," Jack added, "tells her brother that she married a guy named Benjamin Carver."

Ethan nodded. "She knew there would be a public record. She knew that her brother would get a match and come for her."

"Or send some tattooed thugs to find her," Jack said.

"She didn't get married to run away, but to be found." Ethan started pacing, completely consumed. "She's trying to get her brother to come to her. But why? Why would she concoct such an elaborate system to keep him away and then lure him to her? Why would she move to Big Sur and preach mindfulness and balance to tech entrepreneurs and put such a value on privacy?"

"And there's something about the way she was so involved with Hounddog's company culture," Sean added, "and the way she avoided yours."

"She never wanted to discuss Stalker business," Ethan agreed. "She only expressed her concern. But why? What did our site do to threaten her safety that Hounddog didn't?"

Sean walked across the room slowly, taking some time before he answered. "At Stalker you use biometrics primarily to find people, but at Hounddog we use biometrics mostly for privacy. We find ways to block a trail and send false leads. Much of that came from Brooke. She led us down that path. Stalker and Hounddog are basically using the same technology but for opposite purposes."

"She supported technology that helped protect privacy, for people like herself that needed to hide. Anna Gopnik told me that Brooke had put tracking devices in our phones. Brooke warned me that the police were coming for me. She sent me texts and told me where to hide. That's how I ran into Anna—"

"The tracking apps we created for her were spec concepts never meant to go to market," Sean said. "Our guys love working on extracurricular projects, and we encourage it as long as they get their work done. I believed her when she told me they would only be used to help people that had no other options. But I didn't ask enough questions."

"This explains the missing people in Big Sur," Ethan said. "When she lived there, she was hiding, right? Maybe she also helped other people on the run. She got cozy with tech companies that could help her develop tools to do just that."

"To hide people who deserved a second chance," Sean blurted. "She once told me that thousands of people drop off the grid every year, cutting all ties, changing their identities, hiding their money. Maybe that was her concept for Dancing Rabbit... The people who live there valued privacy so much. Maybe she had us develop apps to help some of them turn into ghosts."

"That sounds more like her, helping people who deserved a second chance, a second lease on life, living mindfully. She always talked about people looking through different prisms, how there are always two sides, a paradox. Maybe the reason was because she deserved another chance. I can't imagine what kind of justification there is for killing her father, but until we hear her side..." Ethan's wheels were spinning, and he turned to Sean. "Any chance you have the book *Tropic of Cancer* by Henry Miller?"

"I don't think so."

"Why is that relevant?" Jack asked.

"When I was running from the police," Ethan explained, "the text told me to go inside the Henry Miller library. Anna Gopnik was hiding there. I asked her why she was faking her death. She told me that no one shares how or why they disappear. That's how they prevent any leaks. She told me that Brooke knew that I might come looking for her. And she gave me a copy of *Tropic of Cancer*. Brooke's copy. Brooke had underlined a weird passage. I thought Brooke was trying to send me a message."

Sean grabbed his laptop. "I can download the book from Amazon in ten seconds."

Once he did, Ethan found the section that Anna had shown him and read it out loud: "'As soon as a woman loses a front tooth or an eye or a leg she goes on the loose. In America she'd starve to death if she had nothing to recommend her but mutilation.'" Ethan looked up at Jack and Sean.

They shook their heads.

"She's not missing a tooth or an eye or a leg," Ethan said. "She would starve if she had nothing but what she lost... I asked Anna, was Brooke trying to help me? Was she trying to keep me away or on a leash?"

"What do you think?" Jack asked.

Ethan's smile returned. "I think she's trying to tell me to shed my devices—and vices—like she told me when we were at Dancing Rabbit the first time. Remember when she took my phone away? She wants me to be the one to disconnect. Unplug."

"I don't understand," Jack said. "Where did you get that?"

"If she only had what she lost, which must be her family, her broken heart, she'd die. But she has me now. And I can't get to her with the FBI tracking me, or whoever else is listening in on this thing. Her brother was using technology to find her. He even sent goons to look for me, right? He'll do anything to find her. He's dangerous. That's why she wanted me to stay away. But there's another side to her story and I'm going to find out what it is." Ethan set his iPhone on Sean's coffee table. "I have to find her. Unplugged."

"Without your phone?" Jack asked, incredulous. "How can you go without your phone?"

Ethan smiled. "They call it mindfulness."

Just as he was about to make his dramatic exit, he stopped, froze, and groaned. "Oh damn!"

"What?" Jack asked.

"My car only has a few miles' worth of charge left."

Jack laughed. "Told you that car was a bad idea."

"You can't take your car anyway," Sean said, approaching. "If she really does want you to come for her—unplugged—she doesn't want you bringing cops and FBI agents, and they know what you've been driving." Sean tossed his car keys to Ethan. "Take mine."

Ethan saw the Maserati symbol on the keychain. "Much more discreet," he grinned, unable to hide his love for fast and fancy cars.

Sean's love for cars was even deeper. "It's a special edition and only came in one very discreet color called deep plum. You'll be fine."

"Thanks. I'll try not to scratch it."

Jack grabbed Ethan's shoulder just as he turned. "We won't be able to get in touch with you. Be careful. Please."

"I will."

"And just for the record," Jack added, "I'm glad you know about me, that there are no more secrets—"

"Just for the record," Ethan cut him off, "I'm happy for you. For you both."

"Thanks." Jack smiled as if an enormous weight had lifted, or more like an amputated leg had just grown back. "Now go find your girl."

CHAPTER 33

A FIELD AGENT WAS waiting for Matz and Shu as they pulled up to the curb at the international terminal. "I'm Agent Dempsey, San Francisco division. You requested this phone from the murder victim in Santa Monica—"

"Hang on," Shu told the field agent as he shouted at the baggage handler at curbside check-in. "Hey, you! Yeah, you. I'm a federal officer...FBI. I need the gate for flight five-eight-five. Pronto."

The baggage handler shouted back, "Flight five-eight-five to Grand Cayman departs in five minutes. C-four. That's terminal C, gate four."

"Let's go," Matz said as she got out of the car.

Shu grabbed for Bailey's iPhone, but the field agent pulled it back. "I need you to sign for it."

"Christ, where?"

The field agent handed Shu a form and a pen.

Matz turned back. "What the hell are you doing?"

"I requested the murder victim's cell phone."

"Why?" Matz said. "Why would you do that?"

"So I can sift through all his personal data—photos, phone calls, text messages, emails—and get clues. I'm good with technology."

"We have experts to do all that."

"We don't have time to wait for those hacks. I know what I'm doing." Shu handed the pen back to the field agent. "Are we done here? Can I have it now?"

The field agent let Shu take the phone and the agents headed for C4, hoping to stop Brooke and Rufus before their plane took off.

From the moment Shu took possession of Bailey's phone, Brooke was able to hear the entire FBI search through her Pocket Dialer app. She hated to invade, but she also professed that when you're on the run, you must know who's coming for you and where they are at all times. "You have to hound like a hound dog, stalk like a stalker," she often told her Rabbits.

Now she was able to listen to the FBI agents who were coming after the newest Rabbit, Rufus Wall.

She heard Shu shout, "FBI. Do not close that door!"

Agent Matz said, "We're looking for these passengers."

The gate agent at C4 said, "I don't recognize them."

Shu told him, "Take another look."

"What are their names? I'll see if they've boarded."

Shu said, "Benjamin Carver and Brooke Shaw."

The gate agent punched the names into the computer. "Sorry. No."

"Shit!" Shu slammed the counter like a passenger that just missed his flight. "Can you tell if they canceled or rebooked on a different flight?"

"I can't retrieve that information. I'm sorry—"

"They could be flying under different names," Matz said. "We'll have to check the plane."

"You heard her," Shu snapped.

The gate agent announced with urgency, "Federal agents coming aboard."

As they walked down the loading bridge, Matz whispered to Shu, "Settle down, Sparky. A little sugar goes a long way."

"What did I say?"

"It's the way you said it. Check the bathrooms," Matz ordered Shu.

Agent Shu saw another gate agent come aboard, this one female, her Venusian form swaying back and forth as she moved down the aisle counting passengers.

Matz noticed Shu staring and snapped, "Stop drooling, Shu. Check the bathrooms."

"She's holding a list of the passengers, we should check—"

"The can, Shu. I'll check with her."

Shu headed to the back of the plane while Matz showed the striking gate agent the picture of Brooke and Benjamin. "We're looking for this couple…?"

She took a look and smirked. "I know him, yeah."

"Where is he?"

"He was on the last flight to Grand Cayman that departed a few hours ago."

"A few hours ago?" Matz held the photo up again. "What about this woman?"

"Nope. He was alone."

"Take another look, please."

"He wasn't with anyone," the stunner said with a giggle. "He was on our standby list, trying to get a seat on the last flight, which was full. He tried slipping me cash. We don't take bribes. But he was funny."

"Why? Why was he funny?"

"He kept coming up to the counter to check on his status, and every time he would explain how he just got married and had to meet his new wife on their honeymoon and desperately needed to get on the plane. But he was just making that all up."

"Why do you say that?"

"By the third time he came up to the counter, he had already asked me out four times. We don't take bribes and we don't accept invitations to meet customers in the Cayman Islands for all-expense paid holidays. But he took the rejection well and he literally hugged me when a seat became available and he got on the flight."

Matz shouted at the back of the plane, "Let's go, Shu, we're outta here!"

———

BROOKE SHUT OFF THE Pocket Dialer app and sent a confirmation to Benjamin Carver's email. She had set up an email account on the iPhone she was using (registered under a Dancing Rabbit employee) as "Administration Notification." He knew to look in his junk mail, where Administration Notifications were usually sent. When he saw her heading, "Congratulations, you won a free trip," he would know that he had been set free.

———

AGENTS MATZ AND SHU ran back to their car, not speaking a word until they were on the highway. Rufus Wall may have slipped away, but he didn't leave with their real target: Stella Godeaux. She had to still be in the US. And their only hope was that she wouldn't leave without their bait: Ethan Stone.

Matz asked her digitally savvy protégé to check their own tracking device that was monitoring the GPS on Ethan's phone. "Where is he now?"

"He's still at Sean McQueen's home. Just sitting on his ass."

"Call him."

"What should I say?"

"Ask him why he's not looking for her."

Shu dialed Ethan's phone. It rang four times until he got an answer. "H'llo?"

"Why are you sitting on your ass?" Shu whined. "You're wasting valuable time—"

"You must be looking for Ethan," Jack said. "This is his brother."

"Put him on. This is the FBI."

"He's not here."

"Where is he?"

"I...I don't know."

Shu mumbled to Matz, "He's not there."

"What do you mean he's not there?" Matz asked.

"What do you mean he's not there?" Shu repeated.

"He's looking for his girlfriend."

"Without his phone?"

"He left it here," Jack said.

Shu covered his mouthpiece and told Matz, "He left his phone there."

"Goddamnit! He must have known you put a tracking device in it... How the hell are we going to find him if he doesn't have his phone?"

"I don't know, ma'am. Is that rhetorical?"

"No, it's a hemorrhage. Ask the brother where the hell he is now."

Shu asked Jack, "Where is he now?"

Jack said, "No idea."

"Goddamnit!" Shu said. "Have him call us as soon as you hear from him. Or you call us. Call us from this phone...from his phone—"

"He gets the point," Matz said.

"I'll call you if I hear from him," Jack agreed, "from this phone."

It's true what they say about law enforcement: 10 percent shear fear, 90 percent boredom.

Ergo, the agents spent the next hour in silence.

———

AN HOUR LATER, ETHAN's phone rang again. Jack ran over and checked the caller ID.

"It's Emily Tak. She's a programmer at Stalker."

"Go ahead, answer it," Sean said.

"Hey, Emily, it's Jack."

There was a pause while Emily checked the number she had dialed. "Hey, killer." Her voice was more ornery than usual.

"It was self-defense," Jack explained.

"I know," she said, without asking for him to elaborate. "I'm looking for Ethan."

"He's not here, what's up?"

"Why are you answering his phone?"

"He left it here."

"Where's here?"

"I'm in San Francisco."

"Working for the enemy," Emily whispered, as if it were worse than killing a man. "I heard. Just have him call me as soon as he comes back."

"Okay."

"Wait!" Emily blurted.

"I'm still here."

"Do you know where I can reach him now?"

"You can't," Jack told her. "He doesn't want anyone to know where he is."

"Why not?"

"He's looking for Brooke. He thinks she's in some kind of trouble, and he's being tracked by his phone, this phone...so he left it here with me."

"That could be a trap," she warned.

"What are you talking about?"

"You've got to find him. He's in danger...oh God—!"

The thought had crossed Jack's mind, too. What if Brooke was setting Ethan up? Ethan, Sean, and Jack wanted Brooke to be innocent so badly that they all encouraged Ethan's search for her, regardless of the risks. Without a phone, no one could get to him.

"I understand your concern," Jack said, "but I don't know what to do about it now."

She burst out crying. "Bailey's dead!"

Jack went silent.

"He was shot at the beach," Emily explained. "I'm in the office now. Police are still questioning us. The FBI was here—"

Sean saw Jack's expression and approached.

Jack whispered, "Bailey was killed."

"Ask her what the police think. Do they have a suspect?"

"Who's that?" Emily asked. "Who are you talking to?"

"Just a friend of mine."

Sean rolled his eyes.

"Actually, it's my boyfriend," Jack told Emily. "I guess this is as good of a time as any...I moved up here to be with him. I'm gay."

"*Mazel tov*," she sniffled, "it's about *freakin'* time."

"You knew?"

"I suspected."

She knew. Everyone probably knew.

But now it was out there. Jack was out. It was his first time saying it out loud without fear, and it felt great. His life would never be the same, but Bailey's life was over.

Perspective!

"What the hell was Bailey doing at the beach?" Jack asked. "He hates the sun."

"I don't know," Emily said. "He came to the office really early, before anyone was here, like he usually did. His mocha was on his desk. But he must have taken a walk to the beach for some reason because they found him shot dead under the Santa Monica Pier."

"Do the police have a suspect?"

"If they do, they're not telling us," Emily said. "They're confiscating all our computers. I think they're shutting us down."

Jack said, "Ethan told me about the guy you found that had an account and was looking for Brooke."

"C. G."

"Did you tell the cops?"

"Yes, but we still don't know who C. G. is."

"Yes, we do," Jack told her. "Ethan and Bailey talked about it early this morning. Probably right before he was killed..."

"Is it her husband?" Emily asked. "Was Brooke married like I thought?"

"No. It's her brother. CG is Clinton Godeaux. Tell them. Tell the cops."

"I will."

"Okay, Emily, stay strong."

Jack was about to hang up when Emily said, "You know what I said to Bailey last night? I told him to bugger off. He was bugging me so I told him to bugger the fuck off! Nice, huh?" Emily cried harder. "That's the last thing I said to him."

"I know you and Bailey had your differences, but you spent a lot of time together, and he really liked you. He just had a funny way of expressing himself sometimes."

"I know," Emily confessed, "I've been shagging the bastard for the past two years!"

"No kidding," Jack said gibingly.

"You knew?"

"I suspected."

"Tell me the truth, did anyone else think so?"

Jack smiled. "Everyone."

And they shared a laugh.

CHAPTER 34

E THAN DOWNSHIFTED, ACCELERATED, AND then winced when the gears shrieked. He hadn't driven a stick-shift car since high school, and taking a refresher course on a $100,000 borrowed sports car while thinking that the love of his life was about to get killed was not a good combination. He drove like a cautious maniac, trying to navigate his conflicting emotions. When he had left Los Angeles and headed up to Big Sur, he thought his brother and girlfriend had run off together. Now he was driving down to Big Sur from San Francisco with new information about Brooke and a new reality for his brother. Even his opinion about Sean McQueen had changed from prejudices about his rumored business practices to the acceptance of him as his brother's lover.

Fucking perspective.

Ethan thought about his brother's lifelong secret, the courage it took to come out, and the truth about their best friend, Barry. That was a lot to process in and of itself. But compounded with the possibilities of what Brooke was still up against was causing his mind to race out of control. Brooke had often teased him about his American ambitions, how he was never satisfied and always wanting more than he had. She'd used every phase of Stalker as a perfect example: He had had a commercial idea, but he needed to convince his brother. Once he had talked Jack into being the lead programmer, he needed financing. Once Bailey had showed up with an angel investor looking to fund a tracking app that used biometrics, he needed to get online before anyone else came up with a similar idea. Once competitors had shown up, he had needed to be better and grow faster.

Brooke often said things like, "It's all about the journey, not the destination," but Ethan couldn't quite grasp that concept. He always wanted to get to the next phase, never spending enough time appreciating what he already had. Now he wondered if he took the things he loved for granted, like his loyal partner, Bailey, his talented brother, Jack, and his loving girlfriend, Brooke. Were they all trying to tell him that he had lost perspective?

From now on he was going to appreciate what he had, he decided. He was going to broaden his view of his ambitions and the effects they had on other people. He was going to be more thoughtful about the consequences Stalker technology could result in—and make changes accordingly. He was going to transform. And he was going to start with doing whatever he could to get his love back. Losing Brooke trumped everything, and he needed to find her so he could tell her so. He felt a pang of optimism, a recharged purpose. He was also starting to feel pretty good about his command of McQueen's Maserati GranTurismo, now hugging the winding curves with precise control, going a bit fast, and then he quickly sobered and slowed. He approached Dancing Rabbit—ground zero for the transformers.

And Brooke.

He glimpsed a dark sedan parked in the driveway and the two white-haired detectives who were kicked out of his interrogation room by the FBI, Johnson and Ramsey. He imagined them on stakeout, chomping on donuts, waiting for missing Rabbits to reappear—which they never would—while he sped by with a deafening roar, unseen. He glanced his rearview, and they didn't pull out after him. So he parked McQueen's joyride behind a cluster of large trees just down the road.

The chimes rang when he entered the Henry Miller library, just like before. But he didn't hear Anna's voice when he walked inside this time. Instead, he was greeted by a woman with drooping eyelids, unkempt straw-colored hair, and an aging rock 'n' roller's swagger, as if she were channeling Joni Mitchell.

"Welcome to The Henry Miller Library," said with a singsong flair, revealing miles of wear on her jagged boned face. "Name's Sasha. How may I be of service?"

"I'm looking for somebody, actually—"

Sasha giggled. "Aren't we all?"

"Are you the 'real' shopkeeper?" Ethan asked, trying to determine whether or not she really worked there, or like Anna Gopnik, was just hiding out.

"I'm not only the shopkeeper," Sasha told him. "I'm a librarian, historian, writer, and expert on every famous author who ever called Big Sur their home."

"Can you name all three?" Ethan joked.

"Jack Kerouac's 1962 novel, aptly titled *Big Sur*, best explained why this area is so inspiring and transformative to creative people," she said, revving up for a seemingly well-rehearsed dissertation on everything literary within a fifty-mile stretch and the last fifty years. "But it didn't begin with the beat generation," she droned on, "American poet Robinson Jeffers meditated about Big Sur's 'wine-hearted solitude, our mother the wilderness' in poems like *Bixby's Landing*—"

Ethan cut her off, "I'm here to see Anna."

Her smile faded. "Who?"

"Anna Gopnik, unless she goes by a different name by now."

"No one else is here besides me now."

Ethan wondered if he needed a password or something. "It's okay," he said with a conspiratorial wink. "I'm a friend. I know she's hiding, and transitioning. I was here yesterday—"

"We close in ten minutes," Sasha warned as she walked behind the counter and busied herself with her cash register. "You're welcome to peruse until then."

Peruse? Ethan wondered if that was code for snoop through the bookshelves or back room. "Last time I was here, Anna showed me a passage from *Tropic of Cancer*—"

"That one?" Sasha pointed to a quote on the wall. Sasha's eyes glazed over as if she were reciting a prayer. *"We are all alone here and we are dead.* It's about the necessity to change course radically, to start completely over from scratch."

"Like a Dancing Rabbit?" Ethan asked. "Are you a Rabbit or do you just help them hide?"

Sasha stared back concernedly. "Are you feeling well, son?"

This lady's no Rabbit, Ethan decided, and just then, he noticed a large watercolor paining over Sasha's shoulder of a French château. It was one of Brooke's. It wasn't her usual landscape of Napa, looking out from the church, but rather a close-up of the château with the church in the distance. Ethan stepped closer. "That painting wasn't here yesterday."

"That's correct," Sasha said. "It came just this morning."

"Where did you get it?"

"It was donated."

"By who?"

"By whom," Sasha corrected. "It was donated anonymously, a deliveryman just dropped it off."

"There had to be a name or organization—"

"There wasn't."

"Then how do you know it was a donation?"

"It came with a note."

"What did the note say?"

"That the painting was a donation to the Henry Miller Memorial Library," she said, irritated with his line of questioning. "Are you a detective?"

"No, I'm not a detective," he assured her. "Have there been any detectives here lately?"

She didn't answer.

"Can I see the note?" he pressed.

"I just told you what the note said."

"Please," he tried to sound desperate, because he was, and because he thought she had empathetic eyes. "It's really important to me."

She reached in the garbage can, pulled out a FedEx slip, and handed it to him.

Ethan read, "'For the wall next to the clock.'"

"See," Sasha pointed at the slip. "No signature, and no name. Most of our things are donated this way. Rarely do donors want a receipt, although we do that for tax purposes if any of them should ask—"

"This was obviously sent from someone who has been here recently. She knew you had a clock up there."

Sasha showed no reaction.

"That painting was done by Brooke Shaw."

Still no reaction.

"Stella Godeaux," Ethan tried.

"I don't know all of our visitors. Most are just passing through."

Ethan noticed there was a return address on the FedEx form. He reached for her laptop on the counter. "Do you mind if I just look this up?"

She grabbed Ethan's hand. "I do, actually."

"Please," he pleaded, "I'm pretty sure that the person who sent this knew I would be coming here to look for her."

Sasha looked at him skeptically.

"She's the love of my life," he said, "and I won't stop looking until I find her."

"What makes you so sure this is from her?"

"The estate in that painting looks like a house in Napa Valley that she often painted—"

"It's a French château," Sasha countered, ever the expert. "We must assume it's a scene in France."

There was a crumpled up newspaper inside the FedEx box and Ethan noticed a photograph that looked just like the painting. "What's that, inside the box?"

Sasha lifted the box. "Just old newspapers used to protect the painting."

Ethan pulled the newspaper out and smoothed out the creases. Sure enough, it was a photograph of the château with a title: Highpoint Estate. Ethan remembered their angel investor's mysterious shell company: Highpoint Corp.

Just below the photo, there was an article:

NAPA VALLEY REGISTER
House Of Mystery

Napa Valley's largest private house was built 1993 on a forty-eight-acre plot on Highpoint, a wealthy hilltop neighborhood on the north side, with the loveliest views from nearly every vantage. First owned by British tycoon Arthur Godeaux, the mansion boasts eighteen bedrooms, a ballroom, and a glass rotunda. Arthur Godeaux passed away last year and was survived by his children, the will and testament has been contested, leaving the property in a state of flux. The city of Napa has been unable to determine who is now the rightful owner. Recent activity on the property has forged speculation and controversy to the region. The British government has disallowed the Godeaux children to take possession of the estate and there is speculation that the property has been subsequently sold.

A recent report by the *Financial Times* has found that offshore companies own more than $100 billion worth of real estate in California. The state's property market has become a form of legalized international money laundering, according to a former editor of the *San Francisco Chronicle*.

For Napa residents, worries about the lack of transparency in the purchase of the Godeaux property have become a real concern, with insinuations ranging from a possible mafia hideaway to Russian oligarchs using the property to get money out of their country...

After Ethan read it, he turned it to show Sasha the photo of the French château-style manse. "It wasn't about me, or us. It's about this!"

Sasha looked uncertain how to react. "I'm happy for you," she said reluctantly. "Does that mean she wants you to go find her or stay away?"

Sasha had a point. Ethan remembered how he felt after he first read the passage from *Tropic of Cancer;* he had wondered if she had put a tracker on his phone to keep him away or on a leash. And when he was at Sean McQueen's house, he was so sure that she wanted him to come for her, unplugged. The article most likely explained why her brother was looking for her, something to do with who would take possession of the Highpoint Estate, but it didn't mention murder, the reason why she was running away, or if she wanted him to stay away from her entanglements or come for her. He still didn't know.

"I have no idea," he admitted, but when he looked up at Sasha, he found his answer. His eyes drew wide and he reached slowly for her neck.

She jumped back. "What are you doing—?"

Sasha was wearing the antique necklace that Ethan had bought Brooke at the little jewelry store on Abbot Kinney Boulevard in Venice Beach.

"That's my girlfriend's pendant. It's a handmade one of a kind. I would know it anywhere."

Sasha nodded. "It also came in the package today." She unhooked it and handed it to him.

Ethan snapped open the heart-shaped lavaliere, and sure enough there was a folded-up note inside. He read it out loud, "'I love you always.'"

"Thank you!" He kissed her on the cheek, ran out, and shouted, "I'm coming for you, baby!"

As the door shut behind, Ethan heard Sasha say, "We get all the crazies."

CHAPTER 35

JACK AND SEAN USED all of the Stalker and Hounddog search tools to look for Brooke and her brother Clinton. They went full on, full throttle, full court press.

They worked on separate laptops in the living room, but Jack had trouble focusing, his mind still reeling from everything that had happened in the last twenty-four hours. He was trying to process that Bailey, his friend and former business partner, was dead. He was also thinking about finally coming out to his brother, and Ethan's reaction. And he still couldn't shun the image of a man dying right in front of him. The altercation with the tattooed bounty hunters played back in his mind—the fight, the gunshot, his escape. It looped in his mind until Sean snapped him out.

"Take a look!" Sean called out as he turned his computer around. "I'm using our institution tool to see if they have any affiliations, and I found this." He showed Jack a list of church patrons. "The Godeaux family was a longtime member of St. Francis Church in Napa Valley."

"I wonder if that's the church Ethan called me from," Jack said, "where Brooke got married."

"I bet it was. There's a Godeaux library and a Godeaux preschool. Looks like they were big donors—" Sean noticed Jack's stress face, his worried look. "Are you okay?"

"I don't know."

"You've been through a lot."

"And my brother's out there looking for Brooke with no way to be contacted, and very possibly heading into a trap."

"It is concerning," Sean agreed. "We're doing everything we can, though."

Then Jack smiled. "He took it exceptionally well, don't you think? About us."

"Amazingly well."

"Maybe I should have told him sooner."

"We do it when we're ready."

"He was really cool about it," Jack went on. "Really cool. I mean, this was a really big deal."

Sean smiled. "They say twins are more intuitive with each other. Maybe he always knew but didn't want to say anything until you did."

"Maybe. Now I feel bad about not having more faith. He never wavers from the things he believes in, and I doubt everything."

Sean laughed. "You do have an issue there, I won't argue with that. What made you turn atheist? Did you have a bad experience or something?"

Jack started his stock answer, "The idea of faith in something no one will ever prove—all the manipulations, the ridiculous, antiquated mythologies—just keep the world from breaking down the barriers of differences."

Sean smiled. "And you're supposed to be a chosen one."

"Let's look into the Godeaux family's involvement in this church," Jack said to change the subject. "We can chat about the end of times and other great fiction another time."

As they both looked back down at their computers and continued searching for clues, Jack thought about the many discussions he had had with his brother about faith, and why Jack rejected it. Ethan had tolerated Sunday school, but Jack was always turned off by the Bible's intolerance, knowing then that he was different, and that he wouldn't change, or couldn't.

When the twins turned thirteen, they had a double bar mitzvah—a symbolic ritual when young Jewish boys enter adulthood by chanting a section of the Torah in front of their family, friends, and an entire congregation. It was a turning point for Jack, but not for the usual reasons. He realized something about himself and his brother that he would never forget.

———

JACK WAS SITTING IN a chair behind the podium, watching Ethan singing his *haftorah* proudly, assuredly. Once Ethan completed his portion, the rabbi continued on in Hebrew and Ethan took the seat beside Jack.

"I can't do this," Jack whispered to Ethan.

"Yes you can. You're well prepared. You'll be fine."

"That's not why. I don't believe in any of this. I don't understand a word of the Hebrew. I don't want to start my manhood as a hypocrite."

"Get over it," Ethan hissed.

"I have to be true to who I am."

"You'll break Dad's heart. Look at him."

They both turned to look at their father sitting on the opposite side of the *bima*. He had a frozen squinty smile, a jubilant gaze, and never looked more proud. He was an older dad with thinning gray hair and thick bifocals. And in spite of being a first-generation American whose parents had perished in the Holocaust, he never lost his faith, never held a grudge for a God who would turn his back while millions were slaughtered.

Jack knew that Ethan wasn't going to let him break their father's heart just because he was being a sanctimonious, smug little prick.

"You're going to have to man up," Ethan told him.

"I don't believe in God."

"You're not the first."

"And I don't believe this ceremony makes us men. We're just thirteen years old, for Christ's sake."

"Leave Christ out of it today."

Jack didn't laugh and began to stand up.

Ethan pulled Jack back down. "Don't take it all so seriously. It's just symbolic, a rite of passage. That's all."

"I don't believe in symbolism or rites of passages," Jack continued relentlessly. "I really don't want to do this."

Ethan got the rabbi's attention, pointed off stage, and whispered, "Bathroom?"

The rabbi nodded and Ethan nudged Jack away.

Behind the stage curtain, Ethan began taking off his grey suit. "Switch," he ordered Jack. "And hurry!"

"What are you doing?"

"Becoming you. Gimme your pants. Now. Let's go!"

Jack pulled down his trousers and put on Ethan's. "You don't have to do this."

"I want to."

They switched jackets.

Jack said, "Going through it twice isn't going to make you twice the man or anything like that."

"Shut up and give me your tie."

"Dad will understand."

"I'm not only doing this for Dad," Ethan said. "I'm doing it for you."

"Why?"

"Because someday you might have regrets."

"I won't. I know what I believe—"

"Someday you might grow up and believe in something, or someone. You can't see it now, but I know this—"

"You're not going to hold this over me in years to come, are you?" Jack asked as Ethan handed over his navy coat to complete Jack's transition into him.

"I'll never even bring it up, ever," Ethan promised. "Now get back up there."

They walked back on the *bima* and took their seats just in time for the rabbi to call Jack up.

Ethan sang Jack's portion of the *haftorah* and the twins pulled off their first major bait and switch. Jack didn't feel like a total hypocrite and their father didn't have a heart attack. No one ever knew what they had done, and Ethan never brought it up again, as promised.

—

"My brother has always had my back," Jack told Sean. "He always comes through for me, and I never show him any gratitude."

"Never too late to start," Sean said. "He needs you now. Let's check this place out, this church. Maybe the priest that married Brooke knows something."

"You gave Ethan your car," Jack reminded him.

Sean got up. He was grinning. "I have others."

"Where?"

"In the garage."

"I didn't know you had a garage. You always park out front."

"It's not actually a garage," Sean said, "more like a shrine."

Jack followed him down some steps and through a door leading from his maid's quarters. They entered a two-thousand-square-foot, pristine man cave—a car collector's reverie—with a dozen of the most luxurious sports cars Jack had ever seen. Jack was no car aficionado like his brother was, but he recognized a McLaren, a Ferrari, and a gorgeous Singer 911.

"You should have shown this to my brother," Jack said. "You would have won him over in a heartbeat."

"That's not how I want to win people over."

"Is that why you've never brought me in here?"

Sean climbed inside a bright yellow Lamborghini Gallardo and backed it out like he was handling a newborn. Jack got inside and buckled up. He couldn't contain his smile as the V10 petrol engine purred.

"Is it—?" Jack asked over the grinding din.

Sean shouted back, "I didn't want you to fall in love with me for the wrong reasons."

And he peeled out like a bolt of lightening.

CHAPTER 36

E THAN CHARGED BACK UP north, the Maserati engine growling as he steered around the steep bend and passed the Dancing Rabbit entrance once again. He was in such a hurry, he had forgotten about the detectives in the black sedan waiting in the driveway who were, by the way, not gobbling donuts and trying to explain their Bermuda Triangle conundrum.

The last thing Ethan wanted to do was attract attention, but that's what cars like McQueen's GranTurismo do, especially plum-colored ones. When it had raced past Dancing Rabbit the first time around, with its deafening roar, the seasoned detectives had the fortitude to snap a photo of the license plate and do some due diligence. They learned that the owner, Sean McQueen of San Francisco, had a clean record. A simple search informed them that he was a rock star in the Silicon Valley tech scene.

"There are two likely reasons his car would be dipping in and out of Big Sur in such a hurry," Ramsey told his partner. "McQueen was either dropping off something illegal or picking up something illegal."

"Or a third option," Johnson said. "That car was just stolen."

"Any of those prospects worthy of a tail?"

Johnson shrugged and Ramsey drove out of the Dancing Rabbit driveway. They followed the Maserati for five miles, and then Johnson picked up his phone. "He's leaving our jurisdiction, I'll phone it into the next county."

"Don't do that," Ramsey said.

"That's protocol."

"Fuck protocol. When we were taking down gangs in LA, we bent a lot of rules. We did what we had to do."

"We're six months from retirement," Johnson said. "I don't want to screw it up now. We lose our pension, and then what?"

"I don't know about you, but I won't feel right about leaving this department in worse shape than when we arrived. Sergeant Cruz is a good guy. He's done right by us. He deserves our best, especially now. There are missing people involved here."

"After what we've been through, we deserve something, too."

"You're right. We've been through a lot, you and me. That should count for something. I'll only keep going if you're in agreement."

Johnson glanced his own image in the side mirror. His balding head and leathered skin reflected back a ghost of the cop he used to be. "Let's do this then," he told Ramsey.

"You sure?"

"I'm sure."

—

ETHAN WAS HEADED ONTO the part of Highway 1 that merges with the 101 when he noticed the detectives' car weaving multiple lane congestions behind. They hadn't used their siren and lights but he was sure they were following him. He slowed to the speed limit, but his mind raced: *Could they possibly know I'm inside this monster car? Had Sasha called them after I left the Henry Miller Library? Were they in contact with the FBI agents who were hoping I would lead them to Brooke?*

He glanced in his rearview and figured he ought to be able to lose them in a car like McQueen's Maserati GranTurismo. Why have a car like this unless you show what it can do?

He shifted gears, put pedal to the metal, and charged toward Napa Valley like a bat out of hell.

—

FBI AGENTS SHU AND Matz had no idea where Ethan was. Their APB was searching for the Tesla that was sitting behind Sean McQueen's gated driveway, not a plum Maserati. So when their third-party tracking app suddenly pinged and showed a glowing line moving up the 101, they were able to track Jack, hopefully to Ethan.

"Ethan's on the move," Shu told Matz, "heading north."

Matz glanced the map. "You mean the brother is heading north," Matz corrected. "Remember the brother, Jack, has Ethan's phone."

"Assuming he told the truth," Shu said. "They could have pulled a bait and switch."

Matz rolled her eyes.

"Can you imagine what it would be like to be a twin?" Shu mused. "Think of the possibilities of being in two places at once."

"Call and find out," Matz said. "See which one answers."

"They sound a lot alike."

Matz rolled her eyes again and Shu dialed Ethan's phone. It rang four times and then the voicemail picked up. "I told you."

"You told me what?"

"They're not answering. Bait and switch."

"Give me their fucking twenty," Matz snapped.

Shu watched the blue line on his map turn right. "Elyse exit, off of Highway twenty-nine."

"That's the exit to Napa, isn't it?"

"Yep."

Agent Matz hit the gas.

———

THE BRIGHT YELLOW LAMBORGHINI Gallardo headed north toward the least touristy cluster of Napa, through Yountville, Oakville, and Ruthford, where the landscape is more majestic. Jack looked out the window at the unspoiled rolling knolls and watched a salient blood-orange sunset drop away.

"It's hard not to feel starry-eyed when you move through such a sanguine place," Jack told Sean.

Sean agreed. "It's an instant reminder that there are other choices besides rat races and treadmills. Makes you imagine all the possibilities." Sean turned down a Sugar Pine–lined street peppered with four-star restaurants and artisan shops and searched for street signs. "Did you say we're looking for Sonoma Street?"

"Yeah." Jack checked Google Maps again. "No, sorry, Sonoma Road. It's a winding road that runs up to the church on the top of the hill."

"I think I might have missed the turn."

"Why don't we stop at one of these places up ahead and ask?" Jack suggested. "I could use a bathroom."

"Good idea." Sean pulled up in front of a sophisticated-looking tavern called Carpe Diem.

After Jack did his business, he found Sean at the bar being served by Fritz, the handsome bartender who had practiced his French on Brooke, and was now practicing his pickup lines on Sean, unabashedly. Fritz poured Sean a glass of wine and droned on about it, as if he were a master sommelier. "This heavenly grape is from a top-notch, small producer dedicated solely to super-premium Bordeaux-style reds, incredibly opulent fruit-driven reds that age for decades, like—"

Enter Jack. "We should get going."

"One for the road won't kill you," Fritz said.

"Isn't that the DMV slogan?" Jack smirked.

Sean laughed. "One for the road won't kill you. Good one."

Sean's phone pinged, but he ignored it.

"This is one of California's best reds ever," Fritz said as he topped off Sean's glass and winked. "Tell me I'm wrong."

Sean savored a healthy sip. "Napa bartenders make everything sound so good it almost doesn't matter what the wine tastes like. But this one is truly amazing. Thank you."

Sean's phone pinged again. But he still didn't look.

"Come back anytime," Fritz said, meaning Sean, not Jack. And he moved on to other customers.

Sean's phone pinged once more.

Jack asked, "Aren't you going to see who that is?"

"It's my Grindr app," Sean admitted. "It goes crazy in places like this."

Jack looked around and saw a lot of hopeful men. "This place is gayer than a fruit salad," Jack joked, with a twinge of jealousy in his voice. "Why do you still have a Grindr account?"

"I forgot to cancel—"

Just then, a tall man with curly hair approached Jack and said, "You look just like that guy on TV."

"I can't go anywhere with you, and this is why." Now Sean was the one that sounded jealous.

"I'm serious," the curly-haired man said. "You're that guy—"

"Yeah? What guy?" Jack asked, humored by the attention he was drawing.

"The guy that was on the news." He pointed at the TV above the bar. "You shot some dude and ran away."

Not the kind of attention Jack wanted.

Curly Hair went on and on, "I just saw the follow-up." He pointed to the TV again. "They said it was self-defense and the guy you killed was an escaped convict. You're a hero!"

"Have another drink and I'll look like Channing Tatum," Jack teased Curly Hair.

"You kind of do look like Channing Tatum," Sean said, amused.

Jack grabbed Sean's arm, "We really do have to get going."

Jack hadn't been out in public with Sean much, at least not socially. In Silicon Valley, Sean is a public person who likes to be private, and since Jack had been in the closet, he avoided socializing in places like this, or using apps like Grindr—which signaled other gays that you were in the same area for potential meet-ups—for fear of being found out.

Jack knew he had been a self-loathing closeted gay man, and just then, as he passed by the Carpe Diem clientele, he decided that he wouldn't be a self-loathing out-of-the-closet gay man. He wanted to be proud of who he was.

Jack's first love was Barry, and it ended badly: in death did they part. Brooke had told Jack that he wouldn't be able to have a healthy relationship until he stopped blaming himself, until he truly believed that Barry didn't kill himself because of him. She also told Jack that happiness stems from faith.

And perspective.

They got back into the Lamborghini and Jack said, "True acceptance is thinking less about yourself and more about the self."

Sean laughed. "What?"

"Nothing. Did you get the bartender's number?"

"Sorry to disappoint you, but I'm taken."

Jack grinned. "Good answer." He decided then to have faith in Sean, just like he had decided to have faith in his brother, just like he had told his brother to have faith in Brooke.

And Jack and Sean headed for church.

CHAPTER 37

They drove up the narrow, snaking road leading up to St. Francis. The sanctuary doors were open and it was empty, lit only by dimmed candelabras. Father Oliver came through the back entrance, intending to lock the doors for the day.

"Looks like we caught you just in time," Jack said as they headed toward the priest. "We just have a few questions."

Father Oliver frowned as Jack came into the light, thinking that he was Ethan. "I already told you everything," he said. "I haven't heard from her since you were last here, and I don't know where she is—"

"That was my brother that you spoke with," Jack explained. "Ethan Stone. I'm Jack. Jack Stone."

The priest took a long look, and then nodded. "Your brother told me he was a twin."

"And this is my...friend, Sean."

"We think Brooke is in trouble," Sean said, "and you might be able to help—"

"Stella," Jack said. "You probably know her as Stella Godeaux."

Father Oliver locked the sanctuary doors and said, "Come with me."

They followed him down the long hallway, just as Ethan had.

Jack broke the silence midway. "We know that her family, the Godeaux family, were members here for many years, and that they were big donors."

"Your library and preschool are named after them," Sean added.

"They were our only donors," Father Oliver mumbled, without elaborating.

They entered his study. Father Oliver took a seat behind his cluttered desk and looked up at a painting on the wall of Jacob's ladder ascending to heaven. "Last Sunday, when your brother was here, I gave a sermon about the most famous twin rivalry of all. Did your brother mention it?"

Jack shook his head.

"I spoke of Jacob wrestling with the Angel of God when Esau showed forgiveness in spite of their conflict. Your brother's biggest fear was that you had run off with his girlfriend. He seemed relieved when I told him that was not the case—"

"It was a ridiculous assumption, just a mistake," Jack said.

"There are no mistakes," Father Oliver said with a clip, his heavy Parisian accent making everything sound more dramatic. "You and your brother need to communicate better. Twins have challenges others do not."

"My brother and I don't have a twin rivalry and I'm not into Bible metaphors," Jack said. "We just want to make sure that Brooke... Stella, is safe."

Sean nudged Jack before he could say something more insulting. "No disrespect," Sean said, "but we just need to find out what you know about her. We're concerned. The FBI is looking for her. They think she did something horrible. And it doesn't seem like the woman we know her to be."

Father Oliver's head dipped, seemingly conflicted, and before he could speak, Sean pointed at a painting on the adjacent wall and blurted, "Is that Brooke as a young girl?"

It was a family portrait: mother, father, older son, younger son, and daughter—little Stella and the Codeaux clan, no doubt—all positioned under a large oak with a vineyard and stately château in the background.

Jack recognized the landscape from the paintings Brooke couldn't stop recreating in their Santa Monica bungalow.   .

Father Oliver smiled. "I just put it up today."

Jack asked, "Why today?"

"Because I just received it."

Jack turned to the priest. "Brooke was here today?"

"No. It came by FedEx," Father Oliver said. "Yesterday, actually."

"A gift to thank you for officiating her wedding?" Sean asked.

"Or for hiding her?" Jack said.

Father Oliver didn't like the accusation. "She wanted me to care for the portrait. It had been in their home for many years and had sentimental value..." He looked at Jack hard and said, "I just realized that your brother had a beard, just like Esau, the hairy one, and you're smooth, like Jacob."

Jack scoffed, "Just because he wears a beard doesn't make him more hairy."

"Don't be so literal, son, or you'll keep missing the point. Faith grounds us when things go awry—*quand les choses vont mal*—and things always go awry, don't they?"

"Wait a second..." Sean said, stepping closer to the portrait. "She has two brothers—"

"She had two brothers." Father Oliver said sullenly. "They lost their firstborn son, probably not long after that portrait was painted. His name was Arthur The Second, named after his father. The boy was ten. The twins were only seven."

"Twins?!" Sean and Jack blurted at the same time.

"That's what I was getting at," the priest said, "Stella and her brother Clinton are also twins. As Arthur used to say, '*Twins courent dans notre famille*,' Twins run in the family, '*C'est la vie!*'"

Jack stepped closer to the painting and saw that Clinton and Stella had the same face. "Identical twins," he muttered. "How could she have hidden that from us?"

"Unfortunately, Stella and Clinton were like water and oil," Father Oliver said with a somber gaze, "just like Jacob and Esau. 'Body and spirit are twins; God only knows which is which.'"

Sean put his hand on Jack's shoulder before he could offend the priest. "How did he die?" Sean asked. "Arthur The Second...the older brother. What happened? Please tell us."

"There was an accident..." Father Oliver looked reflective as he stared out his window at the incredible panorama. "It happened when they were here that summer. That's the Godeaux family property down there."

"You mean that mansion?" Jack asked.

"I mean all of it," Father Oliver told them. "From those mountains to those streams, including that mansion, the vineyards, the horse ranch. All of it."

Jack and Sean looked at each other. That much land in Napa was worth a fortune.

"What kind of accident?" Sean asked. "What happened?"

"The two boys were playing on the roof," Father Oliver explained. "Arthur fell to his death. Clinton said that his older brother had jumped off like Superman." Father Oliver looked conflicted.

"Do you think it may have been suicide?" Jack asked.

"I don't, no," Father Oliver said. "Arthur was a wonderful boy, a truly spirited child. But we only had Clinton's story to go on."

Jack and Sean exchanged a look.

"You think Clinton pushed him," Jack said. "Don't you?"

"That's what his father believed, until his dying day. Clinton was a troubled boy, and the family was never the same after...Arthur and Beatrice's marriage was never the same." Father Oliver wiped a tear. "Beatrice died of lung cancer, shortly after, and Arthur died of heart failure...a broken heart."

"Arthur died of cyanide poisoning," Jack said. "The FBI thinks that Brooke—sorry, Stella—killed her father, and that's why she's running."

Father Oliver snapped, "Is that what you think?"

"No," Jack said. "We're here because we don't."

"Did Stella have any animosity toward her father?" Sean asked.

"Not at all," Father Oliver said. "They were very close. Stella was his pride and joy. He groomed her in business."

"It just doesn't make sense then," Sean said.

"But she's running," Jack reminded him. "And Ethan said that he saw a security video showing her injecting some kind of syringe into her father's IV—"

"She couldn't tell me why she was running," Father Oliver said, "but she assured me that her actions were justified, and promised me a full confession when it's all over."

"She promised you a confession?" Jack sputtered. "Then she's basically admitting that she's guilty!"

"Not all confessions reveal wrongdoing," the priest said defensively. "There are many reasons people wish to keep things hidden."

"Like lies or murder—?"

"Like love," the priest said. "I choose to trust her before I make unfounded assumptions. I suggest that you do the same."

CHAPTER 38

OUTDOOR SPOTLIGHTS STREAMED UPON the stately baroque-style château. It was truly magnificent and Jack could easily see why it possessed Brooke and her paintings.

As they approached the towering wrought-iron double gates, Sean mused, "Do you have any idea what a property like this in prime Napa Valley goes for?"

"Enough to make a super unicorn jealous?" Jack teased.

"Maybe even enough to make a greedy sociopath deadly," Sean said. "Do you know anything about English primogeniture laws?"

"I've streamed every season of *The Tudors* and *Downton Abbey*," Jack admitted. "I know their inheritance laws favor the firstborn child."

"Right. It's all about birth order. If the eldest dies before they transfer their property from one generation to the next, it goes to the second child. Clinton and Stella were twins, they would have to split the estate, right?"

"I suppose, why?"

"There's a lot at stake here," Sean said, as Jack peered through the iron gates at the massive property. "This place is enormous."

"I'm going inside." Jack walked over to a bronze lion pillar and peered over.

"I'm sure there's an alarm," Sean warned. "A place like this would have dogs and armed guards."

Jack hoisted himself up. "I don't hear any dogs. I don't see anything either. I'm going in. If you want to wait in the car, I totally understand."

Sean watched Jack hop over and land on the grassy knoll. There was about an acre leading up to the home, but it was dark.

"I know I'm going to regret this," Sean said as he reluctantly joined Jack on the other side.

"Just look at this place," Jack said.

The traditional English gardens were glorious, rich in immaculate topiary forms, with splendid herbaceous borders and thick rosebushes, which lined the pathways leading around the grounds, a lovely maze peppered with ancient marble statues and fountains.

"It's spectacular," Sean agreed. "Imagine what it costs to keep this place up."

"Probably quite a bit," a husky voice answered from the driveway. The iron gates opened easily and two frumpy older men in ruffled tweed suits came through. "I always prefer to walk through the front door than scale a wall," Detective Ramsey said. "It's much easier and less likely someone will shoot you."

Detective Johnson pulled out his badge. "Big Sur Police Department. What are you doing here?"

"We might ask you the same thing," Jack said. "What are Big Sur cops doing all the way up in Napa?"

Ramsey walked closer to Jack. "This is the twin brother, the one that shaves." He turned back to his partner. "This is our killer."

Jack took a few steps back. "The FBI cleared me. Call them—"

"It was already on the news," Sean told them, assuming Curly Hair in Carpe Diem bar was right.

Johnson put his hand up to his ear as if he were making a call. "Hello FBI, is it true? Did you decide that it was self-defense? No trial? Can we bring them in for breaking and entering then? Great, thank you so much for letting us do our job."

"What are you doing here?" Ramsey asked again. "This is private property—"

Just as Jack was about to answer, a gun fired.

Detective Johnson's head cocked. Blood splattered. His knees buckled. He went down.

And out.

Sean tried to scream but nothing came out.

"Get down!" Jack ordered.

Sean tried but his legs wouldn't move.

Ramsey pulled his gun and took cover behind a tree.

Jack grabbed Sean's arm and pulled him behind the nearest cluster of bushes, just as another shot rang out.

Jack put his finger to his lips and they waited. It was quiet, but Jack heard a pounding sound. His head throbbed and he felt disoriented. At first he thought it was from seeing another man die. But then he felt a sharp pain in his shoulder. When he looked up at Sean's face, he knew he'd been hit. Sean grabbed Jack's good arm and propped him up against a marble garden statue. Jack looked up and smiled. "An angel cherub is staring at me. Not a good sign."

"Don't make jokes now," Sean said as he searched the yard.

"Am I dying?"

"It just grazed you," Sean assured him as he examined his wound. "You're going to be fine."

"You look like George Clooney on ER," Jack teased "You should have gone to medical school."

"No money in the doctor game," Sean said as he peeked around the cherub. "There are two guys behind that fountain in the garden. They look like skinheads, covered in tattoos."

Jack pulled himself up and took a look. "Those are the guys that jumped me, from the van. The one with the shaved head was the driver, they called him Ace. The other one is Dale."

They heard Ramsey shout from behind the tree: "This is the police. Come out with your hands up—"

Ace and Dale fired.

Ramsey responded like a trapped animal. He burst out with a guttural cry and fired back.

Ace was hit square in the chest and fell face-first. He twitched like he was being electrocuted, then exhaled his last breath.

"He got the driver," Sean whispered.

"Good riddance," Jack whispered back.

Dale didn't go to help his fallen comrade. He did an about-face and slid back behind the garden like he was caught trying to steal a base.

"My gun is aimed at you," Ramsey announced. "Come out, hands up, or I'll spray you with bullets."

Dale didn't like either option so he tried the same Kamikaze-style warrior cry and charged at Ramsey, firing haphazardly, wildly.

Ramsey squeezed his trigger in rapid succession.

These were front row seats Jack never wanted.

Bullets discharged and pummeled both men; Ramsey tumbled; Dale flailed. It seemed to take forever, like it was slow motion, until they both collapsed, and then everything went still.

Dead quiet.

Sean couldn't speak. Jack didn't want to. Then they both noticed something near the entryway.

The front door was ajar.

"Maybe she's inside," Jack suggested.

Sean found his voice. "Unless it's her brother."

"Let's find out."

"You're hurt," Sean reminded him.

"Details," Jack said, heading inside.

———

ETHAN HAD BEEN WAITING inside the sprawling labyrinth for nearly an hour earlier, hopeful that Brooke would eventually come. When he heard the gunshots, he prayed that she hadn't. He peered out the window in the servants' quarters, just off the kitchen, and searched the massive lawn. He couldn't see anything, or anyone, so he moved through the kitchen pass-through where he had a view of the front door. He felt relieved when he saw Jack and Sean come through, and just as he was about to call out to them, there was a loud thumping noise from around the corner. Someone else was inside. Ethan tucked behind the kitchen door.

Jack and Sean scrambled into the first room on the left—a study with high bookshelves and large paintings of kings and queens who seemed to be watching.

"I knew this was a bad idea," Sean whispered.

"It might have come from upstairs," Jack said, noticing that the foyer ended with a grand winding staircase leading up to a second and third floor.

"God knows how many rooms are in this place," Sean said as if it were an inconvenience. He noticed that Jack's hand was on his wound and he was losing blood. "Let's get out of here," Sean said. "Put your arm around my shoulder and we'll make a run for the door—"

Just then, a dark shadow emerged from behind the giant armoire in the living room, and a thickly accented Englishman spoke: "I am Clinton Godeaux. And you are trespassing." With that introduction and his affected highbrow British idioms, he sounded just like a James Bond villain. "I have the right to keep and bear arms and defend myself and my home…"

The engorged full moon shedding through the high windows above formed a giant gun shape on the wall as Clinton raised his arm and stepped into view.

"God bless this beautiful country."

And he gripped the trigger.

CHAPTER 39

DON'T SHOOT!" SEAN BEGGED. "We're not trespassing. We're hurt. See? He's bleeding."

Ethan watched through the hinge crack, waiting for Clinton to turn away so he could jump and disarm him.

"We need to call an ambulance," Sean continued. "We just want to use your phone, and then we'll leave—"

"You have a phone," Clinton said, pointing his gun at Jack.

Sean looked down. Jack was gripping Ethan's iPhone.

"It's out of juice," Sean lied.

"Let me see." Clinton started toward them, which made Ethan's surprise attack especially difficult since the gun was aimed at and getting closer to Jack.

"I know why you're doing this," Jack blurted. "I know why you're looking for your sister. I'm a twin, too. I know what it's like."

Clinton froze. The moonlight coming through the window streaked across his face. And Ethan couldn't believe his own eyes. He could see Clinton's face now, and it was the spitting image of Brooke—a larger male version, of course—but an uncanny resemblance. And being the first time Ethan learned that Brooke was a twin, it took everything in his power not to react.

How could she have hidden that from me?

He stared at Clinton in the same way people so often stared at him and Jack, stunned by the sameness, the reason he had always sported a beard. The only distinguishing differences he could see were that

Clinton wore short-cropped hair and he had a cleft chin, an apparent dimple that Brooke didn't have.

Otherwise identical.

"The twin dilemma is more complex than regular siblings," Jack went on. "People assume you're the same, but you're not, you're not alike at all, even opposites in many ways. We defy nature versus nurture studies, when twins who are separated at birth and are raised in different environments turn out the same, or when twins who are born and bred analogously turn out yin and yang. Because the answer to the nature versus nurture argument is always both. We don't realize how people can be so alike and yet so different—"

"My sister sent a Freudian, did she?" Clinton laughed.

Jack continued, "It's a connection like no other. Two people, the same, but different. We wonder if we're born equal or not. If we're bred the same or not. If we're liked as much or not. We grow up under a scope. People have expectations. Your twin puts that pressure on you—"

"That's right, they do," Clinton agreed, mockingly. "All references made on a presumption. It often made me feel inferior, less than. Now where is she, my better half?"

No one answered.

No one knew.

Jack said, "You and your sister have a discrepancy about your inheritance, but it's nothing that can't be worked out, or shared."

"Inheritance can be a knotty affair amongst siblings," Clinton said as he moved toward the stairs, certain his sister was already in the house somewhere—watching, waiting, listening. He added, "But nothing compares to the complexities that arise when twins are beneficiaries, especially when greed divides kindred souls..."

Clinton's jeering jabber gave Ethan an opportunity to sneak into the foyer and tuck behind a grandfather clock where he had a better view.

"Did you know that you can't actually own land in England?" Clinton projected loudly so that his sister would hear if she were in one of the rooms upstairs. "Land tenure only means that you hold land,

and our father didn't like that rule. He always wanted to find a place that he could build and own for himself, and for future generations."

"So he bought this mansion?" Jack prodded.

"He bought this mansion and built the entire community around here—the church, school, equestrian center, performing arts building, vineyard... Over the years, his immense success allowed him to acquire over forty-five acres in prime Napa, and he called it Highpoint. We spent every summer here."

"That's what you named your shell company," Jack said. "You financed Stalker through Highpoint Corporation—"

"Yes. I funded Stalker to find my sister. It took longer than I expected, but it will be worth it."

"Because you think this place should be your birthright?" Jack pressed.

"It *is* my birthright," Clinton shot back.

"And your sister's," Jack said. "Twins have to split if there's no firstborn."

"One would think! Most families with twins would treat them equally. But not mine." Clinton's face tensed and he spoke in an angry murmur, "Because my father claimed that she was born seconds before me."

Ethan peered out, realizing the weight of this. Jack saw his brother and made eye contact. Ethan rolled his finger to signal that Jack keep talking.

Jack spoke louder, more assured. "If your sister is the eldest child, this is all rightfully hers. Your father was just abiding by English primogeniture laws—"

"Twins are twins!" Clinton seethed. "Even Mum always told us that there were complications in the delivery room and no one was certain who was born first. I'm sure one of my father's lavish lawyers came up with some horseshit contract that stated a false birth order so he could change his will, and screw me out of what is rightfully mine."

"Why?" Jack asked, already knowing the answer. "Why would he go to all that trouble to make sure your sister got everything and you nothing?"

"Because he hated me."

"Why?"

"Must have been second-child syndrome, Freud," Clinton said assiduously. "Sometimes, they praise the obedience of the first child and wonder what went wrong with the second one. Or maybe it was twin syndrome, if there is such a thing. Maybe he expected my sister and me to be the same because we looked alike, and when he realized that we couldn't be more different, he was disappointed. Or maybe it was post-traumatic God syndrome because my father saw himself as a supreme being—"

Jack cut him off, "Or maybe it could have been because you threw your father's firstborn son off the roof when you were a kid because you didn't like the idea of being the second son, and because your father knew it was no accident. Arthur The Second was poised to benefit much more from the family name than you were. Killing him put you in first position, or so you thought. Your father made sure that you never murdered your way into inheriting his fortune. Nobody could ever prove that it wasn't an accident, but your father knew—"

Clinton's face contorted and he boiled, "He can't control this from the grave!"

Clinton fired the gun. The shot rang out in a deafening, echoing ring.

Jack and Sean scurried on their hands and knees back into the living room and tucked behind a sofa.

It went quiet again.

Ethan was about to make his move, but Clinton started up the stairs, out of his view again.

Jack shouted from behind the couch, "What do you want from your sister?"

"This all sits in probate until I turn her in," Clinton said, ascending the stairs slowly. "I'm coming for you, Stella...I know you're here...I saw that you've replaced the family portrait with that garish rabbit statue on the mantel, but no matter what you do, you can't erase us!"

Ethan moved across the foyer.

"I get it," Jack continued. "You want to turn your sister in so she could be tried for the murder of your father. If they convict her, then the property goes to the next child in line. You."

Clinton nodded ardently. "You can't take possession if you're a murderer."

"But she didn't kill him, did she?" Jack pressed. "They were close. Your father taught her the family business. She had no reason to kill him."

"No one cares why she did it!" Clinton snapped, "There's a security video from the hospital that shows her sneaking into my father's hospital room and giving him a dose of cyanide. Case closed!"

"But she didn't do it," Jack tried again.

"My sister and I play very clever games."

Clinton turned onto the first landing on the stairs and out of Ethan's view again. If Brooke was hiding upstairs, Ethan couldn't allow Clinton to get to her. So he stepped out into the light of the anteroom and announced: "Mummy and Daddy loved her more. Deal with it!"

Clinton looked over the banister and grinned. "Am I seeing double?"

"That joke never gets old," Ethan said as he slowly moved toward the stairs, hoping to engage Clinton until he would be close enough to make a move.

"I know only too well," Clinton said.

"Framing your sister might allow you to take possession of Highpoint," Ethan continued, "but it certainly won't make anyone love you."

Ethan's verbal attack seemed to be working. Clinton started back down the stairs. "You just brought a big mouth to a gun fight, did you? At least your twin brought some Freudian clichés and his fey lover to back him up. But unarmed witnesses are easy to deal with. Let me show you." Clinton turned and pointed his gun at the sofa Jack and Sean were hiding behind.

Ethan screamed, "No!"

Clinton fired two shots.

Jack grabbed his leg and keeled over, reeling in pain. As Ethan started to go to his brother, Clinton turned the gun on him and said, "Do not take another step."

Ethan stopped.

"Twins," Clinton spewed like it was a curse, pointing the gun back and forth, from Ethan to Jack, as if deciding who to shoot next. "Most can't live without the other. I wasn't one of those—"

"What a tragedy for your sister," Ethan said.

Clinton laughed. "Did you hear the one about the twins who were born and given up for adoption? One of them went to a family in Egypt and was named Amal. The other went to a family in Spain, and they named him Juan. Years later, Juan sent a picture of himself to his mum. Upon receiving the picture, she told her husband that she wished that she also had a picture of Amal. Her husband threw his hands up and said, 'They're twins. If you've seen Juan, you've seen Amal.'" Clinton let out a guttural laugh and drew closer. "Your brother was right about one thing: twins feel each other's pain, don't we?" He aimed his gun at Ethan and said, "Let's see if your brother feels this—"

A scream came from up the second floor. "Stop!"

It was Brooke.

"If you don't shoot him," she said. "I'll come down."

Clinton revealed an arrhythmic smile. "I told you that she and I play clever games."

CHAPTER 40

S HE APPEARED ON THE second-floor landing, in a dark shadow. "Let them go and I'll come with you. You can turn me in and have all of this. Everything."

"Game over," Clinton said with a grin. "Only you're in no position to negotiate."

"Don't take another step!" she shouted. "I also have a gun."

"You won't use it," Clinton said. "You didn't get that gene."

"He's not going to let you confess to anything," Ethan said. "He doesn't want to bring you back to London to be tried. It's easier to kill you. If you're dead, the property goes to him and there's no chance anyone will ever learn the truth."

Clinton agreed. "Justice served."

"I'm begging you," she pleaded. "For once, do the right thing. Let's end all of this now."

"Good idea," Clinton said as he fired a shot in the direction of her voice.

The bullet splintered the banister, she screamed, and Ethan bolted toward the stairs. Clinton turned the gun at him and fired. The bullet ricocheted off the marble floor.

Ethan charged up the stairs to wipe the grin off his face. Clinton got a shot off. Ethan heard the bullet skim just over his head and penetrate one of the front windows, making a crackling sound. Ethan slammed into Clinton, a full-throttle football tackle. Their combined weight slammed into the bannister and they both tumbled down the stairs. Clinton's gun flew out of his hand and slid across the marble foyer floor.

Ethan rolled on top and slugged Clinton in the head repeatedly. The Brit knew how to take a punch, one after the other, blood oozing, and he had a taunting grin that wouldn't go away, as if he were drawing strength from each and every hit.

His knee went into Ethan's groin. As Ethan keeled, Clinton ducked out of his grasp and spit in his face.

They wrestled and traded blows, both trying to get the upper hand. Clinton went for Ethan's jugular and squeezed, with a malefic smile. Ethan gasped for air and saw Jack behind the couch on the floor, his leg twitching. His brother was in tremendous pain. And so was Sean. He was holding the side of his stomach, and Ethan knew that one of the bullets must have hit him too.

Clinton's hand was a thick, tenacious vise Ethan couldn't escape. Ethan lashed from side to side, trying to break free, when he saw Brooke coming down the stairs, the vision he longed for. Their eyes met, an assured look that told them both that they would do whatever it took to get out of this situation so they could be together again.

Whatever it took.

She was holding a gun, shaking, frightened. When she winced, Ethan knew that he must have been purple from Clinton's grasp.

"Is this the twin you loved?" Clinton asked her, preparing to snap Ethan's neck.

"I will shoot you!" she shouted at Clinton.

Ethan flailed and thrashed, fighting for his life. Clinton struggled to hold his grip and grunted, "I don't think you will —"

Ethan slammed Clinton's chin with an upper thrust, forcing him to fall back and release his grip. As Ethan gasped for air, Clinton dove for the gun. Ethan jumped on him and tried to wrestle the weapon arm down. Clinton headbutted him. Ethan went back. Clinton gripped the gun and—

Ethan's next move was pure instinct, and brilliant. He rolled away, pushed off his hands, and released a snap kick.

He knew he made contact with Clinton's face, and he saw the gun sliding across the marble floor. Clinton crawled after it, but Ethan lunged at him. They wrestled until Ethan finally overtook him, punching him senseless, until he heard Brooke's voice: "Stop!"

Ethan stopped. He climbed off Clinton, caught his breath, and wiped blood off his fists. Clinton was glaring up past him, a crooked smirk as if he had another surprise. "Go ahead...shoot me," he gushed at his sister. "Finish this."

"Like you said," she lowered her gun, "I can't."

"Too bad." Blood oozed from his mouth and he stared at her, raw puissance, pure hate. "I win. I've thought this through better than you." He started to get up, but fell back, and then tried again.

"You're sick," she cried. "Watching you self-destruct is like dying myself, and a part of me certainly has. I could have removed you like a cancerous limb long ago, but I always loved you. I always had hope for you."

"You'll never turn this around. There's evidence that proves that you killed Father—"

"I didn't do it!" she shrieked.

"But I made it look like you did." Clinton finally got to his feet and smiled. "And I'll never confess."

"You just did," she told him. "Everyone's cell phone here records audio—"

"No one will leave here with their cell phones." He wiped more blood away. "No one will leave here alive."

Brooke shook her head. "That thing I replaced our family portrait with, on the mantel, which you called a 'garish rabbit statue,' also videotaped everything."

Clinton limped over to the mantel, grabbed the statue, and slammed it on the ground. The porcelain rabbit shattered into pieces. "Not anymore!"

"That won't make a difference. The digital tape goes through an app on my phone. It's set to nine-one-one Mode, which means it's already gone out."

No one had to ask where 911 Mode sent the video.

"This wasn't a game I ever wanted to play," Brooke told Clinton. "But I win."

There was a car driving up the driveway, the headlights glimpsing through the still-open front door, certain to illuminate the fallen bodies on the lawn.

"That's the FBI," Jack said, looking out the window, still gripping Ethan's iPhone. "They must've tracked us here."

"They did," Brooke explained. "I was able to hear their conversation because they have Bailey's phone connected to..." She paused, knowing that her technology saved her life, but wishing she didn't have to use it. "It's all over," she told Clinton. "There's no way out now."

Clinton seethed with unbound rage.

They heard car doors shut outside and turned. Clinton didn't hesitate. He scrambled through the kitchen, and the back door shut behind him.

Ethan went after him just as the FBI charged inside the house.

"Freeze!" Agent Shu told Ethan, pointing a gun.

"He's getting away!" Ethan shouted back.

"I told you to freeze—" Shu reiterated.

Jack crawled out from behind the sofa and yelled, "We've both been shot! We need an ambulance!"

When Shu turned, Ethan took off through the kitchen and ran after Clinton.

"Dammit!" Agent Shu went after Ethan.

Ethan burst through the back kitchen door and heard a gun fire. It came from the front yard. He ran around the side of the estate as fast as he could.

Brooke went to the front window and looked out. She saw Ethan standing in the front garden with a sorrowful gaze. Agent Shu approached from behind, seemingly resolved.

Brooke knew immediately what had happened, and wept.

Clinton Godeaux was dead on the front lawn, a bullet through his head, shot at close range.

Agent Shu moved closer to confirm that Clinton was killed with Detective Ramsey's gun. It looked as though Detective Ramsey still had a little life left in him, saw Clinton run out of the house, and shot him, dead. Then died himself.

But Brooke knew what had really happened.

When Clinton ran out and saw Detective Ramsey sprawled out on the grass, already dead, he lifted Ramsey's gun to his own head and pulled the trigger.

It was suicide.

Clinton knew there was no way out of this mess. At the very best he would get a life sentence in prison. At the very least, his sister would have won, and he couldn't accept that.

He didn't get that gene.

CHAPTER 41

A REPRESENTATIVE FROM BRITAIN'S MI6, Agent Ray Arnold, joined the FBI to interview Ethan, Brooke, Jack, and Sean—separately and together. Their stories corroborated and both detectives Ramsey and Johnson were credited for the capture of Clinton Godeaux and his return to the motherland in a body bag.

The two convicted felons lain dead on the front lawn of Highpoint manor, Andrew Lipshitz (aka "Ace") and Dale Norton, were originally assumed responsible for the murder of Bailey Duff since the bullet that had killed Bailey had come from the gun in Ace's hand. But when Brooke showed the FBI agents how to use her Black Box feature on Bailey's phone, they played back the audio of the murder under the Santa Monica Pier, and the record was set straight. Clinton Godeaux was determined the killer.

As if it mattered. They were all dead.

But the Godeaux case was far from being wrapped up. There was still the matter of the Arthur Godeaux's death-by-cyanide conundrum and the indisputable, incriminating evidence that revealed Stella Godeaux as the murderess.

"I'm sorry for your loss," the MI6 agent said after he and the FBI completed debriefing Brooke. "I will escort you back to London tomorrow. You will have an arraignment right away, and then plenty of time to prepare for trial."

"You can finally go home," Ethan said, with a heavy pit in his stomach. "You can go back to being Stella Godeaux."

"I don't want to go back," she said, clearly grief-stricken, and even more discomfited. She turned to Arnold and pleaded, "I didn't kill my father, I promise you. I loved him very much."

"I'm sure you did," Arnold said. "You will have a fair trial, but frankly, the evidence against you is insurmountable. The hospital security tape shows you injecting cyanide into your father's IV."

"It has to be faked somehow," Brooke professed, even though she had never seen the footage. It had only been shared with the British Secret Service, FBI, Interpol, and investigating police.

And Ethan.

"The security tape was authentic," Arnold told her. "Our experts confirmed that it had not been tampered with. And you still have no alibi."

"You just heard my brother's confession, which I recorded on my rabbit statue, my custom-made apps, and you just heard everything from four surviving witnesses, you have to believe me—"

"Still," the MI6 agent concluded, "our evidence shows otherwise."

Just then it hit Ethan like a ton of bricks and he was sure he knew how Clinton framed Brooke. He jumped up and told agent Shu, "Play the tape again."

"We've already showed it to you," Shu complained. "And James Bond here just told you that the tape had not been tampered with."

"Clinton killed their father," Ethan said assuredly.

"Innocent people don't run—"

"Shut up, Shu," Matz snapped. "Just play the video."

"If you insist," Agent Shu said. "It never gets old for me." Shu held up his iPad so everyone could see and played the hospital security footage.

Ethan said, "Go back to where she looks at the camera and pause it."

Shu hit rewind and stopped on her face.

Ethan smiled. "She's innocent," he said, glaring at Shu. "She ran because she's a twin. Giving up on her brother would be giving up on herself. She never gave up hope for Clinton. She believed he would eventually do the right thing."

Brooke smiled at Ethan with a look of gratitude, not only because he was about to save her a lifetime in prison for a crime she did not commit, but also because he understood her and her twin dilemma. She repeated what Father Oliver had told her when she had promised to confess her reasons, "'Body and spirit are twins; God only knows which is which.'" She got up, kissed Ethan on the head, and whispered in his ear, "I love you."

"Back on planet earth," Shu said.

Everyone in the room waited for an explanation.

"That's not her in that video," Ethan told them.

"That's not me," she agreed.

"Prove it," Shu said.

"We had this problem with our face recognition feature," Ethan explained. "Face Match Mode would light up whenever it had a ninety-nine-percent match. But the details in that tiny one percent can make all the difference in the world. Expand the image."

Agent Shu pinched the picture and it expanded. It was still hard to make out because the video was so grainy.

And because the twins' faces looked so much alike.

But with the blown-up image, there was one clear difference. "The person in this video has a cleft chin." Ethan pointed at the lower jaw of the face on the screen, and then turned to Brooke, and touched her smooth, round chin. "She doesn't… See, no indent. Her brother is the murderer."

Shu played the video clip once more.

"That's her brother wearing a dress and a black wig," Ethan explained. "The long raincoat makes it impossible to see his size—"

"Good enough for me," Arnold said, completely convinced.

Brooke couldn't help herself and gave her countryman a big hug. "Thank you!"

Shu turned to Matz and said, "Told you, bait and switch!" as if it were her fault.

"You sure did." Matz slapped Shu on the back. "Well done. Now let's get out of here."

Agent Shu played the security footage one more time, unable to relent so easily. "Unless...she altered this to make it look like a bait and switch—"

"Shut up, Shu," Matz said. "Agent Arnold just told us that it hadn't been tampered with."

"Maybe that's true, but she still has to go back to England." Shu's face brightened with a gotcha grin. "She's been living here without a visa. And there's the matter of using a false identity."

The room went quiet. Shu had a point.

Agent Arnold was the first to speak, "Maybe that can be overlooked—"

"No way," Shu inserted, like a dagger, or a prick.

Ethan beamed. "Unless—"

"She can't stay here," Shu pressed. "Visitor visas only permit her to be here for six months. She's been here more than two years. The law's the law."

"What were you going to say?" Matz asked Ethan.

Ethan blushed and turned to look in Brooke's eyes. "Could she stay if she married an American?"

Brooke's face lit up.

"Is that a proposal?" Agent Arnold asked the room.

"Is it?" Brooke asked Ethan.

"You bet it is."

Arnold stepped forward and said, "She'd need to confirm."

Brooke wrapped her arms around Ethan and shrieked, "I do!"

Arnold grabbed Ethan's shoulder. "If we're going to let her stay, she'll need a diamond ring."

"Don't you worry," Ethan assured the agent with a conspiratorial wink. "I've already been shopping for a rather large one."

Agent Matz and Agent Arnold applauded. "Congratulations!"

"What about false identity charges?" Shu whined, aggrieved by the injustice.

"Shut up, Shu," Matz said, grabbing her protégé and dragging him out.

Agent Arnold followed.

Ethan and Brooke stayed behind and kissed for a long time, deeply, like their very first time. Ethan felt it throughout his body and knew his life would never be the same, and apparently so did she.

"Now I know why my father warned me about falling for the most charming guy in the room," she said. *"L'amour nous fait faire des choses folles.* Love makes us do crazy things."

He kissed her again, longer and harder, this time rendering her speechless.

———

IN THE DAYS THAT followed, they prepared to start their future together, but not the way they had originally intended. Not exactly. Not yet.

First they had to share their pasts.

They discussed everything, the sacred and the profane. Once all the missing pieces were filled in and the hazy layers peeled away, they both agreed that knowing the truth made them love each other more.

And it set them free.

EPILOGUE
ONE YEAR LATER

VALLEY REGISTER
HOUSE OF STONE

Much of the mystery behind the stewardship of Napa Valley's largest private house has been solved after years of speculation. As reported last November when a deadly shootout took the lives of two Big Sur Police detectives and one of the property's potential beneficiaries, the estate has finally been settled. Stella Godeaux-Stone—daughter of the original owner, Arthur Godeaux—has been named the sole beneficiary of the forty-five-acre estate that features the Godeaux manor, an equestrian stable, the Highpoint vineyard, St. Francis Church, St. Francis Community Center, and St. Francis K-6 elementary school.

Stella Godeaux-Stone, who has recently married Ethan Stone, an American technology entrepreneur, was unavailable for questioning. When *The Register* first reported on the renowned Highpoint estate, the City of Napa had been unable to determine who was the rightful owner. Arthur Godeaux had recently died of heart failure and was survived by his daughter, Stella, and son, Clinton, but the will and testament had been contested and the property was in a state of flux.

British courts further complicated matters by putting a freeze on the Godeaux trusts while they were investigating foul play in Arthur Godeaux's death.

According to Oliver Godeaux—the twin brother of Arthur Godeaux and head priest at St. Francis Church in north Napa Valley—Stella Godeaux-Stone and her new husband, Ethan, do not plan on living in the Highpoint manor at this time. Father Oliver told The Register that the recent tragedies that took place on the property hold too many bad memories and the young couple has sought a fresh start for their new family.

The priest has overseen all aspects of St. Francis Church since his brother purchased the property in 1993, including the elementary school and community center. The priest now supervises the maintenance of the Highpoint manor for the new owner as well.

"It has been a challenging time for my niece," Father Oliver explained, "and I pray that she can live in peace, wherever she chooses to settle. The Highpoint estate will continue on as a respected pillar of the Napa Valley community."

There are still many unknown details about why Mrs. Godeaux-Stone was originally suspected of foul play in her father's death, why she fled England, and why the murder charges were placed onto her brother Clinton.

As reported last year, Big Sur detectives tracked Clinton Godeaux down at the Highpoint manor and were killed in a shootout on the property, as was Clinton Godeaux.

Since there was no trial, neither British nor American authorities ever released evidence used to settle the case, and Father Oliver refused to answer any questions regarding his nephew's assumed betrayal. "'Let us forget what lies behind and strain forward to what lies ahead,'" the priest responded, quoting the Bible. "'The old has passed away; behold, the new has come.'"

So it seems that the entire truth about the estate will forever remain shrouded in mystery.

———

AT LONG LAST, GENERATIONS of primogeniture dramas ended, like many family traditions; well-intended security became onerous and thorny;

jealousies spawning a web of secrets and lies; vengeance ultimately destroying it all.

Arthur Godeaux would often spout the Parisian idiom: *"Le sort du verre est de briser."*

The fate of glass is to break.

But the patriarch of the family had also prepared for such a fate. Well aware of Clinton's acrimonious inclinations, he bestowed the Godeaux legacy to his daughter, and entrusted his own twin brother, Oliver, to be the trustee. When Arthur bought the Napa Valley property years ago, he had asked his brother not only to build the church and community, but to oversee all operations of the entire Highpoint estate should he survive him. The good priest never let Arthur down. Even now, Father Oliver turns the other cheek when it comes to Rabbit activity at the estate.

Highpoint is still used as one of the many temporary holding cells for Rabbits awaiting their escape strategies, where they stay off-line until sent to their final destination offshore. Like Saint Peter's Pearly Gates to heaven, such Rabbits wait for their haven, where they will eventually be sent.

Permanently.

———

SERGEANT CRUZ WAS OVERWHELMED by the loss of two of his finest detectives, Ramsey and Johnson, but he once again felt proud of the police department he had promised his father and grandfather he would carry on. Elvis recently hosted a Native American ceremony at Dancing Rabbit to officially change Sergeant Cruz's Ohlone family name back to Costeños and bring honor back to the region.

Dancing Rabbit continued to be the flora and fauna getaway for refocusing and refreshing stressed tech execs. The retreats that Brooke had set up remained their main source of income. The property was once again in the black, and the owners were thrilled. However, none of the Dancing Rabbit owners or staff ever heard from Brooke, or any of the missing Rabbits, again.

—

As soon as Brooke was cleared of all charges, her marriage to Benjamin Carver was annulled so that she could marry Ethan and become Stella Godeaux-Stone. Once she received her green card and was granted authorization to live and work in the United States on a permanent basis, she and Ethan quietly slipped away to an exquisite, remote island hamlet in the eastern Caribbean known as Pelican Cove.

You won't find it on a map and you can't Google it. It's only for people in the know, and on the go.

Literally.

Pelican Cove harbored the largest network of expatriates in the world, sheltering their money, changing their identities, and placing them in the most impenetrable safe havens in the world, from the Caribbean throughout the Pacific, off the South American and European coasts, all around Asia, and Australia, too.

Think there aren't others with dreams of starting over completely on their own terms, committing suicide without killing themselves, and becoming an anonymous person in the netherworld of being on the run?

The International Monetary Fund estimated expatriate cash in foreign banking institutions to be in excess of seven trillion dollars.

Seven trillion!

Ethan had always contended that solving a simple human desire is how great businesses begin. When he learned about how Brooke made Rabbits, how she helped people cut all ties and be truly free, come what may, he pitched her the idea of merging the Stalker and Rabbit concepts, to help people who deserved a second chance by using intricate planning and state-of-the-art technology.

He wanted to make Rabbits with her.

They couldn't do it on the Dancing Rabbit property, though. The Big Sur police were already incensed by the number of missing persons in the region, and it would only be a matter of time before they closed in. Rabbits needed a safe base to operate from that couldn't be regulated or investigated.

Brooke knew just the place. She had already masterminded an eloquent, impenetrable design so they too could enjoy life in seclusion, without being secluded. And she had sent Benjamin Carver there to get things started.

—

Ethan and Benjamin now run the transformation division at Pelican Cove. They help Pelicans run, and teach Rabbits to fly. On the wall above Ethan's desk is a sign with a quote from Albert Einstein: "Try not to become a man of success, but rather try to become a man of value."

Ethan and Stella Godeaux-Stone live near Pelican Cove offices in a Spanish-style home on top of an exquisite, unspoiled archipelago, with breathtaking views of the azure sea and pristine beaches from the front, and lush landscape and mountains from the back. They have a loving marriage with unparalleled appreciation for each other. Ethan often tells her that the worst days of his life were when he thought he had lost her. Stella promises that they will never again be apart, now that they are family.

Now that they're making little bunnies of their own.

She got pregnant the first week they arrived at Pelican Cove.

Jack and Sean visit them often. Jack found faith in himself and in their relationship. On the good days, he even shows signs of optimism.

Hounddog is thriving. Sean, the Wizard of Silicon, bought Stalker from Ethan when he got married, and Jack now oversees it as a separate division within the Hounddog offices.

Ethan is happy that it's staying in the family. Never in his wildest dreams would Ethan have believed that he would never be going back to Stalker or Santa Monica or Silicon Beach. But sometimes dreams change.

Especially the wild ones.

When Ethan and Stella were in the ob-gyn's office getting an ultrasound and seeing their offspring for the first time, they were both taken by surprise when the doctor announced: "There are two!"

Sure enough, two embryonic forms appeared through black-and-white grain on the monitor.

Ethan smiled ear to ear.

Stella wiped a tear and spoke her father's words: *"Twins courent dans notre famille. C'est la vie."*

Twins run in our family. Such is life.

Six months later, Stella gave birth to two beautiful, healthy boys.

They looked identical to everyone, but not to the parents. Confusion in the delivery room prevented the doctors from being able to record who was born first. Ethan and Stella both know, but they'll never tell.

Birth order and birthrights shouldn't matter, but they always do.

The End.

Acknowledgments

FIRST, ALWAYS FIRST, I thank my wife and children, for your love and support. Next, I thank Tyson Cornell, Julia Callahan, Hailie Johnson, Guy Intoci, Jake Levens, Sydney Lopez, and all the great folks at Rare Bird, for publishing this book, and my next. Big thanks to my awesome agent, Paula Munier, for your guidance and dedication. Special thanks to Naomi Weiss, Lenore Weiss, Mittie Arnold, Troy Arnold, David Rocklin, Rhoda Weber, and everyone who gave me inspiration and encouragement. And much gratitude to the International Thriller Writers community and all the teachers, mentors, and muses that taught me the craft of storytelling and the value of discipline and persistence.

I don't necessarily write what I know, but I do write what I love—mysteries and thrillers set in fascinating places, where complex characters find the depth of their courage, and thematically, at their core, examine the layers within us all that reveal themselves when our world turns upside down, inside out, and out of control. I also like to explore how technology and transparency affects human behavior—as I did in this book—and how cultural evolution, for better and for worse, changes us. Which brings me to the biggest thanks of all: To you, dear reader—for picking up *The Second Son*. I sincerely hope you find it as compelling to read as it was for me to write. For more information about this book, or my forthcoming novel, *Flamingo Coast*, please visit martinishotfilms.tv, and connect with me on Twitter (@martinjayweiss) and Facebook (martinjayweiss).

A Sneak Peak of
FLAMINGO COAST

Chapter One

JENNIFER MORTON HAD JUST seen her father for the last time. The look on his face—their shared countenance—already haunted her. He was once her *raison d'être,* her anchor; now he was the reason she was on a runaway power cruiser seeking retribution.

The yacht hit a set of pounding whitecap swells and the unmanned wheel shuttered. Jennifer braced herself and watched the island lights fade away as they charged out to sea. There was no turning back, even if she wanted to. Two men were hunkered down somewhere in the bulwarks, planning their attack. It was time to make her move.

She slipped through a teak hatch, hopefully unseen, found her way into the engine room, and went to work. As she rigged a detonator to the fuse box, her mind drifted back to her earliest memory of her dear old dad, when she was barely five years old and he had taken her for a joyride on his most prized possession—a vintage mahogany Chris-Craft Capri—befittingly christened *The Great Escape.* She remembered how the classic Italian speedboat shimmered from endless pampering as it cut through the rippled surface of the sea like a skimming stone, the warm summer breeze flowing through her long auburn curls, and how safe she had felt as her father preached life lessons: *"When it comes to money, people will do unthinkable things…"*

She was too young back then to know that The Great Escape was more of a decision than a desire, or to understand the scope of her father's betrayals. Three decades later, it was payback time. She would soon feel safe again, or so she hoped.

She set the time delay. She had two minutes, which seemed like an eternity, so she tucked behind two bolted-down ice chests and prayed for the first time in years. She asked to be forgiven for the sin she was about to commit. It was a big one, she silently confessed, but justifiable, and well deserved.

The hatch door sprung loose and she saw one of the men approaching through the relentless rain, then the other, and they were both about to fire their sanctioned Glock 23 pistols when the cruiser crushed a crestless six-foot swell, lifting them off their feet. They both landed face down. The yacht shimmied through a series of whitecap rolls, sending them back to the quarterdeck.

Jennifer checked the timer.

Twenty seconds left.

Her father's deep, throaty voice continued to echo in her head as she pulled herself back through the porthole: *"Whatever you desire—love, money revenge—doesn't matter…"*

One of the men noticed her and fired.

Jennifer dived behind the downriggers.

The yacht struck another enormous wave and knocked the shooter back down.

Jennifer climbed up to the ledge.

Ten seconds left.

The islet lights were barely visible now. The cruiser had drifted too far out for anyone to see them. Jennifer shut her eyes and her father's final words resounded: *"The more you have, the more you want. And the more you get, the harder it is to protect yourself. Unless, you take it all and disappear…"*

Everything that had been murky was now perfectly clear.

Jennifer leapt, jackknifed into the raging sea, and descended into the ink-black void.

"…And there is only one way to truly disappear."

A thunderous explosion bellowed above.

Weiss Martin Jay

Second Son

MART
direct
televi
Illino
in Ch